Praise for
The Recital

"With his characteristic mix of humor and heart, Robert Elmer delivers another gem in *The Recital*. Read it and be warmed."

—JAMES SCOTT BELL, best-selling author of *Presumed Guilty*

"Robert Elmer writes a great love story, not a romance, but a real make you laugh and make you cry love story based on a twist of the old 'whither thou goest' principle. In *The Recital*, we meet real live characters who take you with them on their journey to make love work. From country small town to big city life, I was rooting for Gerrit and Joan all the way. Thanks Bob for a great story."

—LAURAINE SNELLING, author of *Saturday Morning* and *Brushstrokes Legacy*

"Robert Elmer has another winner! His characters come alive and make you feel as though you are catching a glimpse of the lives of real people."

—PATRICIA H. RUSHFORD, author of the Angel Delaney Mysteries

"Robert Elmer's mastery of dialogue captures his characters on paper, whether they be a Dutch descendant farmer, a concert pianist, or a Chinese student in Chicago. He also captures their hearts and reveals them to the reader. *The Recital* is engaging and compelling, speaking the everyday language of the Christian walk. A must-read!"

—DONITA K. PAUL, author of the Dragon Keeper Chronicles: *DragonSpell, DragonQuest,* and *DragonKnight*

THE RECITAL

THE RECITAL

A NOVEL

ROBERT ELMER

WATERBROOK
PRESS

THE RECITAL
PUBLISHED BY WATERBROOK PRESS
12265 Oracle Boulevard, Suite 200
Colorado Springs, Colorado 80921
A division of Random House Inc.

Scripture quotations and paraphrases are taken from the King James Version and the Holy Bible, New International Version®. NIV®. Copyright © 1973, 1978, 1984 by International Bible Society. Used by permission of Zondervan Publishing House. All rights reserved.

Hymn lyrics in chapter 33 are taken from S. Trevor Francis, "O the Deep, Deep Love of Jesus," public domain.

The poem in chapter 20 is taken from William Shakespeare, Sonnet 18, "Shall I Compare Thee to a Summer's Day," public domain.

The characters and events in this book are fictional, and any resemblance to actual persons or events is coincidental.

ISBN 1-4000-7164-X

Published in association with the literary agency of Alive Communications, Inc., 7680 Goddard Street, Suite 200, Colorado Springs, CO 80920, www.alivecommunications.com.

Library of Congress Cataloging-in-Publication Data
Elmer, Robert.
The recital / Robert Elmer.—1st ed.
p. cm.
Sequel to: The duet.
ISBN 1-4000-7164-X
1. Women music teachers—Fiction. 2. Dairy farmers—Fiction. 3. Widowers—Fiction.
4. Domestic fiction. I. Title.
PS3555.L44R43 2006
813'.54—dc22

2006002560

Printed in the United States of America
2006—First Edition

10 9 8 7 6 5 4 3 2 1

To my daughter Danica, whose recital inspired my stories

Chapter 1

What Women Want: To be loved, to be listened to, to be desired,
to be respected, to be needed, to be trusted, and sometimes, just to
be held. What Men Want: Tickets for the World Series.
—DAVE BARRY

"Are you okay, Mrs. Horton?"

"Oh!" The question yanked Joan from her brooding daydream. "Of course. Sure."

She almost bit her tongue at the lie. Little Anna DeBoer looked up at her sideways from her perch on the piano bench, her cute little feet not quite reaching the pedals.

"When I get that way," said Anna, eyes wide and innocent, "my mom tells me that I need more sleep and that I should get to bed."

"Smart mom you have." Joan smiled and returned her attention to the lesson. If daydreams were felonies, she would soon be under arrest. "So why don't you try the right hand through to measure six this time?"

Her youngest piano student willingly attacked the keyboard, blending sour notes with sweet. Mostly sour. This time Joan did her best to keep time as Anna struggled through "Itsy Bitsy Yellow Bug," a simple tune in *Anderson's Basic Piano: Book One.*

So sorry, Anna, but today your piano teacher can concentrate on only one thing at a time: you, the lesson, or the letter. Not all three at once.

Thoughts of the letter threatened to take over every minute of her time. Joan glanced furtively down at her watch and wondered how in the world her concentration had eroded so much and so quickly this afternoon.

Is this what happens to multitasking when people approach sixty? Never mind.

She would survive this lesson, the last of a terrible, horrible, no good, very bad day—as a well-loved children's book put it. Then she would finish heating the Cajun chicken-and-sausage casserole she'd started and enjoy a nice dinner with Gerrit. Or as nice as it could be, given the circumstances. In any case, Gerrit would probably show up at her doorstep any minute now. But no matter what, she would *not* let herself worry about how she would respond to the letter, the offer she'd received in the mail this afternoon. Not now; not today.

"We're getting it right, aren't we?" Anna had no idea how close her teacher was to screaming.

"Almost." Joan couldn't help wincing at the C-natural that should have been a C-sharp.

"Stop?" asked Anna.

While stopping would have been wonderful, Joan shook her head. "No, no," she told her student. "Keep going, please."

As Anna continued, Joan battled her own poor attitude. *God grant me the serenity to accept the things I cannot change,* she prayed. Anna, for her part, still couldn't seem to get the rhythm down. She sniffed and looked around, mightily distracted herself. Joan wondered for a moment if they shouldn't just end the lesson a few merciful minutes early after all and call it a day. Enough damage had already been done.

"Do you smell something burning, Mrs. Horton?"

Joan turned the page and paused. Anna's mother charged through the front door just then, punctual as usual. Instead of her usual polite smile, though, Mrs. DeBoer wore a panicked expression as she dashed in and grabbed her daughter.

"Where's the fire?" cried Mrs. DeBoer.

"Oh *no!*" Joan leaped to her feet at the sound of the smoke alarm, nearly knocking Anna down. The music book flew off its perch. "My dinner!"

Joan was too busy rushing into her smoke-filled kitchen to answer Mrs. DeBoer's questions. All she could think to do was open the oven to find out what was going on, which turned out to be Mistake Number One.

A cloud of thick black smoke poured from the oven, hitting Joan in the face.

"Call 911!" shrieked Anna, but her mother held her back.

Smart mom, Joan thought. "No!" Joan said, coughing. She could handle this…maybe. She tried to wave a towel at the disaster, which only splattered smoking Cajun sauce all over the hot oven, making matters worse. She should have closed the oven and shut off the gas, but that would have been a levelheaded response, and at the moment, there were no level heads in Joan Horton's kitchen. Besides, it was too late now. Where was a man when you needed him?

Baking soda! Long ago some home-economics teacher had told her that baking soda would put out a fire like this. Joan covered her mouth and nose with the towel while she tried to remember where the baking soda was. Meanwhile, the smoke alarm kept up its insistent *skreeee*-ing, and little Anna added to the noise level any way she could with unintelligible shouts and yelps. Her mother wasn't much better, skipping at the edge of the linoleum and waving a music book in the air in a feeble attempt to circulate the smoke away from the alarm's sensor.

By this time they had succeeded in attracting the attention of the Van Dalen Fire Department. No doubt Mrs. DeLeeuw next door had called in the alarm. She'd never missed a thing before, especially not after Gerrit had started visiting Joan on occasions other than his own piano lessons and those of his granddaughter, Mallory. Sure enough, even above the smoke alarm, Joan could now hear Van Dalen's finest hurrying up Delft

Street in her direction, coming to the rescue of the poor widow from New York who still didn't know how to cook anything that wasn't store boughten. Oh yes, Joan thought, she was sure to make the front page of the next *Van Dalen Sentinel.*

"*Burned-Out Music Teacher Torches House with Scorched Dinner.*"

Chapter 2

I played, like, a year of piano until I learned the Pink Panther
theme. That was my goal. Once I was good enough, I quit.
Now my music has to have some rock.
—JACK BLACK

Gomer the Truck groaned and protested as Gerrit pressed the gas pedal to the floor and careened around a corner, headed toward town and his dinner date with Joan Horton—a date for which he was terribly late. The thought occurred to him that a ticket with his name on it might be in store for him if Jed Vanderstraat was lying in wait at the city limits in his black-and-white police cruiser. And that made Gerrit ease up on the gas just a little. Joan had probably eaten and washed the dishes by now anyway.

Gomer backfired, and Gerrit patted him on the dashboard. "Not now, old guy."

Now might have been a good time to have one of those cell phones Joan's grown son, Randy, was always saying Gerrit should get. And "only" sixty-five a month for the nationwide plan! No self-respecting Dutchman would pay that much for a toy that had buttons designed for the fingertips of thirteen-year-old girls. Besides, the last thing Gerrit wanted to do was call Joan to say that he was going to be late. *So forget the cell phone for now. Just get to Joan's ASAP.*

Maybe she'd serve him some of her fancy New York–style coffee and one of her "eye-talian" desserts, and they'd laugh about his being late. *One of them senior moments, right?* The two widowed seniors would talk about their kids again, about how much things had changed in the past year since Gerrit had turned sixty, since his heart had started acting up and he'd had to hand over the family farm to his son Warney, who ended up selling the place because he'd gotten himself so deeply in debt.

Gerrit slowed down as he drove by Al Bovenklein's farm. Pretty nice place, actually. The Bovenkleins were Dairy Family of the Year back when people still awarded that kind of thing. They were good Calvinists, faithful attenders of First Dutch Reformed, and they had raised their kids right. In fact, young Darrell was still sticking around the farm to help his dad, which was how life ought to be. Not like his own had been, though a man shouldn't complain about the will of God.

Gerrit rolled down the window to catch the once-familiar sounds of the evening milking in the barn, the lowing of the cows, the whine of the milking machine, the *thrump* of a tractor. The swallows had discovered this place, too, and they looked just as busy here as they had at the tractor dealership where he worked: some catching dinner on the fly, and others looking under the rafters for a nesting place. Which reminded him of the decision he had to make.

Yes or no? He gripped the steering wheel until his knuckles turned white and went once more through his mental loop-the-loops, kind of like the swallows that circled the barn trolling for bugs.

"Is this your will, God?" he asked aloud once again. He figured God must be getting a little tired of the question Gerrit had been asking over the past couple of months—or ever since he'd met Joan Horton, really. The Almighty didn't seem inclined to answer—well, not in ways that Gerrit wished He might.

It made no sense—at least not from the cheap seats where he usually sat—because if he'd set out to find a woman any more different from him, he wouldn't have been able to. Retired dairy farmer—a little rough around the edges—and a sophisticated, big-city piano professor, polished and professional. He was a homebody who'd lived on the farm all his life—

until just recently—and she, a world traveler. He, a true-blue Calvinist, and she…not.

Maybe it was the last thing that bugged him the most. Even though he sometimes wondered whose faith was stronger, Gerrit couldn't decide how much it mattered that they came from such different church backgrounds. Folks from Joan's denomination tended to be a little more chummy with the Holy Spirit than Gerrit figured was proper, and they did a bit of hand waving in their services. He still wasn't quite sure about all that. On the other hand, Gerrit could bank on Joan Horton holding her own every time they argued Scripture.

He loved the way she had treated his granddaughter Mallory before Warney and Liz had moved off to Olympia after the farm sale. He loved Joan's spunk, too. The way she'd come to a small town like Van Dalen by herself a few years after her husband had died, just to be with her pregnant daughter, Alison. He loved the way she didn't just lie down and let life roll over her. He loved the way she threw herself at problems, as if they had no choice but to move away. He loved the way she protected her own, the way she'd been there for her son, Randy. And Gerrit loved the way she made *him* feel—like maybe he wasn't ready for a lifetime membership in the AARP just yet.

He could go on, but would it be enough to outweigh all their differences? More than the stuff on that list, he loved *her,* plain and simple, more than he ever thought he could love someone after his Miriam had died. And it didn't really matter that Joan was beautiful and dark-haired like some kind of Greek goddess, though, of course, he wasn't complaining about that for a minute.

Bottom line was that he loved Joan Horton. Period.

"There," he announced to the world, "does everybody hear that? I love Joan Horton." He raised his voice. "Do you hear me? I LOVE JOAN HORTON!"

And maybe that was enough—or maybe it wasn't.

What about it, Lord? He prayed, trying hard not to close his eyes the way he felt he ought to. God kept quiet.

Thunk! Something hit Gomer's fender from the side, like a stray snowball in winter. Only this was springtime, so Gerrit stopped the truck, backed up, and got out for a look-see.

"Hey, little guy." He knelt down in the middle of the gravel road for a closer look at a young swallow that had connected with the truck. The bird lay face up—panting and stunned, but not dead.

"You're okay." Gerrit cupped his big, rough farm-boy hands and gently scooped up the frightened little bird. For a moment the bird looked as if it knew Gerrit. "Not your time to die yet. You've got a nest to build, huh? Go on."

As if the little bird understood, it fluttered its wings and was gone in a flurry of feathers, one of which remained in Gerrit's hand as a souvenir. He watched the flash of iridescent blue and finally understood the answer to his question.

"Okay, Lord," he whispered, tucking the feather into his shirt pocket as a reminder. "I see Your point. I guess I'm not getting any younger either."

And he knew he would not let another day go by before he found out from Joan, one way or the other. If she said yes, then praise the Lord. If she said no, then praise the Lord anyway. He didn't feel all that comforted at the moment, but it was the best answer he could come up with and probably one that the rest of the deacons at First Church would have approved.

All in favor?

"Aye." He gave the barn one last look as he jumped back in the truck, jammed the gearshift into first, and hurried down Fishtrap Creek Road. He figured he'd better hustle—Jed Vanderstraat or no Jed Vanderstraat— or he'd lose his nerve. Shoot, Jed was probably home eating dinner with his family, not lurking about for speeders. A couple of minutes later, still praying that God had predestined Joan to forget all about his tardiness, Gerrit screeched around the corner onto Joan's street.

"What in the world?" He slammed on the brakes, glad he'd had them serviced recently. Or maybe that had been back when Warney was a little kid. Which, come to think of it, probably meant the brakes had been serviced sometime in the last century and maybe not so recently after all. But he didn't have time to worry about brake jobs just then, focused as he was on not rear-ending the Van Dalen Fire Department's bright red ladder truck. When he saw he couldn't stop in time, he did the next best thing, swerving to the side at the last minute, jumping the curb, and plowing into the corner of Lulu DeLeeuw's tulip bed.

Missing the ladder truck was good. Plowing into Lulu's tulips, not so good.

Even worse than dispatching a few of the neighbor's flowers, though, was the fact that Van Dalen's fire department had surrounded Joan's little house with what seemed to be about every piece of their equipment. Besides the ladder truck, they'd called out the big pumper (new in '72, but still as shiny now as then), the chief's red and white SUV, and an ambulance. Never mind the truck and light display. This was very, very not good.

"Maybe it's just a drill," he told himself as he jumped out of the truck and started running for the house. The black smoke he saw pouring out of Joan's open kitchen window told him otherwise. So did the bevy of neighbors standing on Joan's front lawn. He recognized all of them—including Lulu, of course, and one of Joan's young piano students. One person was even holding an armful of sheet music, as if she'd thought the house were about to burn to the ground. Of course, Lulu came at him first, fire in her eyes. Funny thing was, she didn't even seem to notice what he'd done to her flowers.

"I saw the smoke and just knew something terrible was happening. So

I called 911." Now she was hyperventilating, too. Good thing the ambulance was here already.

Gerrit held up his hand and kept walking.

"Joan!" he shouted even before he'd reached the open front door. Two burly firefighters in full rescue gear met him on their way out.

"Whoa! Hang on there, big guy." The younger of the two put a hand on Gerrit's arm as he pushed up his helmet visor with his other hand. "I think you'd better wait outside."

"No way," Gerrit sputtered, looking for a way around the two rescuers. "I'm not—"

"It's okay, guys!" a voice boomed from inside. "Let him in."

Chief Larry Spoelstra appeared behind the two men, and he waved at Gerrit to enter. At least that meant the house probably wasn't about to burn up. But what, then? The guy who had held him off shrugged and stepped aside.

"Sorry, Grandpa."

Only one little girl was allowed to call him that. The young bucks must have been new on the force, but that was happening more and more these days. Where did all these new people come from? Gerrit let the comment go and hurried into the house.

"Joan?" He could feel all his panic buttons going off and his heart pounding in his ears. "Are you in here, Joan?" And as silly as it was, he couldn't shake the memory of that little swallow gasping for life in the middle of the gravel road.

Joan was sitting at her kitchen table, hands cradling her cheeks and staring at the black mess on the floor that used to be dinner. Fire-extinguisher foam dripped from around the maw of the oven like toothpaste that should have been spit out a long time ago. The last of a cloud of black smoke was still clearing from the room just as the smoke alarm ceased its bleating. Gerrit hadn't even realized it had been on as he rushed to see if Joan was okay.

"I just feel so silly." She clamped on to his hand pretty tightly when he sat down next to her. "I did everything you aren't supposed to do: opened the oven, and then splattered sauce all over the place, and then I knocked the dish over, and it shattered, and the place almost caught fire, and—"

"You sure you're okay?"

"Just embarrassed, that's all… I can't believe all these men came just for a burned casserole." She shook her head. "But I suppose it could have been a lot worse."

"Amen to that." Chief Spoelstra entered, picked up his official-looking fire extinguisher, and headed for the front door. "Next time just make sure you're not late for dinner, Gerrit, so you don't miss all the excitement."

"Right." Gerrit saluted. "Thanks, Chief."

Joan thanked the man too, but Gerrit stared at the floor.

"I'm really sorry, Joan." The apology tumbled out. "But Randy and I got to talking back at the dealership, and I lost track—"

"Shh." She raised a finger for him to stop. "It's my fault, not yours."

"I should have been here a half hour ago."

"No. But you should have seen little Anna in here, screaming her little head off before the neighbor called 911."

"Yeah, I saw Lulu outside." Now he had to grin. "She must have told them the house was burning down."

The laugh was a good way to ease the stress of the moment. And just looking at Joan Horton cracking jokes in her mess of a kitchen made Gerrit all the more sure of his decision.

Chapter 3

I worry that the person who thought up Muzak
may be thinking up something else.
—LILY TOMLIN

*I*t's going to have to wait, Gerrit told himself. But the excuse didn't fly. Because "it" had already waited way too long. Instead, his mind returned to the crazy little swallow knocking itself out on his fender. The bird, the bird…

Oh, please. What does a stunned swallow have to do with anything? Gerrit would not even try to understand. He didn't have to. He knew he could not wait another minute.

"Joan, I—" His tongue got in the way.

"Hold on to that thought," Joan told him, raising a hand. "I need to go find Anna and apologize."

"Sure." He swallowed hard. "Take your time. I'll just clean up a little bit here."

He puttered in the kitchen for a few minutes, scraping something charred out of the foamy mess and flicking it into the garbage. That would have been his dinner, he supposed.

"Okay, now." Joan reappeared at the kitchen doorway. "I'm sorry. Where were we?"

"You look pretty good for someone who just nearly burned down her house."

A smiled flickered at the corners of her mouth, but she wiped at a tear. "It's all fake."

Her shoulders sagged as she said it, and Gerrit knew it was the first genuine Joan he'd seen since he arrived. She took a step toward him, and he wrapped his arms around her shoulders before her knees noodled.

"I'm sorry," he told her again, as her tears started flowing. "I'm really sorry. I should have been here."

"You keep saying that, but it's not true." Her breaths came in ragged puffs, and she let her tears soak into the shoulder of his plaid shirt. Which he didn't mind. "It was strange, but—"

"But what?"

She pulled back her head to look at him. "You're not going to think I'm a crazy non-Reformed Nazarene?"

"I already knew that." He hoped she noticed his grin.

"Well, it was almost as if I could touch God's protection right here in this room."

"Touch it?"

"Even when I was about to burn the house down." She finally pulled away from Gerrit to inspect the mess that was her kitchen. "I mean, I'm supposed to be an educated person, but when the panic took over, I just started doing all the wrong things."

Gerrit looked over her shoulder at the stove again. Boy, had she.

"So I know it's strange," she went on, "but it wasn't just in a fuzzy, far-off sort of way. God seemed to be right here. Do you know what I mean?"

"I don't know about that, Joan." He paused. This wasn't anything the Reverend Jongsma at First Church had ever preached on. "I just know I should have been here."

"There you go again," she told him. "Trying to blame someone, even if it's yourself."

"Well, it's true. If only—"

"If only? That doesn't sound like a good Calvinist talking."

"Thought we agreed not to get into name calling." He was only half joking. They had agreed, after all, weeks ago.

"Sorry." Joan held up her hands. "It just hit me, that's all."

"Besides, I dunno what being a Calvinist has to do with anything."

Well, Joan the Woman with Tears had made her brief appearance. Now Joan the Woman in Control was back. Never mind that it seemed like an awfully strange time to be having a conversation like this.

"I just mean that you weren't here and it's okay and we don't have to go back and beat ourselves up about it. I didn't mean anything theological, really. Except—"

Here it comes. She seemed to study Gerrit before continuing.

"Except it just surprises me you said that. Maybe you're not such a fatalist after all."

"Fatalist? *Hmph.* You make it sound deadly."

"Not deadly. It's just that…"—she looked down at his hands— "well…your *hands* are shaking! Goodness. I thought I was the one who was supposed to be in shock. Are you all right?"

"All right." He took a deep breath and started coughing smoky air. But he knew he had to say it now before things got worse and he didn't get his chance. Before he crashed into somebody's fender and knocked himself silly.

Now! Gerret held her shoulders at arm's length and looked straight in her eyes. Joan blinked back with a puzzled stare, her dark "eye-talian" eyebrows almost looking like question marks. The phone rang, but he wasn't going to let her go. *Nope. No way. Not this time.*

"Er…"—she wiggled a bit beneath his steady grip—"I'd better get that."

"Can you let the machine pick it up?"

Ring number two. Had he ever said that to her before? Not likely. Now her eyebrows *really* arched.

"Listen, Joan, if I don't say this now, it may never come out of my mouth."

Ring number three.

"You're acting really strangely, Gerrit."

"Okay, I know my timing stinks. And I wouldn't ask you this if I thought you were in shock or anything."

The answering machine clicked on at the fourth ring and they heard Joan's pleasant greeting in the other room: "You've reached Joan Horton's music studio. Sorry I can't come to the phone right now…"

The recording continued as Joan looked back at him with a quizzical expression that asked whether he wasn't a little crazy. The machine beeped.

"Gerrit Appeldoorn, what in the world are you talking about? You're not making any sense at all."

"Mom?" Alison's voice came over the answering machine. "If you're there, pick up. Mom? We heard there was a fire at your house. I don't know where you're at, but—"

"Hi, dear." Joan snapped up the phone and smoothed over her daughter's worried questions. No, it had not been a big deal. Yes, the fire department had taken care of everything. And of course Gerrit was here. She would call her back when she had a chance, and, yes, I love you, too.

Joan never took her gaze off Gerrit while she was talking. But once she had hung up the phone, she planted her hands on her hips and looked Gerrit straight in the eye. Funny how this woman went from chirpy "I'm fine" to blubbering female to back in charge, all in less time than it took to click from talk show to soap opera to reality show.

And this was some kind of reality.

"Okay, here's the way I see it." Now Gerrit was committed. He'd started plowing this furrow, and he would finish it. "I don't know how many years I can give you. Five, ten…maybe twenty, God willing. My Oma Lysbet lived to be ninety-seven, you know."

She smiled as if he always cornered her in her kitchen right after a fire and started boasting about how long his ancestors had lived.

"But that's not my point. About Oma, I mean."

She started giggling then, and goodness knows that didn't help matters any.

"I'm not sure what's so funny," he told her, suddenly wishing he could be someplace else.

"*You're* funny, Gerrit. I don't know if I've ever seen you act this way. Reminds me of…"—she giggled even more—"reminds me of Lenny Lockheart asking me to the prom in the tenth grade. That poor boy nearly fainted, he was so nervous. You're not going to faint, are you?"

No guarantees. This was getting ridiculous. Just then Gerrit was pretty sure he knew exactly how Lenny Lockheart had felt. He was almost convinced that Joan Horton knew every word he was trying to say before he said it. But he wasn't finished yet. He stuffed his hands in his jeans pockets to keep them from shaking even more.

"Listen, I've only done this once before in my life, and that was so long ago it doesn't count. So it's not like I have a lot of practice at it."

"That's okay." She shrugged. "I suppose no one's an expert."

An expert in what? Finally he figured out what to do with his hands: he took hers and tried to remember everything he had told the Lord, everything he'd practiced in front of the mirror the night before. *One more breath should get me through this.*

"Joan, listen. I've gone round and round about it, prayed about it till my knees wore out. But the thing is, I love you, and I'd like you to marry me."

Joan caught her breath and looked at him as if there would be more to come. For a long moment a shadow crossed her face, as if she was trying hard to think of a nice way to let him down gently. Here's where she would say: "That's really sweet of you, but…"

He could see it written all over her face. To be honest, it was really no surprise. He knew he wasn't much of a catch. In fact, when a person really thought about it, what would a sophisticated New York City piano professor like Joan Horton see in a washed-up, retired dairy farmer like himself? Really. What was he thinking? Only problem was, this tractor had no reverse. So he cleared his throat and wished he hadn't opened his big mouth and ruined everything. Shoot, it probably hadn't come out quite the way he'd rehearsed it. He'd come this far, though, so he decided to give her a fair chance to turn him down. He dropped her hands and felt the little blue feather in his pocket, thinking maybe it hadn't been a sign from the Lord after all.

"What I mean to say is"—he stumbled on, now in obvious pain and pulling at what was left of his hair. *One last shot*—"no use waiting around while we both get older and older. Alone, I mean. So, you wouldn't consider marrying me, would you?"

"Yes." Joan didn't hesitate this time; she just smiled and nodded. The shadow across her face disappeared like a summer thunderstorm. "Although you've got a lot of nerve, mister, taking advantage of my emotional frailty."

"You didn't say yes?"

"I said yes."

"I mean, you can think on it some if you want. Pray on it."

"I have done both. I just wasn't expecting you to ask tonight. But the answer is still yes."

"If you need more time—"

"Gerrit Appeldoorn!" She roped her arms around his neck and drew him in. "How many times do I have to tell you? Yes. Yes. Yes."

It wasn't supposed to be this easy. And it wasn't that the kiss startled him—or even the warmth behind it. He supposed it was okay to enjoy a kiss with the woman who had just accepted his proposal of marriage. More than okay. But he nearly bit his own lip when a voice boomed through the living room.

"Mrs. Horton? One thing I forgot to—*oh!*"

And Gerrit wasn't sure which was redder, Larry Spoelstra's fire truck or his cheeks. The guy would've spun on his heel and run if Joan hadn't said something.

"That's all right, Chief Spoelstra." Joan took a step back and dropped her arms. Gerrit might have strangled the chief if the man hadn't just come to Joan's rescue.

"Sorry to…uh…interrupt," Larry stuttered and looked at his boots. "The front door was still wide open, and I wanted to check to make sure everything was still out, you know. Sometimes an ember—"

"It's not a problem." Joan still wore the hint of a smile she'd been wearing since Gerrit had arrived, as if she found stuttering men amusing. "It's all out."

"Good." The chief seemed happy enough to leave.

"There is one thing you *can* do." Joan held up a finger as if she'd just remembered. Chief Spoelstra stopped. "You can be the first to congratulate us."

"Sure thing…er…pardon? Congratulations?" The chief wrinkled his brow. "For what?"

Gerrit couldn't just stand there and let her say it all. *Oh, man. Is it going public already?*

"We're getting—" he began.

"Married," Joan finished.

Wasn't that how old married people talked? One person starts the sentence, and the other one finishes?

"Well, how about that?" A grin spread across Chief Spoelstra's face. He grabbed Gerrit's hand and Joan's and pumped both of them up and down. "About time! And how about that? I'm the first to know."

"But not the last," Gerrit muttered.

The chief held up his hand when his radio crackled. "We're UC out here at Horton's, and I'm RTQ," he told the dispatcher, after which his radio squawked and hissed.

Gerrit had no idea how anybody could ever communicate with those contraptions, especially not in those silly codes they used. "Why don't you just say it's 'under control' and you're 'returning to quarters'?" mumbled Gerrit. Under control, he knew, meant a false alarm.

Larry ignored the question or didn't hear. He happened to be the grand poohbah at the local Society of Benevolent Camels, so secret codes probably made a lot more sense to him. Sort of. Larry paused and squeezed the Talk button once again.

"Say, Cheryl, I was just following up the Code 2 with Joan Horton." He pointed at Joan, who was dropping an envelope from her pocket into the trash. "Who I just found out is finally gonna marry Gerrit. Officially, I mean. Funny thing is, she's even A&O."

This is a joke, right? A&O?

"What are you talking about, A&O?" Gerrit challenged him.

"Awake and oriented."

Larry grinned and headed for the door before Gerrit could swat him on the helmet. Within seconds the news would be broadcast to half of Van Dalen, and it probably wouldn't take much longer to reach the other half.

Joan had said yes, all right. But thanks to Larry Spoelstra, this was *not* the way Gerrit had planned it.

Chapter 4

Life can't be all bad when for ten dollars
you can buy all the Beethoven sonatas
and listen to them for ten years.
—WILLIAM F. BUCKLEY JR.

*I*t feels as if we ought to be out celebrating." Joan swiped at a wisp of hair as she picked through the charred mess in her kitchen.

"You mean celebrating that your house didn't burn down?"

"Not exactly."

Gerrit picked up a wad of dripping paper towels and dropped it into her kitchen trash bucket. This was nothing compared to what it could have been. But what a mess! The smoke had probably damaged half the house. He had no idea how people cleaned up after an even bigger fire.

"I meant celebrating. You know, getting engaged, getting married?" She looked at him sideways, and he almost laughed at the black war paint on her cheek and forehead. So he'd just hit sixty, and she was pushing it. But right then, you could have fooled him.

"Here, you've got—" Gerrit reached out to rub the smudge off Joan's cheek with his finger. Only problem was, his finger was just as dirty. "Uh… you've got a little more ash on your face than you did before. Sorry about that."

She peered at her reflection in the chrome handle of her refrigerator, then laughed. "Are you trying to fix my makeup, Mr. Appeldoorn? Because if you are, I don't think it's working."

And now they both had to laugh.

"Dinner at the Windmill?" he asked her, but she had already disappeared for the bathroom.

"All right, then." Now he was talking to himself mostly. "I'll get the rest of this stuff out of here."

Easier said than done. Joan's glass casserole had cracked from the heat, several potholders had blackened, a couple of plastic plates had melted, and three place mats were now full of black holes. All that from an overcooked casserole? The fire-extinguisher foam was another thing altogether. He mopped up as much of that goop as he could with a couple more paper towels before sticking the whole smelly, foam-covered mess in a trash bag and heading outside to the garbage can.

"Remind me never to have a fire," he told himself just as a pickup truck pulled into Joan's driveway. Ben Kootstra rolled down his window.

"Hey, Gerrit!" Ben hollered. "Congratulations!"

"Yeah? Congratulations for what?"

Surely word hadn't gotten around quite *this* fast. But when Gerrit heard the squawk of Ben's scanner, which was mounted on the dash of his truck, he knew exactly what had happened.

Ben grinned. "No secrets around here, you know."

That was for sure. And if everybody in the neighborhood hadn't heard about the engagement yet, Ben Kootstra was going to do his best to change that with his bullhorn voice. Gerrit frowned but didn't answer.

"Oh, come on, Gerrit. I just meant what took you so long to propose?"

"How am I supposed to answer that?" Gerrit tried not to snap as he did his best to keep the trash bag from spilling.

"Whoa there, buddy. Didn't mean anything by it."

Gerrit supposed not. He just wasn't sure he liked the way town gossip spread, or how fast. Probably all the guys down at Karol's Koffee Kup had already been discussing the matter, maybe even taking bets. "Two to one that Gerrit Appeldoorn goes another month before he asks his girlfriend to marry him."

"Hope you didn't lose your shirt," Gerrit mumbled.

"You say something, Gerrit?" Ben stared at him with a blank expression on his face.

"Never mind. I'm just feeling a little out of touch is all. Maybe I should stop by the Kup more often."

"Yeah, you should. You've been spending way too much time at your girlfriend's—I mean your fee-ahn-say's place. Next time you ought to find someone who…" Ben's voice trailed off as he probably bit his tongue.

"There's not going to be a next time, Kootstra. Two weddings in one lifetime is more than enough for this guy. This is it." Gerrit was about to comment on the fact that Ben had been divorced—twice—but decided to let it go.

A little red in the face, Ben put his truck in gear.

He should be embarrassed! Gerrit thought.

Ben saluted as he made his exit, only this time his voice sounded a little relieved. "I believe you, Gerrit. But I just wanted you to know I'll be there for you at the wedding in case you change your mind."

"That's comforting. I think."

"Just don't be taking out the trash *too* often, pal. Don't make her think you're her servant."

"That's not the way I see it, Ben. It's—"

His coffee-break buddy didn't let him finish; Ben just waved as he backed out the driveway and drove off. Gerrit stood alone on the doorstep, wondering how he might have finished his sentence.

"Congratulations again!" Ben's voice trailed away, drowned first by another squawk of the scanner and then the roar of his truck.

"Off to find another emergency, I guess," Gerrit mumbled to himself. "Those guys have a little too much time on their hands." He clamped down on the neck of the little trash bag. Problem was, Joan hadn't bought one of those heavy-duty bags they advertised on television. And just like in the commercial, his little bag had split at the seam and was spewing half its contents onto the driveway.

"Shoot!" He scooped up as much of the mess as he could—mostly crumpled, goopy paper towels—and tossed it into the bigger can. But the return address on a half-torn envelope caught his eye: "Gaylord Conservatory of Music, New York City and Chicago."

Hmm. A letter from the Gaylord Conservatory, a.k.a. the Gaylord School of Music. Well, nobody could ever accuse Gerrit of rummaging through someone else's trash. No way. But wasn't that the place Joan used to teach? *Right.* He fingered the envelope and wondered at the funny feeling in his stomach. Probably just a note about her giving up a cushy department head's job to stay here in Van Dalen. But that was last spring, and this was none of his business. He tossed the envelope back in with the rest of the trash, where it belonged.

Still…

No, he wasn't going to go picking through somebody else's personal stuff, and that was all there was to it. Not even if he was about to marry this person and they were going to start sharing bank accounts, bath towels, and a bed.

So would I care if she saw what was in my trash? Aside from the obvious gross nature of banana peels and coffee grounds and other items that usually ended up in trash buckets? *Probably not.* What would be so mysterious about a crumpled letter? He could guess what it said anyway.

It's either going to say, "Sorry you're not taking the job," or if it's a little older, it's going to say, "Hey, do you want this job?" One or the other.

Either way, it wouldn't be anything classified or top secret. If it had been, she wouldn't have just tossed it like a used tea bag. No, she was obviously just cleaning out her pockets or her desk or whatever. So what was the big deal? He glanced around before rescuing the envelope, wiping off the smudge, and slipping it open. There would be no surprises here.

Surprise Number One: This note wasn't as old as he'd thought. The crisp, crumpled stationery was dated about a week ago. Hmm. As he'd guessed, though, this was a "Hey, do you want this job" letter. Only it wasn't the job offer from New York, the one Gerrit had known about last year.

Which was Surprise Number Two. He reread the letter to make sure he was getting the story straight.

"Dear Joan," he whispered. If he said the words aloud, that would guarantee he wasn't making this all up. "As you know, our Chicago campus has been struggling lately, frankly because we have no one of your caliber on staff. I understand from Dr. Adelstein that you had personal reasons for turning down the New York department-head position last year, and I certainly respect that. However, I think you'll agree that this is the kind of school where your talents can shine once more. At the risk of sounding presumptuous, I believe this is where you belong."

The letter went on to list the benefits of working in Chicago, the piano classes she would teach, and more. But Gerrit couldn't get past the presumptuous line, and he narrowed his eyes at the challenge.

"How does *he* know where she belongs?" He forgot to whisper this time, and he heard Joan's back door squeak open.

"Gerrit? Are you talking to someone out there?"

"What?" He stuffed the letter into his jeans pocket before turning around. "Just myself. I…uh…I made a little bit of a mess here."

She looked at him a little sideways. "I thought I heard a car."

"Ben Kootstra saw me taking out the trash and stopped to harass me. Think he might have heard the announcement on the scanner." Gerrit straightened and clapped his hands together as he replaced the lid on her garbage can.

"On the scanner already? That means—"

"Yeah. People are probably going to be coming up and congratulating us at the restaurant. Sure you still want to go?"

He still wasn't sure she'd heard him before, about going out to dinner, that is.

"Do you remember the kitchen? And you're still asking me?" She smiled and took him by the arm. "Besides, it's not a secret, is it?"

"Well, no. I was just…"

Forget it.

Speaking of secrets… Gerrit patted his pocket to be sure that Joan couldn't see what he'd just hidden there. Probably with all the excitement, she just hadn't found the right time to say anything about the job offer. *That's it. Too much excitement.*

He promised himself he'd let her be the first to bring it up.

Chapter 5

'Twas not my lips you kissed—but my soul.

—JUDY GARLAND

In Jesus's name, amen." Gerrit finished praying over their Windmill Grill dinner plates, and Joan looked up just in time to see a couple at the next table smiling and staring.

"Don't look now," Joan whispered between her teeth, "but do we know those people across the aisle?"

Gerrit didn't even need to look. "Sunday-school superintendent at First Church," he whispered back. "He was my Sunday-school teacher in the third, fourth, and fifth grades."

Joan shook her head. "If I live to be that old, I will still never understand how everybody's connected in this town."

"You've gotten to know a lot of people in just a couple of years," he told her between spoonfuls of his entrée, a Dutch meatball soup called *gehakt* something. It was clearly one of Gerrit's favorites, though Joan would never attempt to pronounce the name. She kept to the other side of the menu, where dishes were described in English. After everything they'd been through that evening, a chicken salad suited her just fine.

"But you're constantly telling me how everyone is related here. Did I tell you about the student I had, the one who didn't realize she was related to the boy who asked her out to the junior prom?"

Gerrit smiled as she went on, as if he'd heard the story before.

"Once they were on their date, they started talking, and it turns out they're second or third cousins." She shuddered. "They're actually *related*. I'm sorry, but that's just creepy to me."

"Happens all the time."

"It's still creepy." Joan looked up just in time to see yet another well-wisher.

"Ve are so happy foor you!" The gal from the Van Dalen Velkom-vagon, an older woman, would probably have pinched Joan's cheek if she'd allowed it. Instead, Joan smiled and leaned just out of reach. Not all Dutch people were this touchy. Of course, she had never married into a family like this. Or, as she was finding out, a community like this. Maybe she was getting more than one man in the bargain. It almost made her homesick for her reserved Italian New York cousins.

"Thanks, Winnie." Gerrit came to the rescue. "Where did you hear?"

Yes, where? Joan listened for the answer.

"Oh, you know." Winnie Vranken winked at them. "Vord gets around."

Apparently it did, just as it had in the days of telegraphs, party lines, and women at the well. Goodness, but these people knew how to spread the vord…er…word. And she and Gerrit had not finished their *oliebollen* pastries—of all the Dutch foods, these Joan could get used to eating—before at least two more people came to the table: a waitress and Reverend Jongsma from Gerrit's family church, First Dutch Reformed. The gray-haired man stopped by the table and rested a hand on each of their shoulders, as if he were blessing confirmands.

"God's richest blessing on you two," he intoned.

Joan wasn't sure what to say in response except "Thank you." And maybe the reverend didn't expect anything in particular, but he looked at Gerrit with a wink, told him he'd be speaking with him again soon, and left.

"You think they'll put out a special edition of the *Sentinel* for this?" Joan was only half joking. "I had no idea people would get so worked up about Gerrit Appeldoorn getting engaged."

"Sorry." Gerrit popped another of the golf-ball-sized puff pastries into his mouth. "I thought you'd be expecting it."

In reality, Joan had expected nothing.

Two hours later Joan peeked out through the curtains in her front room, feeling like a schoolgirl as she watched Gerrit's taillights disappear down Delft Street. No, she wasn't certain about a lot of things. Not like Gerrit was, at least. She had sometimes envied his certainty, but this time? She knew she had not felt this way for goodness knows how long.

Is this how it's supposed to be, Lord? The trembling would not leave her now that she'd finished dinner. What about the peace that passes all understanding? Didn't that come with the deal? Wasn't that supposed to descend on her as soon as she exercised a little faith, as soon as she said yes?

But it hadn't yet. So she settled for the warmth and the smile that this stubborn Dutchman had left her with. She thought of his care and patience, the gentle way he talked to his granddaughter, the gentle way he handled her own heart. One would think that a dairyman with such big hands would be a little more of a bumbling sort. But she couldn't help smiling when she remembered what he had become an expert at handling during his milking days.

"All right, then, Gerrit Appeldoorn. You want to marry me?" She spun around, trying her best not to feel young and foolish but not quite succeeding.

And yet…

And yet she already knew what she'd left behind, back home in New York. She'd known that for a while now. Only that didn't bother her much. She couldn't regret a moment of her past two years in Van Dalen. The time spent with Alison and Shane and little Erin. The time teaching her young piano students, seeing their love of music come alive. The time getting to know a gentle, wonderful man, and falling in love again when she never thought she could.

And yet...

Would it hurt to find out a little more about the job?

"No, silly," she scolded herself. This man had just asked her to marry him. She loved him—no matter how opposite he was to her in nearly every way. She'd said yes, and he lived here in Van Dalen.

She couldn't have it both ways.

And yet...

She paced the front room, leaning on the wonderful old piano that had once belonged to Gerrit's grandmother, the woman who had introduced him to music, a gift that had been reawakened when Gerrit heard Joan play. The spark had become a flame when Gerrit himself decided to take lessons. Now there was a common interest, this love of music, though of course that would not be nearly enough upon which to build a marriage.

Funny how everything ties together, though, from grandmothers to pianos to lessons to lives. How could she even think of trading all this for another teaching job? No, of course she couldn't. No question in her mind. Or if she were a little more honest with herself, not very much of a question. It was that "not very much" that troubled her, though, like a splinter in her finger that she couldn't see. This splinter, no matter how small, could swell and become infected, and she would cut off her arm rather than see that happen.

And yet...

She replaced the keyboard cover on the piano and wiped a bit of dust from the top with her finger. The job offer would remain in the kitchen garbage can, right where it belonged. There was no reason to pursue the offer other than to send a polite refusal. They would understand her position, wouldn't they?

And yet...

She should at least have the courtesy to thank Dr. Chambliss. What was she thinking? He'd been kind enough to offer her another teaching job, even after she'd turned him down before. That had been a generous offer too—like this one.

She could e-mail him back, thank him for his kindness, but politely refuse the offer. She could tell him that she was getting married instead and that she was completely fulfilled here in this small town, teaching first- and second-year students how to place their fingers on the keyboard.

He'd never believe a word of it.

That wasn't her problem. She stepped into her little kitchen once more. It still reeked of charred dinner and that horrible foam the firemen had sprayed all over the fire. *Never mind.* She'd just retrieve the letter, get Dr. Chambliss's e-mail address or perhaps his Chicago mailing address, and send him her note. She did owe him that much. Then that would be the end of it.

She owed Gerrit Appeldoorn so much more. This man who had patiently unlocked her closed heart, helped her laugh once more with his playful jokes and his one-liners. He had taken her for walks around town, listened patiently to her griping, sat for hours in her front room as she played—how could she not love him?

"Oh dear." She peered into the empty trash can under her sink and remembered Gerrit taking out the trash. That was another side of Gerrit she loved, the gentleman who held the door open for her, washed her dishes, and even emptied her kitchen trash can. Only this time…oh well.

Joan retrieved a small flashlight from her kitchen drawer before heading outside. There was no other choice. Feeling like a bit of a traitor for even considering the job offer, she would just have to recover Chambliss's note from the bag outside and send him a polite refusal.

As she opened the back door that opened to her side driveway, she jumped at the sound of a metal lid clattering to the cement driveway.

"Hello?" She leaned outside and called into the darkness. "Who's there?"

Two glowing red eyes greeted her, and one step down the stairs told her that she was looking straight into the face of a young raccoon. Apparently he'd caught the scent of a banana peel or some spoiled lettuce, and the lid must not have been secure.

"Shoo!" Joan stomped her foot and hoped the little masked beast wouldn't turn on her. Raccoons had sharp teeth, didn't they? Rabies, even? "Scoot on out of here!"

Though Joan had backed up just inside the door, the raccoon took one look at her and must have decided that his trash treasure wasn't worth going to war over. Nice that he'd hardly had a chance to really get into the bags and split anything open. He trilled once and exited the way he must have come: the little trellis that screened her garbage can from her next-door neighbor's kitchen window. Right now it looked like the perfect little jungle gym.

Joan counted to twenty-five slowly before she dared step back outside. When she heard no more noises, she descended the stairs to the trash can and gingerly took the edge of the top plastic bag between her fingers, wondering if it was possible to catch rabies without being bitten. She kept playing the flickering beam of the flashlight on the bushes and trellis and beyond to where the animal had disappeared.

"Nice raccoon," she whispered, hoping it would not be close enough to hear her. She held her breath and used the flashlight to dig through the previous day's garbage. That and the charred mess from today's fire fiasco. How she'd escaped without a scratch she honestly wasn't sure, but she had. *Thank You, Jesus.* And despite the fire mess that Gerrit had largely emptied here, finding the note should not have been that hard. The banana peels and the yogurt container were from yesterday, so the crumpled letter ought to be right there, lodged somewhere between them.

"Come on." She poked a little deeper, assuming that the paper had worked its way down a little. Who knew how much Gerrit had shaken the bag when he'd taken it out. And while it was very kind of him to have helped out, at this point she wished maybe he just…hadn't.

"Orange-juice can." She pulled it out carefully, just in case the letter had globbed onto it, then set it aside. She continued with the rest of the garbage, one item at a time. This was getting…

"Oh!" She threw the final item down, a plum pit she'd tossed in the trash more than three or four days ago. It did help to have the light from Lulu's window, however, so she could see a little better.

"Uh-oh." She heard the window slide open above her head and ducked behind the trellis as Lulu DeLeeuw clapped her hands to make noise.

"Shoo!" yelled Lulu. "Get out of there."

Joan froze, not daring to breathe. How much could her neighbor see? Maybe not enough to realize that Joan was not an alley cat or a raccoon. Through the trellis Joan could make out Lulu's frowning face, cheeks slathered with hysterically blue face masque and hair piled high in a turban. For once the woman's appearance matched her equally hysterical name, a nickname that obviously stemmed from her formidable Dutch surname. But as much as Joan wanted to, she could not giggle now. So she waited until her knees started to ache and the window finally rumbled closed. The light remained on, but—

"This is too silly," she declared, finally straightening up. Her neighbor could either see her or she couldn't. What did it really matter? But Joan looked down at the garbage can and sighed. Maybe the raccoon had eaten her letter. Or maybe God was telling her to just forget about it. She could probably find Chambliss's e-mail address someplace else and drop him a line later. She didn't really need the letter anyway.

And besides, she had enough to worry about without digging through horrid garbage cans searching for a letter she obviously shouldn't have been looking for in the first place.

Chapter 6

Lots of people believe in God who are not crazy. Isaac Newton,
Bono, pretty much anyone who wins an award.
—Joan to her therapist in *Joan of Arcadia*

No, she *didn't* call me back!" Alison balanced little Erin on her hip while trying to stir the Hamburger Helper, which probably wasn't such a smart idea on account of the hot stove.

Dinner, at this hour?

She looked at Gerrit with tears in her eyes. "I would have run over there myself, but Shane's not home from work yet, and he has the car. You're saying she's okay, though?"

"I just had dinner with her at the Windmill. She's fine," Gerrit said. "Her kitchen's a mess, but I know she'll call you when she has a chance. But listen, I stopped by 'cause I was wondering if I could ask you—"

"I'm home!" Shane called as he walked in the front door. He smiled when he saw Gerrit standing in the kitchen and opened his arms to hold his daughter.

"Hey, Gerrit. What brings you—?"

"Am I glad you're finally here." Alison walked over and gave Shane a quick kiss. "Erin won't go to sleep until Daddy's home."

"I came at a bad time." Gerrit started for the front door. "Maybe tomorrow."

"No, no." Shane rested a hand on Gerrit's shoulder. "Actually, it's great timing. We've been meaning to ask you about something, haven't we, Alison? Come on and sit down."

"Mom had a fire in her house," announced Alison, but Gerrit tried to play down the drama, doing his best to explain. Shane nodded as he listened to the story.

"Well, I'm glad it wasn't more serious," said Shane. "To tell you the truth, sometimes I wonder if her daughter might burn down our kitchen. Runs in the family, I think."

Alison's face paled.

"The Hamburger—" And she dashed back into the kitchen, leaving the men with Erin in the front room. Their little girl had put on a few good pounds in the past several months, and no wonder, the way Alison fed her.

"Did you burn something?" asked Shane, sniffing the air. Judging from his amused expression, this wasn't the first time that sort of thing had happened.

"No problem," she called back, banging pots and pans. Something sizzled in the sink. "Just a little dry. Gerrit, you're sure you don't want— oh, that's right. You've already eaten."

"Yeah, but thanks." Gerrit looked at his watch. Well, he'd *better* have eaten by now. These kids were on a different schedule.

"Don't worry about it, honey," Shane called into the kitchen once more. "You shouldn't be on your feet so much."

Alison said something about being right there. And Gerrit had to wonder...

"You said you had a question for me?" he asked his future...son-in-law?

"Right." Shane glanced toward the kitchen and shifted in his chair. "But it can wait. Did you...?"

Did Gerrit have something to say? Well, sure, but it could wait a minute.

"No, go ahead." Gerrit held out his hand. "You first."

"You men." Alison now stood in the kitchen doorway, mixing spoon in hand. "Why don't you just come out and say it, Shane?"

Shane paused for a moment, then pulled a letter out of his shirt pocket and tossed it on the coffee table with a sigh. Addressed to county extension agent Shane Nelson. The return address said Bend, Oregon. Looked official.

"I've been offered a promotion for another extension-agent position down in Oregon. It's a real good job, a step up, but—"

"But it would mean moving away from Van Dalen." Alison finished her husband's sentence. "Moving away from Mom and Randy. Oh, and you too, Gerrit."

Oh, thought Gerrit. *So that's what this is all about.*

"Well, yeah, that's all true." Shane took the ball again. "And I told Alison if she really doesn't want to move, I'm not going to force her to do anything she doesn't want to do. But we're thinking it's too good to pass up, and we thought maybe you would have some ideas or...I don't know. Actually, maybe you could tell us how you think Joan will react."

"I get it." Gerrit nodded. "Nice of you to ask me, but don't you think Alison might know her mom better'n me?"

Alison had stepped into the room to scoop up Erin, who was pulling newspapers off the coffee table, and she presented her daughter with a couple of animal crackers instead. This time she let her husband talk.

"We were just hoping for a second opinion, I guess."

They both looked at Gerrit as if they were expecting a word of wisdom.

"Okay." Gerrit leaned back in the couch. Maybe he could get them to talk it through. "So what's the good part about the move?"

"The money, for one thing," Shane replied. "We'd be able to get a bigger house, maybe with another bedroom or two. Prices are good down there. Alison's mother would understand."

Alison wasn't going to let that comment slide.

"That's just it. She'll smile and say it's fine. But it's still not going to be fine," she said.

"Well," added Shane, "at least she has her boyfriend."

Whoops. That earned Shane a disapproving glare from Alison. And by this time, Gerrit was beginning to wish that he hadn't stopped by after all. Now didn't seem like the best time to ask them what they thought of his marrying Joan. Was he just going to casually slip it into the conversation somehow?

"Be serious, Shane." Alison fired back. "We're talking about moving *away*. And what about Randy? He's getting really attached to his little niece. After what he went through—"

"Come on. We can't stay here just because it's good rehab for your brother."

She gave him another look; no one could mistake what she thought of *that* comment.

"Okay, sorry." He backtracked. "I didn't mean that. But remember, we'd be closer to my mom."

"Bend, Oregon, is not closer to anybody. It's farther way from *everybody*."

"I hear the skiing's great there." Shane offered up the comment as if it might convince her.

"Uh, listen." Gerrit raised his hands in a feeble attempt to referee the argument.

"No, really. If you look at a map"—Shane grabbed an envelope off the coffee table and started drawing—"with Oregon up here and Mom down here in San Diego, it's actually closer."

"All right." Alison shifted Erin to the other hip. "Technically it's closer, even though we both know it's really not. So the one pro you can come up with is…"

Alison's voice faded as she held the side of her head and leaned against the wall.

"Alison, what—?" Shane jumped up. "Is it…are you?"

She didn't answer right away, just handed Erin to Shane and lowered herself into the nearest armchair.

"Alison?" Gerrit didn't think she looked right either.

"I'm fine." She took a deep breath and put on a weak smile. "Just on my feet all day. You know how it is with women sometimes."

"You're not supposed to be dizzy." Shane's voice raised a notch, and he set his daughter on the floor. "You weren't dizzy with Erin."

Well, hold on, folks. By this time Gerrit could see what was going on in this home just as well as the next guy. A house with a couple more bedrooms. A dizzy woman. He looked first at Shane to make sure, then to Alison.

"Tell me I'm nosy, but…was that some kind of announcement?"

Shane lifted his eyebrows and looked over at his wife. She smiled shyly and nodded.

"And…" Gerrit went on, "I take it you haven't told your mom you're… expecting?"

She shook her head. "You're the first, actually. We weren't sure until this morning."

"Yeah." Shane grinned. "One of those little in-home test-kit things."

"Well, I sure don't know what you've been waiting for. Congratulations!" Gerrit chuckled and clapped his hands. "I'd say God's in control and His timing is perfect. And I've got a feeling your mother's going to see it that way too."

Little Erin didn't seem to care much about the news. She had been busy stuffing more and more crackers into her mouth. They all looked over just in time to see the sweet little girl lose the mouthful—and much more—all over the coffee table and Shane's promotion letter.

"Oh, sweetheart!" Alison moved in to help. Shane jumped to his feet and watched as if his daughter had just sprouted horns. Gerrit got out of range as quickly as he could and took the cue to head for the front door.

"Like I said…probably wasn't the best time to drop by. But I'm happy for you kids. Really I am. You want to tell your mom yourself or—?"

Alison glanced up from mopping little Erin's face.

"Tell her to call me!"

Right. She'd find out about the engagement from her mother, and that was probably for the best anyway. Gerrit nodded, looked down at his shoe where Erin had left him a souvenir, and let himself out.

They'd find out soon enough.

Chapter 7

I've had plenty of Joe jobs, nothing I'd call a career. Let's just say
I've got a healthy collection of name tags and hair nets.

—WAYNE FROM *Wayne's World*

"This is a joke, right?" A week later Gerrit waved a memo from the dealership's corporate headquarters as he stepped out of the employee lunchroom, which doubled as a conference room. "Tell me this is a joke."

The owner of the local tractor dealership could only shrug and shake his head as they walked down the hall toward the showroom floor.

"Listen, Gerrit, I'm really sorry. I know it's not your favorite thing in the world to do. But corporate says—"

"And that's exactly the problem." By this time Gerrit had found his soapbox, and he wasn't climbing down anytime soon. "I know I'm just your farm-boy sales manager, so what do I know, but seems to me like for the past few months, everything's been corporate this and corporate that. They don't give a fig about us, much less understand a real live customer."

"Gerrit—"

"And this proves it, Dale! How do those suits in Kansas City or Chicago have any *clue* what our farmers need here in Van Dalen? Have they ever even *been* here? Do they even know we don't grow soybeans and milo like they do in Arkansas?"

To which Dale had no answer, of course. Not that Gerrit gave him a chance to respond.

" 'Course not. They don't have a clue. So now they want us to sell our customers *credit cards* with a picture of a tractor on 'em when we answer the *phone?*"

"It's just a suggestion, Gerrit." Dale's voice had quieted to a whisper, and his face had turned a shade of pink. As the local owner, after all, he was the closest thing to corporate they had at Van Breemen's Tractor and Implement.

"Yeah, like 'Good morning, Van Breemen's Tractor and Implement. Gerrit speaking. Can I sign you up for a three-point-nine percent APR Platinum VISA from Elco Agricultural Machinery with a cute picture of a shiny new tractor on it, just like the one you'd really like to buy, except you're already up to your eyeballs in farm debt, but we don't care, so we'll help you get in deeper?' How's that sound?"

"I'll tell you what, Gerrit." Dale paused halfway down the hallway. "I know you have a lot on your mind with the wedding coming up and all."

"It's not the wedding that's bugging me. I've got that figured out, I think." Not that they'd set a date yet. Maybe sometime in August would be good. They still weren't sure.

"Right. But since you feel so strongly about this credit-card thing, just forget about it for now. I'll call corporate and get a...I don't know. We'll figure it out, okay?"

Finally Gerrit took a breath long enough to absorb what his boss had just said. Well, all right. He could live with that—for now. He supposed he was lucky even to *have* this job, though, of course, luck had nothing to do with anything. As Gerrit crumpled the idiotic memo, Dale rested a hand on his shoulder.

"Okay? I don't want my best sales manager having another heart attack on me."

"You mean your *only* sales manager. And the only kind of attack you have to worry about is Clem Vanderzee attacking us here in the showroom if we try to twist his arm with one of these lamebrain offers."

That got a laugh out of Dale, which was a good sign. So, case closed for now. Gerrit checked his watch, which told him it was just about lunchtime. He said good-bye to Dale and went to find Randy. When Gerrit stepped into the showroom, Randy stood up from his desk and came over to him, a huge grin all over his face and a hand raised for a high-five.

"So how do you like this, Mister Manager Man?" He slapped Gerrit's outstretched hand. "I just bagged a signed order for a brand-new 6420 with all the goodies. Haven't figured out my commission yet, but not too shabby, huh?"

"You're catching on."

The kid actually was. Pretty amazing, too, considering how messed up he'd been only a year ago. *Not bad. From suicide attempt to salesman of the month.* So here was a prime example of a prayer-chain success story.

"Thanks to you. I've got to tell you, Gerrit, this has been a good place."

Gerrit followed Randy's gaze out the window to the mountain in the distance. The gravel lot in front was filled with green and red tractors. The new models had been lined up ready to help work the valley's neat, green hay fields and berry farms, apple orchards and dairies. Van Dalen was home—the only home Gerrit had ever known. The same had been true for his father and his grandfather before that. He could understand how a kid like Randy might like it here. Pity the poor people who have to live out their lives anywhere else.

"Has been?" Gerrit wasn't sure whether Randy was trying to tell him something, whether his use of the past tense was intentional. The oversize American flag flapped from a pole just outside the door. Randy shook his head.

"I just want you to know I still appreciate how you got me this job. I really do. And I think it's very cool that you and Mom are getting married."

Gerrit grinned. Randy was a good kid. A little mixed up sometimes, and he still came up with some weird ideas, but a good kid.

"What are you getting at?" Gerrit gazed at the mountain view he never grew tired of seeing. In the distance Mount Baker rose like a giant upside-down snow cone over the lush green fields.

"I don't know... Just wondering." Randy said, gazing at the same view. "You ever thought of living someplace else?"

"Someplace else?" The question caught Gerrit off guard, and he snorted. Good thing there weren't any customers in the showroom. "How could anybody ever leave this place?"

"Oh, I don't know. You already left the farm, right?"

"Well, sort of, but—"

"And I was just thinking that Mom... I mean, this is a terrific little town and everything. But honestly? I just never thought she'd want to stick around here for the rest of her life. She's a city girl."

"People change," Gerrit told Randy, a little less than halfheartedly. He couldn't help thinking of the letter, the job offer. It would have been far better if he'd never seen it. As if Joan might change enough to want to live and die in Van Dalen.

"Oh, I know they do. I have. But I just thought when you get married, you might do new things together. You know?"

Gerrit wished he didn't. And he didn't have an answer, so Randy went on.

"And now that Alison and Shane are moving too—"

"That's not for sure, yet."

"I thought it was."

Gerrit still didn't know how to answer. What Alison and Shane decided was none of his business, really. Instead, he watched a swallow flit under the eaves and back out, showing a flash of color. "Did you see who's back?"

"Who?" Randy apparently didn't see anybody.

"The swallows. That means spring for sure. See?"

Gerrit pointed at the diving birds, their cartwheeling movements more elegant than any ice dance you'd see on television. Not like the Canada geese, who loudly announced when they were leaving town in the fall like noisy party guests laying on the horn as they headed home.

The swallows, on the other hand, were all about hello. *I'm here! Did you miss me?* they seemed to say. Gerrit pointed at one that spun into a tight barrel roll right in front of the dealership window, then flew low and tight over a big used John Deere.

"You ever see those guys close up?"

"Can't say that I have." Randy shook his head. "If you've seen one little bird, you've seen—"

"Nope. Not quite." Gerrit chuckled and held on to the feather in his pocket, the reminder of his own fragile hold on life. "Look. They're almost too quick, but if you don't blink at just the right time, you can see how they fly around with their mouths wide open right through those little swarms of gnats. See?"

Randy squinted at a couple of the new arrivals, then smiled and nodded. "Makes me dizzy to watch. But maybe you're right."

"So imagine that this is the ocean above our heads, and these little blue guys are whales, trawling for krill. Only these birds are a little smaller, and they're trawling for their bug dinner."

"Maybe you should be a science teacher, Gerrit, instead of a farmer. See what I mean? You could do other things. You ever thought of that?"

"I don't think so." But Gerrit smiled at the thought. Now *that* would have been a different life.

"Speaking of dinner, though, I've got a date tonight. I was wondering if it would be okay for me to leave a little early."

"Still seeing Terri Westervelt?"

"What do you mean *still?* We've only been going out since…well, for a few months, anyway."

"So, any plans?" asked Gerrit.

"You mean like tonight? Yeah, I was thinking I'd grab a DVD and—"

"No, no. I meant *plans.* Future stuff. You know."

Gerrit cleared his throat. Funny how he and his own son Warney hardly ever talked like this. Warney had never much shared the kinds of things Randy had shared with him. But Randy didn't seem to mind. He just kept looking out the window as he talked.

"Actually, I was going to ask you. Don't know who else to run it by. Mom would have a cow if I told her."

"Well, there's plenty enough calving going on around here without her—oh, forget it. What would she have a cow about?"

Randy paused. A loaded hay truck rumbled by, leaving behind slender shoots of hay as a sweet air freshener from last fall's second mow. "I was thinking of joining the navy."

"Oh!" Gerrit choked on his spit when he tried to answer, which brought Randy to his side.

"Breathe." Randy pounded his back, a little too hard.

"Easy…" Gerrit gasped, "easy for you to say." By that time he was catching his breath a little better.

"See, that was what I was afraid you'd do."

"No." Gerrit held up his hand. "I didn't mean anything like that. It was just kind of—"

"Random?"

"Maybe." Gerrit nodded and straightened up. "How old are you now?"

"Almost too old."

That made Gerrit chuckle. *This kid's too old? Right.*

"Hey, don't laugh." Randy's face turned dead serious. "I've been thinking about this for a long time. I see things on the news—the Middle East and stuff. And I just want to, I don't know, *do* something. Not just sit around in my La-Z-Boy and complain about things. You know what I mean?"

Gerrit nodded. "I think I do."

"So you think it's a good idea?"

"You're asking me? The old guy who's…uh…*marrying* your mother?"

Randy didn't answer but crossed his arms and waited.

"Okay, then." If the boy wanted advice, Gerrit could give him advice. "I think you've come a long way in the past year, since…you know…since you were in the hospital back in New York."

Gerrit hadn't planned to bring up that subject—not unless Randy did—but it was no use pretending that he didn't remember how the kid had almost killed himself a year ago.

"You know I'm not like that now. Like you said, people change."

Gerrit nodded but thought, *Do they?*

"If you've prayed about it," Gerrit told him, "and you think it's what God wants you to do, then do it. What does Terri think?"

Randy shrugged. "I haven't told her yet. You're the first."

"Oh. I'm honored, but maybe you should run the idea by your lady friend. See how she reacts before you make any decisions. I mean, if you're serious about her, then—"

"Yeah, I know. She might freak out even more than you did."

"I didn't freak out."

"Whatever. Promise you won't tell Mom just yet, okay?"

Gerrit paused a moment, remembering the week-old secret he was still carrying in his pocket, folded up, and he felt heavy with the growing certainty that Joan really needed to think on this opportunity. After all, she was—as her son said—a city girl. But this wasn't Randy's problem. Not even related.

"Got your word on it?" Randy asked.

"Sure." Gerrit shook his head to clear the thought. As long as he didn't have to keep his other secret much longer; one secret at a time was plenty. "My lips are sealed."

But he wished they weren't. Yet maybe there was more than one way to handle these secrets.

∽

"Oh, hey, Joan." Renée Timmerman looked up with a smile from the parts counter when Joan walked in the next afternoon. "He's on the phone, but you can go on back."

"Thanks." Joan smiled and started for Gerrit's little cubicle in the corner of the showroom, hoping he wasn't doing anything for lunch. But the young receptionist didn't let her get that far.

"May I see your ring?"

Joan only hesitated a moment as she felt for her left hand—just to be sure. "Uh…we're planning to exchange rings at the wedding, but—"

"Oh, I'm sorry. I didn't mean to be nosy."

"You're not being nosy at all. We just didn't think an engagement ring was necessary this time around."

And that was about all the explanation the girl was going to get. Renée was young enough to be Joan's daughter. Besides, there wasn't more to offer. Joan smiled and quickened her pace before Renée thought of any more questions.

"So you're saying there's a real possibility?" She heard Gerrit's gravelly voice echo around the room. "How real? I mean, assuming I was interested."

She slipped to the edge of the office partition. She knew better than to lean on it; she'd tried that only once. Gerrit was sitting in his swivel chair with his back to her and was speaking in a low voice.

"Sure I'd like to know more. As soon as you can—"

His voice trailed away when he turned back around to face her. He might have seen her shadow out of the corner of his eye or simply caught her waving her hand to get his attention. Either way, Gerrit would normally have smiled and pointed for her to sit in the chair in front of his desk. This time, though, his eyes widened and his face turned a visible shade of white. And he nearly choked on his next words.

"Okay, okay. Listen, there's someone here I need to talk to. Can I call—can I get back to you about this?" He nodded silently, thanked the caller, and hung up the phone.

"*That* sure sounded mysterious." Joan was smiling, but there was a question in her voice.

"Nothing mysterious about it. Just a…"—Gerrit's face turned even paler—"just a possible deal."

"Really?" She felt nosier than she had a right to. But why was he acting so strangely? "Where are they?"

Which seemed like an innocent question. Judging by Gerrit's reaction, though…

"I'm sorry." She backed up, not sure why. "It's none of my business."

"Chicago." He finally spit out the word as he went to work rearranging the piles of papers on his desk.

What? The thought crossed her mind that this was his strange way of trying to tell her about the missing letter. But no. She could not believe that Gerrit Appeldoorn would go rooting around in her garbage can. So she stood there for a moment while Gerrit's phone buzzed with another call. *Busy day.* He held up his finger and answered it as she tried on a few scenarios for size.

One, he knew nothing about the letter, and she'd just startled him in the middle of a phone conversation with a customer in the Midwest. That's what most certainly had happened.

Two, he'd somehow found the letter and knew all about the job offer at Gaylord, which she could hardly believe. After all, he hadn't said anything to her about it the past week.

Or, three, God was trying to tell her something about Chicago—in an odd, roundabout sort of way. Of course, she'd never known God to act in odd, roundabout ways. Mysterious, maybe. Hard to understand, often. But—

Gerrit held his hand on the phone receiver, obviously on hold for a moment.

"Oh, by the way," he told her, "I just heard back from Reverend Jongsma. He says the church is available."

"The church?" She shook her head, puzzled. "You mean *your* church?"

"Sure."

"Gerrit, we haven't talked about this yet. What about *my* church?"

"Yeah, I know. We can change our minds, but he says it's open July nineteenth. And on this kind of short notice, there was another group that wanted to use the building that day. But the reverend said we had first dibs, and he needed us to tell him pretty soon, so I sort of, kind of made an executive decision."

"What's that supposed to mean?"

"You know. Somebody had to decide."

"I understand that, but before we even talked about it?" This she could hardly believe.

He sputtered a few words in return, not really an answer.

"And what is this? About four months?" she asked. Nobody planned a wedding in that amount of time. Did he have any idea what it would take, even for a simple wedding? What was he thinking? "Are you—was he—kidding?"

"Seemed like plenty of time to me. And I was hoping we could just pencil in that date, but—"

"Gerrit, tell me you're not serious. Even if it is the second time for both of us, we need to do things properly."

"Meaning…"

"Meaning we have to send out invitations, line up bridesmaids and groomsmen, arrange for flowers, get dresses, rent tuxes, book a photographer, buy a cake, talk to a wedding planner… This is crazy, and I don't appreciate—"

He pointed at the telephone and paused before returning to his phone conversation. *How convenient. Now I'm the one on hold.*

"No, sorry," he told the person on the phone. "I was talking to someone else. Actually, we can arrange for delivery on that plow unit in July"— he ran his finger down a calendar—"the twenty-second. No, the nineteenth is my wedding.… Oh, thanks!"

Excuse me? Joan felt her jaw drop just a little, and she tried not to grit her teeth. Given the chance, she might have something to say about this as well. Executive decision?

"Sure, I can hold again." He covered the mouthpiece of his phone and looked up at her. "Did you want to run out and grab a bite to eat so we can talk about it? Or do you just want to elope?"

She ignored his last remark and glanced at her watch. As a matter of fact…

"Actually, I'd better get back. I have another student coming in twenty minutes. Maybe we can talk about it tonight. But you're not going to tell Reverend—"

Gerrit held up his finger and nodded as the person on the other end of the line obviously came back on. "Yeah, no problem. We can do that. And I think you're going to like the warranty it comes with."

Enough of this three-way silliness. She rolled her eyes and turned away just as Randy came up to her with a broad smile.

"Hey, Mom!" If he grinned any wider, his lips would fall off the side of his face. "This is just perfect! I mean, who would have thought that—"

"Do *not* tell me what's perfect and what's not. It is *not* perfect, and that's exactly the problem. No one around here is thinking."

She left him standing there with a gape-mouthed expression. She would deal with him later too. *Men.* Right now she had a piano lesson to teach—and she'd missed lunch besides.

"What's gotten into her?" she heard her son mutter.

And maybe she had a phone call to make—if she could only find the number for Dr. Chambliss. Perhaps he could tell her a little more about the job after all.

Just for curiosity's sake.

Chapter 8

The joy of music should never be interrupted by a commercial.
—LEONARD BERNSTEIN

*L*isten, I'm sorry." Gerrit didn't know how many more times he should say it. As many as it took, he supposed. "I shouldn't have said what I said this afternoon."

"You're right about that." Joan's ravioli was getting cold as they talked, but at least the Windmill Grill served a little bit of the Italian food she liked. The pasta was pretty tasty, and that was a good thing.

"I was just excited about everything, and when the reverend called to tell me that a date had opened up, it seemed like the right thing to do." He wiped a little marinara sauce from his mouth. The Italian food here was okay. Not as good as the good old Dutch stuff, but not bad, he had to admit.

Good thing Joan wasn't staring bullets at him anymore, at least not here in public. She'd finally uncrossed her arms too. He'd learned at the tractor dealership that when a customer finally uncrossed his arms, nine times out of ten he was ready to make a deal. Only this was no customer, and Joan Horton wasn't buying a tractor. *No deal.*

"You can't blame me for being eager about it, can you?" He held his breath and waited, one toe out of the doghouse. And finally…there it was!

The hint of a New York smile. But only a hint.

"I just need to be a part of these decisions, Gerrit. No more of this executive stuff."

"I'm sorry." *One more time.* "Maybe we both need to be more up front with each other."

She started to nod, then seemed to catch herself and look at him a little sideways. He hadn't been planning to slip this in about the secrets and all, but maybe now was the time. He still had the envelope with the letter from Gaylord, after all.

"Listen." He decided to grovel a little. "I know I made a mistake arranging for us to get married at First Church. Maybe we should just have the ceremony out by the log cabins at Pioneer Park."

"No!" Joan's eyes blazed. "I mean, it's important to me that we get married in a church; it's a statement. Don't you think?"

"I don't know if the kids would agree with you, but sure."

"Well, the kids aren't getting married."

"Then how about your church?" Gerrit thought he'd better ask. "I'm willing—"

"That's sweet of you." Finally she smiled and delicately forked a bite of her dinner into her mouth. The ravioli definitely would have tasted better hot. "But I've thought about it. With all the people in town who are related to you, my church isn't going to be big enough. So even if we wanted to, we couldn't have it at Cornerstone Church of the Nazarene."

"Okay." *One down; one more to go.* "So what about July nineteenth?"

"I've thought about that, too."

"And?"

"And I am not interested…"

Uh-oh.

"…in a long engagement either."

"You're not?" He finally breathed. "I mean, of course not. Long engagements are for the birds."

"I agree. Just don't make any more of those executive decisions without talking it over with me first."

So now she was playing with his mind. He reached over and stopped her fork in midair.

"Wait a minute. After all that, now you're okay with getting married in July *and* at First Church?"

"Where you go I will go, and where you stay I will stay." Her eyes sparkled as she recited the verse from the book of Ruth. "Your people will be my people and your God my God. Where you—"

"I get it." He held up his hand. No need to finish the phrase with the part about "Where you die I will die, and there I will be buried." But now that he had the chance, he might as well ask.

"So does that mean I should tell Reverend Jongsma that you're interested in attending a membership class?"

She choked on her ravioli and took a big gulp of water. "That's not what I said, Gerrit."

"Just thought I'd ask."

"Fine." Her eyes narrowed. "But I haven't changed what I believe. I mean, we're on the same page when it comes to the fundamentals of the faith." She ticked them off on her fingers. "The authority of Scripture, who Jesus is, the Virgin Birth, the Trinity—all that. But on so many of the other issues that Christians have always debated, you're on one side and I'm on the other."

Gerrit chewed for a long moment while she went on.

"What I need to know is, if that never changes, are you going to be okay with that? Or do you still think you're going to convert me to Reformed theology?"

The very Dutch-looking older couple at the next table glanced over at them with widened eyes, and Gerrit leaned forward to whisper a warning through his napkin.

"You might want to bring it down a notch, Joan. That's Norm Van Dijk sitting over there."

Her puzzled expression told him she didn't know Norm Van Dijk from Adam.

"He's on staff at Third Reformed. Active in the local pastors' round table."

Joan nodded as she pressed her lips together and rubbed her forehead. Lowering her voice, she continued. "Fine. But I don't want you thinking we're unequally yoked or anything like that."

"I never said such a thing."

"You implied it."

"Okay." He held up his hands in surrender. "We've been around and around the block on this stuff, and I think you're right."

"You do?" She almost dropped her fork.

"I mean, no, I don't think you're *right*-right. Just that you're right that we're probably not going to agree on every point of theology beyond the essentials."

"Well, that's a relief to know. I wasn't sure I wanted to get into another Scripture-throwing contest with you."

"Why not?" He grinned. "Afraid you're going to lose again?"

"Excuse me?"

This is a challenge, right?

"All right, then. So what if I say, 'For many are invited, but few are chosen'—Matthew 22:14. Then you say…"

"That's easy. I just quote you John 3:16—'For God so loved the world that he gave his one and only Son, that whoever believes in him shall not perish but have eternal life.' So there."

"Hmm. Then what if I say 'All that the Father giveth me shall come to me'—John 6:37. Then you say…"

Joan hesitated a moment, as if trying to remember. But finally she smiled and tossed back her quote. "How about God 'wants all men to be saved and to come to a knowledge of the truth.' It's in the Bible some- where. Not sure of the chapter and verse."

"What does that say about women, I wonder?" Gerrit teased.

"I was being serious. Now you're being silly. And your verses are all out of context."

"Sorry. But I suppose we could keep lobbing Scripture at each other or…"

"Or we can find another way to approach this."

"What are you saying?"

Now she leaned forward, not caring that Norm Van Dijk was still watching them out of the corner of his eye. "I'm saying that maybe we need to get rid of the labels. Have you ever looked at it that way?"

Now it was Gerrit's turn to act confused. He shook his head.

"I'm saying that if someone pressed you into a theological corner, you'd call yourself a Calvinist."

"Obviously," he nodded. "Card-carrying, five-point."

She closed her eyes for a second but kept going. "And in the denomination I grew up in, most of the folks would call themselves good Arminians, right?"

"That's what you tell me."

"So what if…just what if you changed your thinking a little bit on one of the points? Could you still call yourself a Calvinist?"

He scratched his head, trying to see where she was going with this. Wasn't sure he liked it. But she wasn't going to let him answer.

"So here's my idea. We drop the labels from now on. I mean, except Christian. We look for the truth in the Bible, wherever that takes us. And we don't worry if we would end up in the Calvinist or the Arminian camp, because in the end it really doesn't matter about camps and clubs and labels and titles, because what good does it do anyway?"

Preach it, sister. For a moment he looked at her and almost wished First Church would allow women preachers. *Almost.* Now she held out her hand, and here was her real challenge. Not the Calvinism-Arminian theological thing. Not at all. This was precisely what he loved about this woman: He didn't know anyone else who would have pushed him this way—and won.

"I'll listen to you," she said. "And I mean *really* listen, not just circle my wagons and hang on to my precious man-made ideas."

"That's it?"

"Half of it. The other half is that you listen to me the same way. Oh, and don't forget. None of those silly labels." She cocked her head to one side. "Deal?"

Gerrit felt Norm's eyes watching him from the other table. Or maybe everyone else in the restaurant was staring too. But Joan made a lot of sense. How else was this relationship going to work, if not like this? She might not always know chapter and verse, but she could fling verses at him just as fast as he could at her, and he was pretty sure he didn't want to live the rest of his life in a stalemate. He reached for her hand and couldn't help grinning.

"Good thing we don't have to raise any children in this mixed marriage. Two confused people are enough in any family." He liked the smooth feel of her hand. Always had. Strong but smooth.

"Children? You mean you don't want to adopt?"

Oh, come on. He dropped her hand and searched her face to see if she could possibly be serious. For a moment her expression didn't crack.

"Just kidding, farmer boy. At this point in our lives, I think grandkids are a much better deal."

"Right." He sighed in relief as she wiped her smile in a plaid napkin.

"You really didn't think I was serious?" When those dark eyes sparkled all over again, it made him glad she wasn't asking him to do anything else just now. Because, honestly, he was pretty sure at that moment he'd say yes, whatever it was. She had him all right. It did make him wonder, though. *What have I just gotten myself into?*

By dessert time, they'd steered well away from their pesky theological argument and settled into a warm slice of three-berry pie with a generous dollop of vanilla ice cream melting atop the golden crust. Gerrit had dug into the pie with gusto while Joan grazed from the sidelines with a long-reaching spoon.

"I thought you said you didn't want any pie?" He tried to fend off her spoon but missed.

"I didn't say that. I just said I wasn't going to order any if you were."

He was learning. Gerrit glanced to the side and noticed that Norm Van Dijk had left, which meant they were more or less alone in that corner of the little restaurant. Probably Norm would be making an emergency report to Reverend Jongsma, but that was okay too. Right now the world looked a lot better from where Gerrit sat—straight across from a beautiful woman who'd agreed to marry him and twelve inches above a thick slice of Windmill pie that was predestined for his stomach. He even thought the piano playing tonight wasn't too bad, as the strains of a show tune drifted down from the meeting room upstairs.

"One of yours?" He lifted his eyebrows with the question and tried not to talk with his mouth full.

Joan picked at a plate of diet low-carb sorbet, which, in a place like this, was nearly a felony. That explained why she'd snitched so many bites of his pie à la mode. She knew what she was missing, and she knew what he meant.

"No. Most of my students are beginners like you, remember?"

He nodded, looking for a way to slide his question into the conversation without making a fuss of it. The easy way would be to just pull the letter out of his pocket right now and lay it on the table. He wouldn't have to say a word; just lay it there and wait. But that sounded more like the way he'd sell a tractor. Lay your offer on the table, shut up, and the first person to speak is the loser.

Nope. He wasn't going to sell any John Deeres to Joan Horton. He'd talk this one through.

"You ever miss teaching people who can give you more—I don't know—more of a run for your money?" He watched her expression. "You know. The advanced students?"

She nodded, just barely. If he had been a lie detector, Gerrit might have recorded that brief instant when Joan looked away, when her eyes flickered. Only for a moment. *Shoot, maybe it's nothing.*

"I enjoy all my students." She licked her spoon. "Even bright second-year students like you. Look how far you've come."

"Who, me? I can barely play 'Chopsticks' without hitting the wrong notes."

"Gerrit Appeldoorn! That's not true and you know it. You're already playing level-three music just fine. You could always practice a little more, but *level three,* Gerrit!"

"How many levels is that from the college kids you used to teach?"

She wrinkled her forehead. "Please! You're not really comparing yourself to college kids, are you? I thought you got over your midlife crisis a long time ago."

He shrugged. If this was a fishing trip to get her to explain about the college job offer, maybe he wasn't using the right bait.

"Naw, don't get me wrong. I just wonder every once in a while. You know, you watch these kids, and they soak it all up. And me, my fingers just get tied up in knots. I mean, even if I had twenty more years to practice—which I probably don't—I'm never going to be a concert pianist."

"Well, that's startling news!" She laughed at that one. "You never told me you had those kinds of aspirations. I thought it was just for the enjoyment, for the love of music."

"It was just an example." He had to chuckle at what he was telling her. "Or maybe I haven't ever really gotten used to getting old. Thinking that I can't do anything I want to."

"First of all, you are not old, mister—unless you're ready to call *me* the same thing."

"Uh…hadn't thought about it like that." *Uh-oh. This could be a buzz saw.*

"But is that why you asked me to marry you now?"

"I almost didn't. Thinking it wasn't fair to you."

"Well, I hope you don't think you're depriving me."

"We're not kids, Joan. I can't offer you a golden anniversary. Probably not a silver one either."

"Is that what you're worried about? Anniversaries?" She took his hand and stared straight at him with that snake-charmer gaze that he couldn't shake if he wanted to. "You know you couldn't promise me that if you were still nineteen years old, my dear."

With that she started laughing, which only made the waitress, who was coming with their bill, pause and stare as if she'd approached them while they were praying for the meal. Joan didn't seem to notice.

"And I thought you were the Calvinist." She shook her head. "The fatalist. What happened to you? I think we've already started to switch chairs, and we're not even married yet."

"Switch chairs?" He took the bill with a nod to Maryanne.

"Musical term, Gerrit. You're playing my song, and I'm playing yours. And sometimes I think neither of us knows it's happening."

"Well, I know one thing." Not the way he'd hoped to steer the conversation. "This is going to be an interesting marriage." *If we can just get to the wedding in one piece.*

Chapter 9

Whatever our souls are made of, his and mine are the same.
—EMILY BRONTË

*Y*ou think this is funny." Gerrit pointed at his son from across the
sanctuary as Warney leaned up against one of the big, arched beams
that spanned the building. Warney straightened up and looked around in
his best Mr. Innocent act.

"Yeah, I'm talking to you." Gerrit wasn't going to let him get away
with it. "What do you say we switch places and you go through all the
dance steps here?"

"Whatever you say, Dad."

Gerrit looked over at his bride-to-be, then at Reverend Jongsma, who
was standing at the front of the church on the other side of the commu-
nion table with the words "In Remembrance of Me" engraved on it. Alison stood just behind and to the left of the reverend, holding Erin. Hadn't
they already gone through all this stuff once before? How many times did
they have to do this?

"On second thought." Gerrit held his ground. "You stay where you
are."

"Okay, everybody." Kirsten Smit clapped her hands to get everyone's
attention. "Let's run through this ceremony just one more time tonight,
and then I think we'll have it."

This young wedding coordinator sure took her job seriously. But
Gerrit supposed somebody had to. Warney sure wasn't.

"Yeah, if Dad can just remember not to come in too early." Warney managed a stage whisper loud enough for everyone to hear, and everybody in the sanctuary giggled. That young man was sure feeling his oats lately.

Well, if that's what it took. Gerrit hadn't been so worried about where he stood and how his feet moved since he and Miriam had signed up for square-dancing lessons. They'd actually been pretty good at dancing. Miriam especially. She hadn't been musical like Joan, but she sure had known how to move. But that must've been a long time ago, when the kids were still…

"Mr. Appeldoorn?" Kirsten broke into his thoughts like an alarm clock busting into an unfinished early-morning dream. "This is where you come in."

"Right." Gerrit shook his head to clear the cobwebs. "I do!"

Which got the biggest laugh of the evening—by accident. Of course, he wasn't going to let on; he smiled with the rest of them. *Yeah, I meant to say that.*

Joan looked at him then the same way she'd looked at him that night at the Windmill, when they'd first talked about the wedding. And he knew right then that he was probably marrying a mind reader.

"Your vows, Mr. Appeldoorn?"

Oh. The wedding coordinator pointed at the piece of paper in Gerrit's hand, the profound little piece of devotion he'd penned earlier that day during his lunch hour.

He folded up the paper and stuffed it into his shirt pocket. "I'll read it tomorrow," he announced. "Not before."

Miss Wedding Coordinator didn't quite know what to do with that.

"Way to go, Gerrit!" Randy yelled from the first row, clapping as if he were cheering on the Seattle Supersonics during a close basketball game. "You're in charge."

Gerrit wasn't so sure, but he knew he didn't want to read the life out of those words until it was time. If it was bad luck to see the bride before the ceremony, it was just as bad to read his speech before its time.

"That's fine." Kirsten turned to the reverend. "Isn't it?"

Reverend Jongsma shrugged and nodded. Give the man a Bible to stand behind, and he came alive. Other times you hardly heard him string together more than ten words at a time. But really it didn't matter much as they finished rehearsing the simple ceremony. The prayer of dedication, snuffing the candles, the special music Joan had picked out. Finally Bonnie Leenstra folded down the cover to the church piano—their signal to break camp.

"Um…before we break for dinner, could I make an announcement, please?" Randy joined the group at the front, his girlfriend, Terri, in tow. Joan and Gerrit parted to let him stand between them, facing the wedding party and Warney's family—Liz and Mallory. Gerrit turned to Joan for a clue, but she could only shake her head and shrug.

Wait a minute. Gerrit looked at the way Randy was holding on to his girlfriend, and now he knew what this was all about. Talk about timing. Maybe his mother getting married had inspired him to do the same.

Hope you know what you're doing, boy. But Gerrit knew he wasn't going to have any say in this.

Randy looked around at everyone as if they'd just caught him with his zipper… Never mind. Everyone waited. Mallory's stomach rumbled loud enough to be heard in the next county, and she clapped a hand over her mouth. Well, it was past suppertime, wasn't it? Gerrit gave his granddaughter a wink. *Just a few more minutes.*

"Uh…" Randy cleared his throat again, and Gerrit supposed he wasn't going for any public-speaking award this time around. "I just wanted to let everybody know…that is…"

He glanced at the waiting faces and tried to scrape a hole in the carpet with his toe. If people couldn't tell by now what the man was trying to say, all they had to do was look at the way Terri watched her man with tears in her eyes. *C'mon, folks. Have a clue.* These kids were getting married too.

"I just wanted everyone to know that I've enlisted in the navy, and I report for training at the Great Lakes Naval Base in a couple months."

Oh. Gerrit tried to keep his face from falling. He glanced at Terri's left hand just in case.

"It was a hard decision," Randy went on, "because the people in this church have been a real family to me. You all have helped me a lot—plus family, of course. But it's time to move on."

There was a pregnant pause.

"Wow, Randy." Warney was the first to pipe up. Give him credit for that. "That's pretty cool. But what about your job?"

"I still have to talk to my boss." He glanced over at Gerrit. "But I want to do something that matters. I want to be a part of something that's bigger than me. Like for my country. Terri and I both think it's a good idea for now."

Yeah, right. Gerrit sure wasn't going to say it aloud, but this made about as much sense as saying you're going to climb Mount Everest in a pair of shorts and a T-shirt. *We're getting married, except I'll be in the navy on one side of the world, and you'll be left here on the other side of the world, wearing your engagement ring.* Only she didn't seem to have the engagement ring just yet. Not even a Cracker Jack prize. How much sense did that make?

"Well." This time Joan just stood there like a boxing referee, holding on to Randy with one hand and Terri with the other. "This is a surprise. I..."

It seemed she'd run out of words, and it was Gerrit's turn to step in. He paused as everyone looked to him for a long, quiet moment.

"If we were at the dinner table, I'd say we should have a toast. So unless there's any other blockbuster announcements, Mallory and I are starving, and we should move down to the tables and get to it."

At that they all broke into applause, while Randy and Terri whispered to each other as if they were trying to decide their next move. Well, it was a little late for that, Gerrit supposed. The motion had already been seconded and carried. And all those in favor were clapping Randy on the back.

"We had no *idea!*" Joan didn't seem to mind being upstaged as she smothered her son with a hug. "When did this... When did you—?"

A quick glance at Gerrit made her stop in midquestion as her mind-reader mode kicked in.

"You knew." She didn't ask. Gerrit figured if he were in one of those churches where people waved their hands a lot they might have tried to tell him she had the gift of prophecy. For now it just felt better to say that she had his number. Or maybe it was just the look on his face, which he had a hard time disguising.

"He's your son," he shot back, and that was as good an answer as any. He managed to trade a knowing look with Randy as they shook hands over the top of the women. But maybe Randy wasn't through with the blockbusters yet.

"Aren't you going to tell them the rest, honey?" Terri wanted him to say more, and Gerrit guessed that this was where the engagement would finally be announced. Sure enough, Randy started to open his mouth as if he was going to speak. But he must have changed his mind—or gotten cold feet.

"I'm hungry too," he finally said and headed for the back door in the direction of the fellowship hall where their dinner waited. Terri clenched her fists, dabbed at her eyes, and hurried for the opposite door toward the restrooms. Joan pulled Gerrit to the side of the sanctuary by the folding seats in the overflow section.

Before speaking, she looked around to make sure that no one could hear them. "She's pregnant."

Just like that. How did she know? Terri wasn't showing. "Is that what you were looking at her for?"

"I hope it wasn't that obvious. But she is."

"How can you be sure?"

She bit her lip and the tears pooled in her eyes. "I wish I was wrong. Really I do. But I'm not. Can't you tell?"

"Nope." Gerrit shook his head. He wasn't the prophet around here.

"But did you think they were going to tell everyone they were getting married, too?"

"Well, sure. Maybe they just decided not to make a big announcement of it tonight."

"I don't think so." She dabbed at her eyes to keep her makeup from smudging.

Gerrit was glad he didn't have to deal with that stuff. Tears or makeup.

"All right. Here's the deal." Gerrit hoped it wasn't coming across as another executive decision, but somebody had to say it. "We don't know for sure, all right? And unless that changes, we just treat them like…well, like we always do. Right?"

Joan swallowed hard and crumpled her tissue. Gerrit took it from her and stuffed it in his pocket. Finally she nodded and closed her eyes.

"It's between them and the Lord. They're big kids, and for now we give them the benefit of the doubt. Okay?"

So there you have it. Gerrit wasn't at all sure whether he was doing the right thing, but did Joan have any better suggestion?

"Hey, you two!" Alison approached them. "I hope you didn't forget that this is your rehearsal dinner. We're starving."

Mallory came running over to her grandfather and put her arms around his waist.

"Are you kidding?" He squeezed Joan's elbow as he turned to the others with a big, quick smile. "You're not near as hungry as me. And we're having my all-time favorite dinner tonight!"

Which is what again? He turned back to Joan for help, but by this time he could already smell what was cooking in the basement church kitchen.

Right. Lasagna.

He took his granddaughter by the hand and headed for the stairs.

"So, come on, princess. You're sitting by your grandpa tonight, and we'll chow down on Italian."

And just for tonight they'd forget about all the secrets everyone would rather not know.

Chapter 10

Without love, what are we worth? Eighty-nine cents!
Eighty-nine cents worth of chemicals walking around lonely.
—HAWKEYE IN *MASH*

So he was a sixty-year-old farmer-turned-tractor-salesman whose farm had failed after his son took over. So his hair was thinning a little on top, and it looked a little like a weather vane when the breeze picked up. So he looked more comfortable wearing muddy black waders than a pressed black suit. Joan was almost surprised that he hadn't shown up for his wedding in his old milking uniform.

But today none of that mattered. This man was hers, and to tell the truth, he cleaned up pretty good. The trade-off? Well, it wasn't really a trade-off at all. *How could anyone compare the job offer of a lifetime to a lifetime with Gerrit? Ha!* Hers was the bargain, and she hadn't thought of the letter from Porter Chambliss in weeks. Or, to be honest, she'd tried not to. Not after she'd tried to find the man's phone number in a fit of exasperation.

But none of that, not on her wedding day. She smiled as she waited her turn to enter the cedar-ringed meadow at the center of Pioneer Park. As she looked out over the small sea of faces, she imagined that they were back in her own church home, back in the sanctuary. Never mind that gray clouds overhead threatened showers. Surely God would hold off the rain at least until this was all over.

"I can't think of a more beautiful place to get married, Joan." Shane bounced little Erin in his arms while Alison stood up at the front as the matron of honor. "And I'm glad Gerrit changed his mind about having the wedding here."

Meanwhile, the toddler was probably weighing heavily in her daddy's arms. Last time Joan had tried to pick up her granddaughter, she'd almost collapsed. Standing tall in his best black suit under an archway entwined with roses and morning glories, Joan's handsome husband-to-be waited in front with the reverend. His best man, Warney, stood waiting as well.

Shane was right. It *was* a nice place for a wedding, despite the overcast sky. Old-growth cedars hemmed them in on all sides, sending the notes of Bethany Klassen's flute soaring in a cascade to the center of the field, which was lightly sprinkled with wild daisies and dandelions. The campers standing off at the edge of the clearing must have thought so too. Joan noticed a mom holding her two little ones back in the shadow of the play set. Or maybe they were just disappointed they couldn't play softball in the field this afternoon. Well, they were welcome to stay for refreshments if they liked. Women from her church and Gerrit's had set up a half-dozen folding tables in a semicircle around the picnic shelter, and she could see the large cake unveiled on the shelf above the row of built-in barbeques.

Just beyond the shelter, she could hear the soft gurgle of Kelsey Creek, which widened out here after passing Gerrit's old homestead a few miles upstream. (Of course, everyone still called his farm the Appeldoorn place, no matter who owned it now.) The creek ran a little deeper here, which made it the perfect place for summer dips and baptisms. In fact, if anyone needed a good baptizing, she imagined it could be taken care of just fine. Her pastor, Kevin Gardener, sat in the third row back. He'd dunked his share of new believers here in the past couple of years. Of course, the groom's crowd on the left side of the grassy aisle wouldn't go in for any dunkings, but that was okay.

Beyond the creek a winding trail led to the edge of the woods and beyond that to the Middelkoops' berry fields, already nearly picked clean for the summer. Even now she could make out the lovely scent of raspberries, which reminded her more of a good milkshake than what it probably reminded Gerrit of. But that was the difference between the city girl and the country boy, wasn't it?

"You're next, remember," Shane whispered. It was a good thing to have her son-in-law here too. "You look great, by the way."

Oh! Delia Meijer at Delft Square Formals thought the light peach gown went well with Joan's complexion. Delia said she'd been jealous that Joan didn't need to go to a tanning booth with that Mediterranean complexion none of the Dutch girls had. Well, Joan supposed that's what God had given her, and she supposed it came in handy once in a while. Like now.

Randy strolled up from the side with a smile on his face, and Joan took his elbow the way they had practiced. She could not keep her mind from racing, from imagining little Randy as a four-year-old. The way his little hand used to feel in hers. *But my, his hand has grown over the years, hasn't it?* Now as he cupped his hand over hers, she honestly had no idea what had happened to the decades. The moves, the jobs, the Little League games…

Your father would have liked this place. She almost said the words but couldn't, and the stab of guilt at the unexpected thought made her catch her breath. But it was true, and she could almost imagine her Jim in the clearing, playing Frisbee with the dog, rolling in the grass like the camping kids on the fringes of the wedding, getting himself muddy in the creek. Like a kid himself, like Randy. And when she saw her son, she saw her Jim, so she let her mind drift for just a moment back to a small Nazarene church in upstate New York where Jim, with an impish grin and that sparkle in his blue eyes, was waiting for her in a white tux.

"You okay, Mom?" Randy whispered into her ear as he held on to her arm. This time it was Gerrit waiting for her, not Jim.

"Perfect." Joan answered truthfully, waiting for the music that would announce the bride's arrival. And the memory faded.

She closed her eyes and listened to Reverend Jongsma praying, his soft

Dutch accent echoing over the field as the flute had done earlier. Then he spoke about the joy and the *loaf* they shared here. That would be the *love*, but she'd grown used to the quaint way he said things. A few of her friends on the Cornerstone Church of the Nazarene side nodded and said "amen," which drew a couple of curious looks from the good folks on the First Dutch Reformed side. At least no one was getting carried away with "Yes, Lords." *Yet.* Joan could almost imagine some of the staid Reformed saints fearing a slaying in the Spirit, which would never have happened in her fellowship, but they didn't know that. She almost giggled at the thought. And with the final amen came Ashley Schoenmaker's soft classical guitar with the notes Joan had been waiting for—along with a screech she had not been anticipating at all. *What?*

Joan's heart leaped to her throat when she saw an exceptionally large crow soar with a hair-raising squawk from his perch in the trees straight toward the three-tiered cake with its little topper couple. *Please, no!* She opened her mouth and pointed, but nothing came out. And what could she do anyway? Thankfully, old Mrs. Norris noticed at about the same time. Joan had never seen the snow-haired reception coordinator for Cornerstone Church move so quickly.

"Shoo!" The older woman hissed and waved at the intruder. "Get out of there!"

No match for Mrs. Norris, the crow changed course at the last minute and returned to his perch to watch for another chance. Funny thing was, only a couple of people sitting in the back rows even noticed. Randy looked from the cake to the groom and back again at his mother.

"Would've been a bummer if he'd flown off with your cake, huh?" He smiled and cupped his free left hand over hers. "But right now I think somebody's expecting you up front."

Right. Mrs. Norris would protect the cake from bird attacks.

Joan swallowed hard and nodded, and they slowly stepped out onto the field as 150 witnesses rose to their feet. But she was far from counting.

She simply cut off the circulation in her son's arm and fixed her eyes on Gerrit Appeldoorn standing there in front of this mixed congregation in his dapper black tuxedo and charcoal gray tie, which was only a little bit crooked. But my, did he look good. And the music—well, they could have been playing "Tonight's the Night," and she wouldn't have known the difference. Not any more. She simply floated down the rollout carpet.

"You're shaking, Mom." Leave it to Randy to remind her of the obvious. She didn't answer but just smiled and nodded in a sideways kind of way at the people lining their way. And as much as she tried, she could not record the moment for posterity, could not focus on anything but the groom. And she knew she had not felt this way for a very, very long time.

"Wait till after the ceremony, Mom." Randy whispered in her ear. "You're going to like the surprise I have for you."

As her mind spun, Joan had no idea what Randy was talking about. Meanwhile, she was vaguely aware that Randy had kissed her on the cheek, and for a moment she couldn't let go of him as he embraced her. But eventually he steered her over to her spot on the platform, just as they'd rehearsed the evening before at the church.

What else did she remember? Precious little, except for the part where Gerrit was supposed to read his vows, the ones he'd taken so much care to write. She'd already read hers barely above a whisper, a short six or seven lines about how he had taught her the meaning of faithfulness, how much she loved him—just the way he was—and how much she saw the light of Jesus in him. She meant every word of it, but it was just as well that the guests couldn't hear much of it. This was between her and God and Gerrit Appeldoorn.

But now it was Gerrit's turn. She knew for a fact that he had sweated over his own little speech for hours, and, yes, that was sweet. But when Reverend Jongsma nodded at him to go ahead with it, Gerrit's face went pale and he patted his pockets.

"Uh...uh..." he mumbled, and it only made Joan more nervous than she already was, if that was indeed possible. "Dumb tux has too many pockets in all the wrong places."

From his right pants pocket he came up with his trusty Swiss army knife, which didn't help much in a situation like this. Warney gave him a moment and finally held out a folded scrap of paper.

"This what you're looking for?"

"There we go." Gerrit replaced his pocketknife and took the paper. "Trying to make me sweat, huh?"

A couple of people chuckled from the front row, but that didn't stop Gerrit from unfolding his script and clearing his throat. It was his turn to read.

"Joan, I'm not a writer, so I'm not sure I can really describe in writing what you mean to me. And it puzzles me sometimes when I wonder, what does a lady like you have to do with a hayseed like me?"

That brought a laugh from the audience, but Gerrit didn't look up. He only gripped his paper more tightly until it ripped around the edges and went on.

"Maybe I'll never understand the deep things of marriage, but I do know one thing: God brought us together, even if we came from different parts of the world, from different families, from different churches. None of those differences matter much today. What matters is that we share the same Lord and that He's given us a love we can share."

By this time the tissues were starting to come out. Still he went on.

"Joan, you brought the music back into my life in a way I never thought I'd hear it again. And while you know I can't promise you years, I can promise you all my devotion while we are still breathing. So in front of all these folks, let me tell you that I will always take care of you, no matter what. I will always protect you and honor you, and I will give my life for yours, no matter how old we become, no matter what we end up looking like. I promise you my heart—what's left of it. And wherever the Lord and the music take us, that'll be our home."

Oh, my. By that time Joan was trying unsuccessfully to keep the tears from smudging her makeup, and Alison handed her yet another tissue. The music, the rings, the prayer, the words from Reverend Jongsma—all of it seemed to blur until the part when the reverend told them, "By the authority of God and the laws of the state of Washington, I now pronounce you husband and wife."

There. Now all Joan could see was the sparkle in her man's eye. All she could hear was the unshaken promise in his voice when he leaned closer to whisper, "I love you, Mrs. Appeldoorn." And all she could feel was his gentle kiss...and the promise of more.

But this wedding wasn't over yet. Far from it. As the sun finally peeked out from behind the clouds, the newlyweds led their guests to the picnic shelter where Mrs. Norris had been guarding their cake against marauding crows and hungry children. The crow had apparently flown off to find another party to crash, and their guests enjoyed their fill of cake, meatballs, veggies, chips and dip, little pastries, sausages, and thick local ice cream topped with fresh local strawberries.

Everyone had to have a photo of the bride and groom feeding each other cake, and when the time came to toss the bouquet, Joan made very sure that all the girls discreetly backed away so Terri could catch it. She winked at her husband when all the bachelors did the same, leaving Randy to catch the garter. *There, how's that for a hint?*

Randy came by after a while with a well-loaded plate, and he smiled and shrugged. "Don't even think of sneaking off. Not before you see my present."

So it's apparently not one of the brightly wrapped presents piled on the nearby tables.

"You're not going to tell us?" Gerrit asked. He fished a bit for hints, but it did no good.

"Nope." Randy popped a strawberry in his mouth. "Not until it's time."

They had no idea when that would be, so Joan chatted with their guests and pushed thoughts of Randy's present to the back of her mind. Gerrit discreetly whispered people's names in her ear as they approached so she knew whom she was hugging. The process was so absorbing that she hardly noticed Randy and Terri stepping out into the green field and kicking off their shoes. That, it seemed, was Bethany and Ashley's cue to start the music once more.

Joan turned to see what was happening. "That's not what we practiced at the rehearsal."

It wasn't. Someone had discarded J. S. Bach in favor of a fast-moving Irish jig that would not allow anyone to stand still or just watch. The girls seemed to know just what to play for this occasion, and Joan noticed even Mrs. Norris nodding her head in time to the music.

"Do Dutch Reformed dance Irish jigs?" Joan wondered aloud. *And more to the point, does Gerrit?*

"Maybe we should find out." Gerrit held her hand as they stepped into the sweet-smelling meadow fringed with lush, green ferns. And to the happy sound of flute and guitar, they swung each other around, laughing. Their first dance as Mr. and Mrs. Gerrit Appeldoorn.

Even a gentle mist could not dampen their spirits. Dancing with her father, Mallory pointed up at a full rainbow now arched and sparkling overhead—a blessing God seemed to have created just for the occasion. Joan caught her breath in wonder. And as others joined the dizzying dance, she breathed in the colors of the rainbow, allowed the mist to kiss her cheeks, and smiled up at the face of God.

The quartet of big Belgian draft horses didn't seem to mind a little mist in the late afternoon air. And besides, Randy had rigged a canopy over the backseats of the big-wheeled wagon. Big scripted letters on the side read *B. Klopstra & Sons, Feed Delivery.*

They probably didn't deliver in this wagon, but Gerrit had to admit that it would be a classy ride for the couple of miles to the Windmill Inn, where they'd be staying the night. The *real* honeymoon trip—the one Gerrit had been planning for a couple of months—would start the next day. For now, though, how could he not look forward to their first night together?

"So, this is the surprise you told us about?" Joan asked her son as she looked up at the wagon.

"You're surprised, right?" Randy looked about as proud as a guy taking the wheel of a new hundred-thousand-dollar tractor. This one, though, came with just four horsepower and more reins than most guys knew what to do with.

"How'd you talk the Klopstra brothers out of their team?" Gerrit wanted to know. Bernie Klopstra usually won a ribbon each year at the Holland Days Parade, and most folks said he never let his babies out of his sight.

"I made him a deal." Randy grinned down at them from his perch. "He needed some work done on his old 3140, and I needed to rent a team of big horses and a wagon for a special occasion."

"Oh, great. So the dealership is paying to work on his tractor?"

"Don't worry, Gerrit." Randy held out his hand. "I've got it covered. All you have to do is help your wife get up here."

Gerrit could do that, even through the rain of birdseed. He winked at Shane, who was recording the whole event with his digital camera, and held Joan's hand as she climbed into the wagon. Gerrit clambered up after her and waved at Mallory. By this time his granddaughter was crying and laughing at the same time, but so was everyone else.

"Have a great trip!" Alison waved at them, and Joan reached down from her perch to take her daughter's hand.

"Do you know where he's taking me?" she asked.

Alison only zipped a finger across her smiling lips. "We've been sworn to secrecy."

"Hmm." Joan settled into her place with a mock frown. "Too many secrets around here."

Gerrit might have agreed, though this was one of his better secrets. She'd find out soon enough. The question now was, did Randy know how to control these four big beasts?

"They look like elephants." Joan held on to Gerrit with one hand and the wagon seat with the other. Gerrit had to agree. Though he'd grown up seeing these animals at the farm down the road, Gerrit still couldn't get over their tree-trunk proportions—the huge hairy hoofs and legs, their massive bodies and heads, the majestic way they moved. Then they did move, responding to Randy's shake of the reins with a flick of their giant tails and a jerk of their heads.

"Relax, you two." Randy wore his sure-I-can-do-it smirk when he looked back over his shoulder at them. "I can handle this. We'll have you at the inn before you know it."

"I hope so." Gerrit wasn't as sure, and the horses probably didn't appreciate the flashes going off in their faces. Of course, they probably didn't appreciate the shower of birdseed either. The Belgians snorted their disapproval and shook their manes.

"Isn't birdseed supposed to be some kind of fertility thing?" asked Randy.

Gerrit could see his bride blush. He poked his new son-in-law in the back. "Just drive, bub."

"No problem." But he still grinned over his shoulder.

Gerrit had to admit that Randy actually wasn't doing too badly with the team. *A little cocky, maybe, but not bad.* So as the horses headed down the county road at a brisk trot, Gerrit leaned back in his seat and let himself chuckle.

"What's funny?" asked Joan. But Gerrit wasn't entirely sure he could explain.

"I don't know. Here I am on my honeymoon with the most beautiful woman in the county. So I'm wondering… If I pinch myself just to be sure, would the wagon turn into a pumpkin?"

"Yeah, and I'm a mouse," added Randy. "So smile for the camera."

A little blue Honda pulled around them, windshield wipers keeping time with the *clippa-cloppa-clop* of the horses' hoofs. Cal De Vries from the *Van Dalen Sentinel* rolled down the passenger window and pointed a thirty-five-millimeter camera at them.

"Smile!" he yelled.

"Oh, great," Gerrit mumbled through his grin. "How did he catch up with us?"

"I called him." Randy waved for the camera.

"You're kidding me. You actually—?"

"Be nice," Joan whispered.

"Yeah, but how many pictures does he have to take?"

Only a few, actually. Cal waved back at them once he'd snapped enough shots for good measure, then he zipped past the wagon. Up ahead they could make out the slowly turning paddles of the Windmill Inn, right on the edge of their little Dutch downtown. Along the way Randy played tour guide.

"On the right, ladies and gentlemen, we're looking at the historic Dutch Cemetery, where they bury all the dead Dutch people. On the other side of the road is where they put all the folks who don't have "vanders" or other Dutch stuff in their last names."

Gerrit chuckled. At least he qualified for admission to the right side. And now, so did Joan—if they stayed here that long. For the first time in his life, he wasn't so sure.

"You'll still be here when we get back, right?" he teased his son-in-law. Fact was, Randy wasn't due to report for basic training at the naval base in Great Lakes until September. And they expected to return from the honeymoon in ten days or less.

"Depends on when you get back," Randy countered.

"You know very well he'll be here, Gerrit," Joan said.

"All right," said Gerrit, "but anything else you want to tell us before we leave?"

"Tell you? Like…?"

"Like if you're going to need anything before basic training, or what's going on between you and Terri. That sort of thing."

"I see what you're getting at." Randy let out the reins a little more so the Belgians picked up steam as they neared downtown. He paused for a minute. "But we don't really want to be talking about *me* now, do we? This is *your* time."

Maybe so, but Gerrit couldn't help feeling that this guy was planning a quiet exit—like he'd slip out the back door this fall without saying good-bye.

Joan gave Gerrit a worried glance but didn't say anything as the horses trotted even faster down Main Street, passing the post office—the Postkantoor—and the Amsterdam Lanes Bowling Alley.

"Whoa." Gerrit finally had to raise his voice over the *clop-clop* of hoofs. "No hurry."

Randy obliged by pulling back on the reins to slow the team. By that time they'd nearly reached the front of the Windmill Inn, a half-sized replica of a real Dutch windmill in Kinderdijk, Holland.

"Actually, Terri and I are fine with the way things are going. We're not in a hurry, either." He brought the team to a halt, pulled back on the brake, and turned on his bench to face them. "That was what you were getting at, wasn't it?"

Gerrit grabbed him playfully around the neck as they stepped down. "Can't blame a father-in-law for asking, can you?"

"I don't mind." Randy wrapped his arms around the older man in a fierce hug. "And I'm going to miss you guys when I go. But you're going to take care of my mom from now on for me, right?"

"You bet," Gerrit couldn't keep his voice from breaking as he slipped an arm around his bride. "We'll be praying for you, too."

This kid would need all the prayer he could get.

For that matter, so would Gerrit.

Chapter 12

When you realize you want to spend the rest
of your life with somebody, you want the rest
of your life to start as soon as possible.
—HARRY IN *When Harry Met Sally*

*J*oan wasn't thinking about the ferry sinking as it plowed through emerald waters toward Vancouver Island the next afternoon. She stood behind an elevated railing of the foredeck with the man she had just married, soaking in the tangy salt air and letting her dark hair fly back in the wind as she admired the view. Forested islands dotted the waters on all sides, set like jewels in a larger-than-life seascape. A pair of gulls escorted them on either side, surfing an invisible wind wave. What was it she was supposed to do now? Stretch out her hands and shout, "I'm the queen of the world"?

Instead, she snuggled under Gerrit's arm, using him as a windbreak. She squinted at the gold of an afternoon sun leading them on a path through the islands. She was afraid that she herself was probably glowing, perhaps so much so that people would be able to look at her and realize what she'd been doing the night before. She turned her face upward to Gerrit's. "Is this how all dairy farmers look after a good night's sleep?"

He took the bait. "Good night's sleep? If that was sleep last night, girl, then sign me up for more."

"I knew it." By this time she couldn't hold back her grin. "One-track mind."

He responded by wrapping his arms around her, and she knew she could have been a teenager trapped in the body of an over-the-hill music teacher. She closed her eyes and let him squeeze her for a bit. When he finally let go, he told her that he would bring her a cup of coffee from the little onboard snack bar.

As she waited, she wondered if he might have a tube of the lip balm she'd seen him use. Probably in his backpack—the one he used as a camera bag. She unzipped the outside pocket and rummaged around inside. Sunglasses. A wadded-up Seattle Mariners navy blue Windbreaker. A Louis L'Amour novel yet to be read. (The book had been Joan's idea, and he'd reluctantly agreed.)

She stopped at the sight of a crumpled envelope with a familiar return address, bit her lip, and almost couldn't touch it.

No. The letter with the offer she'd promised herself she could never accept. The either-or proposition she thought she'd put behind her weeks ago.

Either spend the rest of your life in Small Town, USA, or run back to city life.

Either marry this man or accept the job.

Either say yes to love or say yes to music.

She knew she couldn't have both, but why had God dangled the possibility in front of her? And now—even worse—why had this letter suddenly reappeared? And in Gerrit's backpack of all places? She jerked the zipper closed, wishing she'd never seen the tattered letter.

One of their gull escorts banked in lower, perhaps thinking she had a handout he didn't want to miss. Come to think of it, maybe she did. Without thinking it through, she unzipped the pack again, grabbed the letter, ripped it in half and then in half again, then held it up in the air for the gull to see.

"Piece of bread for you, guy."

If the gulls didn't eat it, the waves would swallow this reminder of her past, and then maybe she could *really* leave it behind. But tears stung her eyes, and she couldn't let go just yet.

What's wrong with me, Father? She didn't ask God for a miracle; just an answer. A small clue would be better than nothing. Even now she couldn't release the letter into the wind, couldn't feed it to the birds. Maybe Jesus would help her, but she couldn't do it alone.

"You sure you want to toss that?"

She turned to face Gerrit, who stood behind her with two foam cups of steaming coffee in his hands. He held out one to her.

"Where did you get this?" she asked. She knew, of course; she just wanted him to say. She wanted him to apologize for snooping in her garbage, for poking his nose into business that was none of his own. *Imagine the nerve!* She'd read about people like this, identity thieves and such, and wondered how he could have stooped so low.

"Take this before I drop it, would you, please?"

"I need to know." She could be as stubborn as the next person. Especially now.

"I'm sorry, Joan. I've been wanting to talk to you about it, but it never seemed like the right time. I was kind of hoping you would bring it up first."

"Nothing to bring up."

He raised his eyebrows, but she was not going to let him turn this around, put it on her. Who dug this letter out of the trash in the first place? He had had no right.

"I know how crazy the past few weeks have been," he finally admitted. "Neither of us has stopped running until now, what with the wedding, your students, Randy joining the navy, my job. And I guess I'm not a very good communicator. But maybe we can talk about it now, if you want."

"If I want, Gerrit? You still haven't told me how you got your hands on the letter in the first place."

So he explained how he'd found the letter, why he'd kept it, why he'd said nothing for weeks. As he spoke, her silly flash of anger drained away. She stuffed the ripped pieces of letter into the envelope and turned to the railing once more.

"It just seemed like something you would want to do. I mean, did you ever get back to him about it? What was his name? Chambers?"

"Chambliss. Dr. Porter Chambliss."

"Yeah. Quite a name. Sounds like a real blue blood. Did you ever talk to him?"

She sighed. "I tried to call once. Left a voice mail. Told his secretary I would get back to him, but that's been weeks ago."

"So he's still waiting on you."

"I don't know. Surely the position would have been filled by now."

Gerrit looked for a place to set down his two steaming coffee cups, gave up, and extended them to a passing woman.

"Would you hold these for a minute, ma'am?" He smiled at her and gave her no chance to refuse. Then he turned back to Joan and took her by the shoulders. "Listen to me, Joan. I've been thinking about this, praying about it."

Joan would have backed up in surprise if Gerrit hadn't looked so earnest—or if he hadn't been gripping her shoulders.

"About the job offer, you mean?" She was almost afraid to mention it. What was this man thinking?

He nodded before answering. The woman holding their coffee fidgeted and looked around the deck.

"Uh..." the woman began, "are you still going to want—"

But Gerrit didn't seem to hear, and his eyes stayed locked on Joan's. "Here's what I'm thinking, so just hear me out, okay? The other day I talked with the main office, and they say there's a regional sales-rep job based out of their office in...in Chicago that's mine if I want it."

What is he saying? Joan started to open her mouth, but he touched her lips with a finger.

"Now let me get through this, all right? They want to interview me after we move, but from what I hear it's just a formality."

"I can't believe you would ever want to do that," she finally managed to say.

"Probably wouldn't be forever, you know. It'd be a good job."

"But it's not in Van Dalen. I mean, you're...you wouldn't—"

"What? You think I'm so stuck in the mud, I'd never leave?" He grinned. "Well, all that changed as of two o'clock yesterday afternoon."

She wasn't following him.

"Listen, I said it yesterday so the whole world could hear, and now I'll tell you again so you won't forget." He took a deep breath as if he'd been rehearsing the words. And if she knew Gerrit, he probably had. "From now on, *you're* my hometown, Joan. You understand? *You're* where I belong. I'm not sure I totally understand yet how that's going to work or how tough it's going to be, or even how I'm going to do it. But if God calls us to Chicago, well then, that's where we're going."

Joan squeezed her eyes shut at the absurdity, this bolt out of the blue. The utter irony of this unreal conversation was not lost on her. If anything, she should have been trying to convince *him*. Gerrit had lived in one place, on one farm, his entire life. He thought a trip abroad was driving a few miles over the Canadian border to go to dinner in Vancouver. She, on the other hand, had lost count of the places she'd grown up in as a preacher's kid, the cities she'd lived in. "But I've enjoyed my students here," she finally told him, and the argument sounded weak indeed. "When I married you, I was prepared to stay in Van Dalen a long time."

"I know you have and I know you were, but you can't tell me you don't get a little frustrated with the beginners. And you can't teach college-level piano in Van Dalen."

"But—"

"No buts. You know it's true. Plus, our kids have all flown the coop, so that's not part of the deal anymore. And you're always talking about what a great city Chicago is, how much you liked going to school there."

"Not because I was trying to talk you into anything."

"I know that. You've just got to admit it, though. You're made for this job."

How could she argue what she knew in her heart was true? But Gerrit, no way. She could only remind him of some facts.

"Do you really know what you're saying? Chicago's a big place, Gerrit. You've hardly ever been to Seattle—which is only a fraction of the size—and you hated it there."

"That's different. We could always come back and retire after a few years, if you wanted."

For a minute she turned away to watch the gulls and the foam the ferry churned up as it plowed through the gentle waves. What kind of man had she married, really? A man who said "I do" and then suddenly decided he would trade his life for hers? A seal watched the ferry from a safe distance, and it reminded her of a big brown dog—Mallory's old dog, Missy, who had died before the farm sold.

"It's hard to keep a dog in the city, Gerrit."

"What are you talking about? I never said anything about dogs."

"I was just thinking how much you like animals. Dogs and cows and—"

"Would you hang it up already? I didn't marry a dog or a cow. I married you."

There they could agree. The woman standing behind Gerrit choked on one of the cups of coffee she was sipping. *Never mind her.* Gerrit went on.

"Listen, Joanie, here's the way I see it. The music school really wants you or they wouldn't have offered you another position. And I think God wants you to listen to your heart. You want to go, don't you?"

"How do you know?"

"Can't say I speak for the Lord. I don't think it'd be a sin, necessarily, if you decided you really wanted to stay in Van Dalen, but I know you, Joan. You've gotta do what God made you to do."

Goodness. One day of wedded bliss with this man, and now she felt her world tipping upside down all over again. And it wasn't just the gently rolling deck of the *Spirit of British Columbia.*

"You sound so sure about all this." She tried to read the steely look in his eyes.

"I don't know how to say it any plainer. But if it makes it any easier for you, consider it your wedding present from your new husband. And where I come from, folks don't turn down presents. Will you?"

By this time the woman holding their coffees had finished one and had started on the other. Joan looked at her curiously.

"He's right, you know," the woman told her with a shrug. "You can't say no. If you ask me, I think you should take the job." Then she walked off.

Oh, brother. Joan sighed once more. Two against one. Although in a strange sort of way, she knew she wanted to lose this argument.

"Now approaching Sydney!" The blast of a loudspeaker above their heads made Joan jump. "All passengers please return to your cars."

That would, of course, be Sydney, British Columbia, a short drive from Victoria, where they would explore the Parliament buildings and some of the shops before enjoying tea and crumpets at the grand old Empress Hotel.

Their car was parked under the main deck, so they hurried down narrow green passageways and echoing metal stairs with a herd of other passengers—couples and families, a few businessmen, and truckers. When Joan slipped into her Volvo sedan, she busied herself buckling up and checking the mirror to see what the wind had really done to her hair. Outside their windows she could see the crew in their yellow-striped safety vests scurrying about, and then she felt a dull thud as the ferry snuggled into the arms of a Canadian pier at Swartz Bay, just north of Victoria. Joan knew that she couldn't just leave the discussion hanging. "Can we talk about it some more later?"

"Sure we can." Gerrit nodded as he slipped the key into the ignition, ready to go at the crew's signal. "But how about we...uh...get settled into our hotel room first?"

"Hmm." She smiled. "I was thinking the same thing."

Chapter 13

To achieve great things, two things are needed:
a plan, and not quite enough time.
—LEONARD BERNSTEIN

*Y*eah, I know it was kind of sudden." Gerrit burned his tongue on a sip of steaming church coffee from his mug, the one he'd kept in the kitchen cupboard in the basement of First Church for the past thirty-two years. First time he'd done that in years.

He hid behind the steam coming from his coffee cup and tried to answer Mrs. Jongsma's question in a way that made sense. Reverend Jongsma's wife had only asked the same question everybody else had—and he couldn't say he blamed her. He would have asked himself the same question, and he sometimes did.

So soon? Yes, so soon. Yes, they hadn't been back from their honeymoon that long. Yes, they'd prayed about it.

And yes, Joan's classes were starting next week. She'd already made all the arrangements with Dr. Chambers. *Chambliss,* Gerrit corrected himself. *Porter.* He would never get that name right.

"You know we're going to miss both of you terribly." The reverend's wife blinked her eyes and turned away.

Shoot! He hadn't meant to make anybody cry. But things were getting mushy in a hurry at this Sunday-night, after-the-service going-away party. Gerrit looked across the church basement, tried to get Joan's attention, and wished he could just slip out the back door and pretend this wasn't happening, pretend he wasn't leaving his home. But he guessed that the guest of honor couldn't be the first one to ditch the party. And by this time Joan was pointing with her eyes toward the group assembling around the cake over by the piano. Reverend Jongsma was waving Gerrit over as well. *Uh-oh.*

"Speech!" announced the reverend. There was no escaping, so Gerrit took a deep breath and found his place behind the cake, where people would no doubt fire a steady barrage of questions at him.

"People told us we couldn't get it all together in time." He managed to explain their preparation for moving to the heartland from one of the country's coastal boundaries. When he'd finished, he took another bite of his second piece of cake. This piece included part of the *G,* which might have been from the "Good-By" (no *e*) or from the "Gerrit."

"But you're all ready?" Reverend Jongsma wanted to know.

Gerrit nodded. "Just like we were for the wedding, I guess. Already got rid of most of the good stuff when Warney sold the farm last year, so what was left to do? Pack up my toolbox and my Johnny Cash record collection, throw a toothbrush in my bag, and I'm good to go."

Not entirely true, but pretty close. Tomorrow they'd load up their worldly goods in a small U-Haul truck, hook Joan's Volvo on the back end, and head east. Gerrit didn't expect the packing to take long. Just the easy chair and the television and the stereo and... Oh well. His new wife, on the other hand, had more shoes to pack than most women could wear in a month of Sabbaths, though he didn't dare say anything about it. The only thing left was the family piano that Joan had rescued from the farm auction...

"I still can't believe you and Joan are gifting us this grand old instrument." Reverend Jongsma ran his hand across the oak, polished smooth over several generations. "But I guess that means you'll have to come back from Chicago and play it again sometime."

Bad Casablanca *imitation, Reverend.* Gerrit smiled and studied the instrument his grandfather had bought for his grandmother, the piano she had once played by kerosene light on winter evenings after the milking was done and dinner dishes put away. It belonged here at First Church.

"Me play this thing?" Gerrit smiled. "You mean Joan."

Besides all the lessons he'd taken from Joan, Gerrit couldn't help remembering the times he'd planted his little rear end on that bench as a young boy, and Oma had introduced him to her simple music—folk melodies like *Het vloog een klein wild vogelken* or *Slaat op den trommele*. And he couldn't forget how Joan had played it when she'd first moved to the area and visited his home. Her playing had reeled him in like a fish on a hook.

It's only a piano, for goodness' sake. If it was only a piano, why did he have so much trouble swallowing the goose egg in his throat while standing here like a clown under the "We'll Miss You, Gerrit and Joan" banner stretched across Calvin Hall, which was, after all, just a fancy name for the church basement?

"We will miss you both," Reverend Jongsma said. "You'll visit soon?"

"I'll miss you guys, too." Gerrit had never hugged his pastor before today.

Soon it was time for Gerrit to leave. He needed to walk alone through the quiet streets after dark, to say good-bye his own way. And to pray. After all the good-byes had been said, he figured the empty fairgrounds would be a good enough place to walk. He was right.

"If You want to stop me from making a dumb mistake, God," he prayed aloud, "I need You to show me before it's too late. Please. If You wouldn't mind, that is."

The litter crew still had a bit more work to do to clean up the mess from the past fair day. Oh well. He kicked an empty soda can and begged God for a miracle one more time.

"I know what I told her, Lord." He tried another angle. "And you know I meant every word at the time. But…"

But he hadn't ever intended to leave Van Dalen, not ever, and the realization pained him. He looked inside the empty cow barns where he'd shown a couple of prize winners when he was Mallory's age. Even Warney had done pretty well showing his animals here before he'd grown up. Truth be told, his son's heart was never in it, and Gerrit had gotten over that a long time ago. No use crying about it all over again. No, no, *no*.

He kicked another soda can, sending it spiraling into a cow pen.

No more whining and complaining. But still he couldn't help asking himself, *What have I done?*

Two days later Gerrit was gripping the wheel of the U-Haul truck white-knuckle style and trying to keep from grinding his teeth as much as he was grinding the gears. His leg ached from mashing the gas pedal for so long. This time he ignored the driver who passed them and pointed to the cloud of smoke pouring from the back of the truck.

"You really don't think we should check what's going on?" Joan looked out over her sunglasses from the road map she'd been holding. "Every other car since Missoula has honked at us."

Gerrit shook his head. "It's a diesel. Diesels smoke."

And rattle and shake and sputter.

"I know. But this much?"

Maybe not this much. They'd packed Gerrit's one remaining toolbox somewhere in the depths of the truck, and he had no idea what he was going to do with a full set of socket wrenches in the middle of the city. He just knew he could not throw them away or put them in storage. Here on this lonely stretch of I-90 in the middle of the Rocky Mountains, on the other hand, they might have come in handy. But he wasn't about to unpack the whole confounded truck right now, right there on the side of the road, especially not with all the lunatics flying by them up this hill. If they weren't waving at the stupid cloud of smoke following them, they were—

"Did you see that?" Joan's eyes widened as an SUV whizzed by. "I used to see that hand signal all the time in New York, but never out here."

"Welcome back to the big city, huh?"

That didn't make a lot of sense because they were a long way from just about anywhere. A long way from Van Dalen, for sure, according to the trip odometer. And with each mile, the clouds settled in tighter around Gerrit's heart.

"Come on, you old rustbucket." He might have added a few less-than-complimentary descriptions of the truck if he'd thought it would do any good.

"At least we got a good deal on it." Joan was obviously doing her best to keep a smile on her face and be pleasant. Though it pained him to admit it, getting a good deal on this truck was exactly the problem.

"Yeah, I've got half a mind to turn right around and tell that Dutch-man what I think of his sweet deal."

And, yes, he knew how funny that probably sounded—one Dutch-man calling another Dutchman Dutch. But, hey, the ten percent discount had sounded too sweet to resist. *Fifty bucks is fifty bucks, right?* And he would be doing the dealer a favor by getting the truck out of his district and driving it back east where it belonged, right?

"It says we're coming up on the Continental Divide." Joan pointed to the sign they'd just crawled by in the truck that had a big mural painted on the side, a picture of Niagara Falls. Which was where he would have liked to dump this rattletrap if they hadn't both been riding in it with all their stuff loaded in back. He did his best not to point the truck toward the edge of the next cliff to put the old thing out of its fuel-guzzling misery. He looked down at the gas gauge and tapped it to make sure.

"How many miles back did we fill up?" he wondered aloud.

"Back in Butte, remember? Why?"

"Gas gauge says it's almost empty—again."

Something didn't make sense here, especially with the insane price of diesel at the last gas stop. He'd done a little mental math, and the miles just didn't seem to add up with the miles per gallon—not even for a tired old rig like this. And was that speedometer right? They ought to have been able to climb the pass a lot faster than ten miles an hour. Right now it felt as though they could get out and walk faster than this thing was chugging uphill.

Maybe it's a sign that we need to go back.

Yeah, wouldn't that have been nice? Or maybe a lightning bolt from heaven. Anything like that would have been real fine too.

"Maybe we should pull over at the next rest stop." Joan did her best to keep the panic she felt from creeping into her voice. Not that she was keeping anything from Gerrit. By this time they both knew that something was seriously wrong with their rental truck. For one thing, normal trucks didn't bury all the traffic behind them in a three-alarm thundercloud of smoke. As the next line of cars and trucks pulled around and passed them, Joan ducked her head, then started rummaging in the glove box to find their paperwork. The rental company would have to have some kind of towing deal. At least she hoped it did.

Meanwhile Gerrit pulled off at the rest stop, and they both stepped out to stretch their legs. After nearly a full day of driving, they'd made it only half as far as Joan had hoped they would.

"Dude." A bearded young trucker in a Wal-Mart semi looked down at them from his cab. "You got yourselves a nice fuel leak there."

He pointed to the pool of diesel fuel forming under the cab of their truck. They hadn't noticed that before. And now it didn't take a master mechanic to tell them they weren't going any farther in this truck anytime soon. What would have happened if that fuel had caught fire?

"Shoot!" Gerrit opened the hood, and a white cloud billowed up from the engine. "I should have known it was something like this."

While Gerrit and the trucker puzzled over the engine, Joan inspected the damage to her own car, which was being pulled behind their truck on a little half trailer. The sight of it made her gasp.

"Oh no." She gingerly ran a finger across the hood just to be sure. It was no mistake: Her pretty black Volvo had been completely coated in a slimy layer of diesel oil. And not just the hood, but top to bottom—the glass, the bumpers, the mirrors, everything. She could hardly see inside.

"Gerrit!" She went to look for a tissue to wipe the pungent slime from her hand. Forget the fuel leak and forget the silly truck. This was her car they were talking about now. "I think we have a problem here."

"No kidding." Gerrit never even looked up at her. "When did you figure that out?"

His sarcasm stung like an unexpected wasp. She turned away, tears brimming in her eyes. Had he waited until they were married to talk to her like that?

"Listen, I'm sorry." He came up behind her and rested a greasy hand on her shoulder. "Didn't mean to bite your head off like that."

"My head's still on." She didn't turn to face him but patted the back of his big hand. "Can you fix it?"

"Tools are all packed away somewhere. But even if I did have 'em, I'm not so sure."

"Tow?"

"We'll get one"—he sounded sure of himself—"eventually. And at least we're not lost. See?"

He pointed up at the bright Rocky Mountain sky, studded with stars. Before clouds covered their view, he pointed out some of the constellations he knew: bears and hunters and, of course, Polaris, the North Star.

Eventually. Joan pulled the collar of her pullover up a little higher to fend off the sudden mountain chill. A storm coming? The booth where a local service club usually served coffee was tightly boarded up, but Gerrit trundled off to use the pay phone and contact a towing company. And when she gazed up once more into the slate sky, she caught one of the season's first snowflakes on the tip of her nose. She opened her mouth to taste the falling ice crystals.

No, it wasn't quite like the rainbow at their wedding. But the same God was in control.

And despite herself, she smiled.

Chapter 14

*I am always ready to learn although
I do not always like being taught.*
—WINSTON CHURCHILL

*A*re you sure you don't want me to drive us into the city?"

Gerrit shook his head and gripped the steering wheel even tighter. "Nope. You drove enough yesterday. And besides, didn't I get us out of that snowstorm in the Rockies?"

That, and the towing adventure, and waiting for the mechanic to fix their old rustbucket, and running Joan's car through the Pink Elephant Buggy Wash in Bozeman, Montana, about five times. And they were still married after all that.

"I know you can handle it, dear. It's just that city driving is a little different than pulling a plow through the fields."

"You better ease up on that Farmer Gerrit stuff." He patted her on the leg. Besides, most people thought driving a tractor was a piece of cake. They didn't know it took a fair amount of skill to keep a furrow straight. So could the farm boy drive a truck into the city? *Better believe it.*

"Just wanted to make sure." She smiled and turned back to the window.

Maybe he wasn't prepared to admit it just yet, but he'd never really seen this kind of city up close before. Seattle had a few tall buildings, yeah, but nothing like this. And these crazies on the freeway? Another one zoomed up behind them, and for a moment he almost wished he could push a button and activate the diesel spray again. Joan didn't seem to notice.

"The really tall building is the Sears Tower." She pointed up ahead. "The view from the Skydeck is wonderful."

Great. Gerrit tried to keep his distance from the long white limo just ahead of them, but now the SUV behind them had filled up his rearview mirror. "Give me a break, huh?"

"What did you say?" She gave him that look again.

"Not you. Just talking to the truck."

"Oh. If he talks back, let me know." By now she was smiling and pointing out more landmarks—the big towers, of course, but eventually the old Water Tower and the horse carriages, the waterfront, and some of the restaurants where she used to eat when she was a teenager growing up here in the city.

"There's Pizzeria Uno!" She bounced in her seat like a little girl while Gerrit concentrated on not sideswiping the double-parked cars or running over a woman walking her poodle. "And the Hancock Building! I can't believe it!"

"Me neither." Gerrit inched past Jake's Cleaners and searched for a street sign that read LaSalle, the way Joan had directed him. "Did you say left up here?"

"Right," she answered.

So he wheeled around a construction crew—and directly into a line of oncoming traffic.

"Whoa!" He slammed on the brakes to avoid a little motor scooter, while a taxi screeched to a stop and the driver gestured wildly at him the way folks around here seemed to like to do. Okay, so that helped a lot. Joan wasn't helping any either.

"Gerrit! This is a one-way! I told you to go right."

"I thought you meant I was right," he croaked. They didn't have these kinds of crazy streets back in Van Dalen, and folks back in Van Dalen didn't heat up this quickly. Now a whole lineup of taxis and delivery vans and cars was all honking a chorus at him.

"Hey, I hear you, pal." Gerrit desperately ground the gearshift, looking for reverse. "I'm trying, all right? I'm trying."

But that wasn't good enough for the angry army of city drivers. And by now the traffic from behind swarmed around them like whitewater rapids, keeping Gerrit from backing up as he would have liked. Besides, the car dolly wasn't quite designed for backing up, so it took several tries to keep it from pretzeling itself around the back end of the truck. All the while Joan seemed to sink farther and farther down into her seat.

"Welcome to Chicago, huh?" he whispered under his breath as they finally got straightened around and headed back on LaSalle.

"Welcome to Chicago!" A tall, fifty-something man—with dark hair that shouldn't have been—greeted them in front of the Lake Shore Towers a half hour later.

Gerrit unfolded himself from the seat of the U-Haul and breathed again. Was anybody passing out medals? He'd managed to keep their truck headed the right way this time, and never mind that he'd had to circle the block five times before he finally decided to double-park in front of the Wan Luc Chinese Grocery with his emergency flashers on. Who was going to try to tow him away? *Go ahead and try.* Where was a guy supposed to park his rig in this town anyway? Not in one of those parking garages with the Early Bird Special signs. Joan had already explained that the charge was per *day*, not per month.

All that was pretty hard to believe, but not as hard to believe as this stranger in the designer suit who was kissing his wife on the cheek. Gerrit had to unclench his fist before Joan introduced him and he was forced to hold out his hand.

"Dr. Chambliss," she announced sweetly, "I'd like you to meet my husband."

Chambliss, eh? The headmaster-at-Gaylord-Conservatory, guy-who-had-written-Joan-the-job-offer Chambliss? Gerrit swallowed hard.

"So you're the farmer who finally managed to lasso Joan Horton." The guy's smile looked way too big for his face, his fancy gold ring way too big for his right hand. "Porter Chambliss. I've heard so much about you."

I bet you have.

"Jed Clampett." Gerrit shook the man's soft outstretched hand. "Pleased to meet y'all."

So maybe the Southern accent was a bit over the top. But it was all Gerrit could do not to be ill. The guy's perfume—sorry, *cologne*—turned Gerrit's stomach as well.

"Gerrit?" Joan gave him a puzzled look. "I thought I married a serious farmer, and I really get a—"

"*Beverly Hillbillies*!" Dr. Chambliss snapped his fingers and laughed, a short little machine-gun sound that did nothing to help Gerrit feel any better about him. "That's pretty good. Wasn't Jed Clampett the name of the fellow who played the hillbilly?"

"Actually his real name was Buddy Ebsen, but a lot of people forget."

"Of course." Dr. Chambliss glanced at his expensive-looking Bulova watch, then down the street as if he was waiting for somebody or would rather not be here anymore. He shifted around the sidewalk in his Italian-looking slippers, the kind a woman might look good in.

By this time Gerrit was biting his tongue pretty good, but he figured it was better to remain silent and appear the fool than to open his mouth and remove all doubt. Mark Twain, if he remembered correctly. *Well, it's about time to take some of old Mark's advice,* Gerrit counseled himself. By now the movers—or rather, the unloaders—had arrived to help. A guy in a ripped Student Movers T-shirt stepped out of his van and tapped on his clipboard.

"We got"—he paused to check his watch—"one hour, fifteen minutes to unload. Your stuff in there?"

"We in that much of a hurry?" Gerrit wondered.

"Freight elevator's only ours till three thirty."

Gerrit wasn't quite sure what the guy was talking about, so he helped unlock the back of the truck and grabbed the floor lamp as it tumbled down toward them.

"Whoa there, old timer." Mr. Mover took the lamp from Gerrit and set it down on the sidewalk. "You better let us handle the heavy stuff."

Oh yeah? Gerrit grabbed the nearest box he could find, the one that said "MUSIC BOOKS—HEAVY" on the side, and marched toward the lobby of the building.

"He's right, dear." Joan joined in. "You really ought to let them do the heavy lifting."

"You bet." Move over, Jack La Lanne! And this young kid with the ripped T-shirt probably had no idea who La Lanne was. He balanced the book box in one hand, which nearly killed him, but he would go down with his pride intact. "I'll just walk up with a few of the little things."

One hour and twenty minutes later, Gerrit walked into their two-bedroom apartment on the eighth floor with the last of the "little things"—a box stuffed with paper and Joan's treasured little dead-musician plaster head. *Bach or Beethoven?* Gerrit couldn't remember. Anyway, this one didn't start out heavy, but Gerrit did his best not to limp or stumble into the apartment all hunched over. Every square inch of his body hurt. *And what don't hurt, don't work.* So he stood in the doorway, catching his breath and trying not to groan. All he could really do at this point was hold on to the doorjamb and survey his new world.

From the hallway the front door opened into a fair-sized living room, now crowded with most of their furniture. The nine-foot-high ceiling was decorated with plaster squares, which seemed a little foofy, but this was probably okay in the city. A walk-through kitchen—a little smaller than the kitchen in his old house, but bigger than the one in the Missionary Cottage where he'd been living before Warney sold the farm—flanked the living room. Toward the outside wall, the kitchen widened a bit for a little eating area, which would be kind of nice. A bathroom and one bedroom opened off to the right, and another bedroom to the left. *Not bad.* Then there was a bank of windows on the far wall.

"What do you think of the view, Mr. Appeldoorn?" Joan walked up and slipped her arms around Gerrit's waist.

She meant the peekaboo vista of Lake Michigan and the little park below, which Gerrit would later admit was pretty nice. Okay, so there was nothing like this in Van Dalen, though, of course, Van Dalen offered its own views of Mount Baker. But instead of admiring the cityscape, he turned in Joan's arms to face her.

"From where I stand," he said, "the view is great. In fact—"

This would be his chance to carry his new bride across the threshold, right? So he grabbed her the same way he had the sofa.

"Gerrit, no!" she protested. "You're going to break your back—or worse!"

That might have been true, but he sure wasn't going to admit it. With his wife more or less in his arms, he stumbled through the door, caught her feet on the doorjamb, and nearly bowled over Joan's new boss.

"Whoa, coming through."

Porter Chambliss made a pretty good side step, and Gerrit unloaded his wife next to a pile of boxes. Which only made her blush, of course. But what could he do about it now?

"Thanks for the help, Dr. Chambliss." This time Gerrit didn't try to break the man's hand as he shook it. He couldn't fault Chambliss for hanging around the entire time, though the headmaster had rarely picked up anything heavier than a couch pillow and hadn't even broken a sweat. "I know Joan's looking forward to reporting for duty on Monday."

"Not as much as I'm looking forward to having her." Porter smiled and pulled a handkerchief out of his pocket to dab at an imaginary scuff on his fancy shoes. "Really. You have no idea how much this means to me. To the school, I mean. To the staff. They're all thrilled that Joan is here."

Right. Gerrit narrowed his eyes for a second and decided to take the man at face value—for now. Though maybe he didn't have any idea how much this meant to the school staff. But as Gerrit looked around at his new home, he knew one thing without a doubt. This farm boy was a long way from Van Dalen.

The thought hammered through his head that night as he tried— *tried*—to sleep. Below them the city throbbed and pulsed with life, even at one a.m. Didn't anyone ever go to bed around here? He tried counting sheep and tractors, but it only reminded him of home, and the persistent ache it gave him reminded him of the time he'd cracked his tooth a couple of years back. But a dentist wasn't going to fix this pain.

He probably should have closed the window, but the air conditioning only spewed hot air, and Joan had insisted that the city noise would lull her to sleep. Well, it had, and he could almost see the smile on her face. She looked as if she'd finally come home. Funny, he didn't remember her smiling quite like that back in Van Dalen. But then, he had never seen her face as it hit the pillow back in Van Dalen. He tried to make out her features in the dim light from the open window and kept himself from tracing her lips with his finger.

"Sleep tight," he whispered, and her rhythmic breathing told him she didn't hear his words. So it wouldn't hurt to tell her again.

"You're my home now, Joan." Maybe saying the words would make it so, sort of like "I do" had linked them together, turned the marriage vows from script to reality. Even though everything around him screamed and shouted, even though the horns were giving him a headache and the concrete grated his soul. He waited but nothing changed—not his heart, not his ache. So for now he would have to settle for a simple commitment and leave it there.

"I'm doing this for you," he told her, perhaps too loudly.

For a moment he thought she would awaken. She moaned softly and turned over. But moments later her soft breathing returned. He buried his face as close to her dark hair as he dared, cupped a hand over his ear, and pretended they were falling asleep in a bed of clean hay back in the barn. The noises were just swallows coming and going, or cows shuffling in their stalls. *There.* His eyelids finally grew heavy and closed, but when he finally did doze off, a siren jolted him awake once more, and he sat up straight without quite knowing where he was.

"What?" Maybe the panic in his voice woke Joan.

"Are you all right?" Her whisper sounded husky, far off. He wanted only to slip back into his haystack dream, back to the sweet smell of alfalfa he'd found in her hair. Instead, another siren yanked him right back to Apartment 813, Lake Shore Towers, North Lake Shore Drive, Chicago, Illinois. He looked out the window to get his bearings from the stars, but the lights from a nearby building drowned out all evidence of heaven.

"No stars here." Well, he could live without stars. Without the Big Dipper and the North Star, without Orion the hunter and Cassiopeia the queen. They were just silly legends. What did it all amount to anyway? He tried to roll over, tried to wrap a pillow around his head to block out the city sounds. And if he'd still been a little boy, he knew he would have cried himself to sleep.

Chapter 15

*My first day in Chicago, September 4, 1983. I set foot
in this city, and just walking down the street, it was like
roots, like the motherland. I knew I belonged here.*

—OPRAH WINFREY

Joan glanced up at the ornate facade of Chicago's famous Fine Arts
Building, traced the arches with her eyes, and took a deep breath.
"Okay," she whispered to herself. "Here we go."

She'd been in here before, years ago, for a recital when she was, what,
seventeen years old? *No, eighteen.* But who would have thought then that
she'd be teaching here someday, right here in this wonderful old building
on Michigan Avenue?

And she loved everything about this place, from the wondrous view
of Lake Michigan and the fountain by the shore to the rich art-deco
details inside. Arched, marble-lined hallways, mosaics and lovely paintings
from the 1920s, and a fantastic little sheet-music shop on the fourth
floor—if she remembered correctly—filled with shelf upon incredible
shelf of music by Berlioz, Beethoven, and Bach. Even the quaint little
Artist's Café on the ground floor, crammed with round tables full of students and artists and tourists and musicians enjoying a morning cup of
coffee. She could almost taste the creative buzz, even as she could smell
the coffee. Everywhere the talk was about practice times and treble clefs,
choruses and quarter notes.

Ah, heaven! She had little doubt she could get very, very used to this.

"Oh! Pardon me." She bumped into a young student carrying a

violin case, then navigated through a small crowd and slipped into an old-fashioned lobby elevator. She smiled at the attendant. "Fourth floor, please."

He worked the accordion doors closed and echoed her request.

"Fourth floor. Gaylord Conservatory of Music." They rattled up to her destination, and when the doors opened, she had to pause a moment to take everything in.

"Oh!" When was the last time someone had hung a welcome banner across the high-ceilinged hallway?

"Is right floor?" The elevator man questioned her in his thick Russian accent.

"Yes." She stepped out with a smile. "Is right floor, all right."

And goodness, she wasn't going to correct them, not when they'd gone to so much trouble. Most of the teachers would still know her by her old name, just as it appeared on the banner: "Welcome, Joan Horton!"

They would find out soon enough. And she let herself feel only a brief flicker of disappointment as she greeted Porter Chambliss hurrying down the hall in her direction, hand extended and shoes clicking on the ornate tiled marble floors.

"This is all very nice," she told him. He held on to her outstretched hand just a little too long for comfort. "You shouldn't have."

"Are you kidding?" He led her by the arm down the hall. "I told you everyone was excited about your coming. You haven't really seen the campus before, have you? I'll show you around."

They went first to the main office, where she recognized at least a half-dozen teachers she hadn't seen in years. Orchestra people from New York, old music pros, teachers—these people didn't go away so easily.

"Joan!" A tall African American woman in her early fifties nearly squeezed the breath out of her. "I thought you'd dropped off the face of the earth, girl. Where have you been hiding the past...how many years?"

"I've been teaching a little younger crowd lately, Latisha," She said, catching her breath. "Getting to know my daughter and little grand-daughter. Learning how to milk cows. Getting married."

The question popped up on her friend's face. "You're going to tell me the whole story later. But married? What happened to Jim? Tell me you didn't get divorced?"

Dear, sweet Latisha. Never one to hold back a question.

"No, nothing like that. He died several years ago. I met a man in Van Dalen, Washington, where my daughter lives, and we got married. His name is Gerrit. You'll like him."

"Oh. Well, I'm sorry to hear that…er…actually I'm happy for you. I mean…you know what I'm trying to say."

"I know." Joan returned another hug. "Thanks. It's good to see you, too. It's been, what, eight or nine years since we worked together in New York?"

"Those were the good old days. But tell me about this new fella of yours. I assume he's a musician? What does he play?"

"Johnny Cash records."

They both laughed, and Joan let Latisha wonder if she was being straight with her.

"I tell you what, though." Latisha leaned closer as if she were telling a secret. "It's a good thing you got here when you did. We've been missing a world-class keyboard teacher like you. We've had the basics covered, but we've been really hurting with the most advanced students. Now—"

Dr. Chambliss brought them both back to the now. "We'll all have a chance to talk to Joan at the staff meeting tomorrow, Ms. Carpenter. At this point I'd like to finish showing Joan around the campus."

And what a campus! Students filled several dozen practice rooms equipped with lovely ebony Yamaha U3 practice pianos; their music fil-tered out into the halls. Were they really that good? She'd forgotten how well a twenty-two-year-old advanced student could play. A little heavy on the decrescendo, perhaps, but that could be fixed.

Chambliss turned his head like a dog picking up a scent and grinned. "You're already getting back up to speed, I can tell."

She hoped she didn't look as awestruck as she felt. They peeked into classrooms equipped with video presentation screens and filled with students who looked as if they actually wanted to be there—rather than just having their mommies drag them to their lessons because they thought it was the thing to do. Joan and Dr. Chambliss walked past performance studios and sound-mixing rooms jammed with the sights and sounds of wonderful music being made. And she nearly gasped at the grand, high-ceilinged performance hall, ornamented with carved ceilings and graceful red-velvet curtains swept away to the sides. It looked just as she had remembered it, only even more grand. Behind the platform three floor-to-ceiling windows opened up to that grand view of a sparkling azure Lake Michigan just beyond Buckingham Fountain on the parklike shore.

"You like the view?" asked Dr. Chambliss. "Wait until you see your office. I had to pull a few strings to get it for you. But for Joan Horton— I mean, Appeldoorn. Sorry, I keep forgetting."

"That's all right." With a view like this and in a place like this, just about anything was all right. Dr. Chambliss went on with his tour.

"We can seat about 350 in here for your recitals." His voice echoed slightly as he swept his arm across the empty hall and grinned at her. "See what you've been missing?"

"I see." Joan did her best to keep her jaw off the floor and caught herself wondering now what she would be able to do with these serious, dedicated students in this fantastically creative atmosphere. For certain, no one would be playing "Itsy Bitsy Spider" at the next recital. And the thought of playing *real* music again with kids who could handle it! She couldn't keep the smile off her face and wasn't sure she wanted to.

"I'll show you your office." He led her through the wood-paneled hallways and past another pod of practice rooms to a door with a frosted-glass window. He paused before opening the door—probably for effect—and she ran her finger across the etched-glass lettering.

"My name on the door already?"

"Of course." He inclined his head. "We spelled the name right, I hope."

"You did." She checked once more just to be sure. *Joan Appeldoorn.* At least they'd not made the same mistake as—

"I have to apologize about the welcome banner." Once more he had read her mind, and this time it was a bit unsettling. "Not everyone knows you've remarried. Of course, people in the industry will continue to recognize you as Joan Horton. Your past stays with you around here."

"I know. It's not a problem." Really it wasn't. And neither was the office for that matter. She stood in the open doorway and stared.

"It's just an old thing we dug up for you to use as long as you're here."

Just an old thing? Not quite. The gleaming ebony grand piano commanded the corner, while a black-leather couch, a walnut desk, and an empty oak bookshelf completed the office. Not to mention the picture window looking out on the lake.

"Are you sure this is *my* office?" There had to be some mistake. Did every professor in this school qualify for a hundred-thousand-dollar Bösendorfer?

"Victor Borge played it when he was in town once." Chambliss seemed to be reading her mind again. "He liked it."

"How could he not?" Joan had encountered her share of expensive pianos, even played a few. But never in her own office.

He smiled. "And no one's played it since."

"Now you're pulling my leg."

"I should be so lucky." He let the double entendre drop and quickly changed the subject. "So...feels like home?"

She smiled despite herself. "You have no idea."

He grinned and gently patted her on the back. His hand lingered a split second longer than she might have preferred, but not long enough for anyone to notice. *Some people are just more touchy than others,* she told herself.

"Why don't you take some time to get yourself settled? I'll be back in a few minutes, and we'll get your teaching schedule confirmed."

She thought she answered, though perhaps she was still just staring at the Bösendorfer, which she was a bit afraid of touching, much less playing. Whether or not she answered, Dr. Chambliss disappeared, and the door clicked shut behind him.

She stood in the center of her office, doing a slow Mary Tyler Moore twirl and trying her best to take it all in. The welcome, the piano, the view, the students—fragments of Berlioz and Bach drifting in from several directions. Oh, of course!

"Come on, little man." She pulled out the small ceramic bust of Johann Sebastian Bach, the one her first husband, Jim, had given her on her forty-fifth birthday, just before he died. Since then, little Johann had kept an eye on her wherever she'd played—or taught. He just came with the territory. *There.*

And once more she looked at her name on the frosted glass of the door, backward this time.

Professor Joan Appeldoorn—not Joan Horton. And she felt the new gold wedding band on her finger, a promise from the man who had given her his name, his life. He had traded his life for hers, his home for hers. She wondered how his job interview was going, because deep down she had a feeling that this move was not exactly as easy for Gerrit as he made it sound.

Chapter 16

City life is millions of people being lonesome together.
—HENRY DAVID THOREAU

Gerrit checked his watch again, looked at himself in the little bathroom mirror, and wondered.

"So does my hair make me look too old?" he asked the mirror. He knew he didn't want to do the swoop-across-the-bald-spot thing. Bill, the barber back home, was a little too far away this morning to stop by for a touch-up, and while there had to be a good old barber somewhere in this town, he didn't exactly have time to go roaming around searching.

"Oh well." He pulled a notice out of his pocket, the one he'd pulled off the little bulletin board down by the building mailboxes the night before. "Special Discount for All Lake Shore Towers Residents," it read. *Hmm.* The Dutchman in him saw the word "discount" and really didn't need to read any further. Besides, this Chi Clips place was right here in the lower-level lobby, so he wouldn't have to go out searching all morning for a barber pole. *It'll be fine.*

So he set out in search of the perfect haircut. Probably he'd find the shop down by the exercise room, which he hadn't explored yet. The building manager, a Mrs. Dukakis, who was no relation to the presidential candidate or the actress, told him they used to have an indoor pool down there, but it had gotten too expensive to keep it filled with chemicals and stuff, and they ended up building a floor over the top. She never said whether they had actually filled the pool with cement.

Chi Clips was right where he figured it would be. Only there was no barber pole in front and no males in sight. Three older women whose combined height couldn't have totaled more than a dozen feet, not counting the piled-up silvery blue and rose–colored hair, sat in chairs. He might have thought they were sisters, and maybe two of them were, except the odd one out looked pale as a ghost, as if she hadn't been outside for years. Much more pale than the other two.

What really got him as he stepped inside, though, was the smell—the gagging, cloying perfumed cloud of hair spray and heaven-only-knew-what. His windpipe was clamped up to the point where he nearly started looking for a phone to call 911. He would have turned around and bailed out right then, except one of the old gals circled around behind him and blocked the only way out.

"Can I help you?"

"Yeah. I mean, no. I think I came to the wrong place." He looked down at the crumpled discount flier in his hand and sighed. "Actually, no, I need a haircut."

"Bend over," she commanded.

Her voice reminded him of old Miss Hoogaboom, his ninth-grade English teacher in Van Dalen. You didn't mess around with this lady either, so Gerrit obeyed. Besides, she wouldn't have been able to see his head if he hadn't bent over.

He couldn't tell what she was looking at, but he could hear her clucking over the background noise of a hair dryer. And he jumped when she started pawing through what was left of his hair.

"You think I haven't seen balding old heads before?" She motioned him to the seat closest to the door. "I think we can help you."

Gerrit gulped but shoved the flier at her. "I saw the discount coupon," he croaked, wishing he'd had the courage to outrun this gal while he still had the chance. She snatched the coupon out of his hand as he took a seat, opened a magazine, and held it in front of him like a shield.

"Which one of these?" she asked, pulling out a tiny laminated chart she must have saved from beauty school…back in the '50s. Of course, Gerrit had to pull out his glasses to see the difference between all the styles of hair on the coupon. All of them looked like variations of the Beatles in their early years—not the styles so much as the thick mops.

"You think I really have that much to work with?" He tried to catch a glimpse of his crop in the mirror, but the image only repeated itself off into infinity, which made it hard to really see what was going on.

"You tell us the style you want, and we'll prorate it for how much hair you got."

Great. Maybe they'll prorate the price, too. Fifty percent off, if he was lucky. He pointed to a style that didn't look like a punk rocker, a do called the Continental.

"That okay?" he asked. He wasn't going to start taking any of that hair-growth tonic he'd heard advertised so much on the radio. With his luck, he'd probably grow hair on his elbows and have to start wearing a bra.

His hairdresser frowned and studied his head again as if it was a side of beef.

"I'll see what I can do," she told him with a straight face, pulling out a pair of scissors and a comb and stuffing a drape into his collar. *So this is how it feels to be a side of beef ready for dressing.* Now he was going under for sure, and Joan would only read about it in tomorrow's *Chicago Tribune*—"Customer Strangled During Visit to Lake Shore Beauty Salon."

Yeah, wouldn't that be a handy way to die? From then on, he only caught an occasional word of Spanish as the girl talk shifted into high gear. He supposed one could call it girl talk, though any one of the women looked old enough to be his own mother. And in his case, that was saying a lot.

Turns out his hairdresser's name was Olivia, but he only discovered that when one of the other gals called her by name. The rest of the time he tried to keep his eyes shut, especially when she leaned close enough to remind him why he had always gone to a male barber.

I'm a long way from Bill's place, he told himself as he felt what little hair he had disappear under the flashing scissors of Señora Olivia. He didn't suppose she wanted to talk about grain prices or tractors or the pennant race. But five very long minutes later, she yanked off the shroud "ta-da" style. Or maybe it was more like one of those magicians who yanked a tablecloth off a set table, leaving everything standing. He checked his ears to make sure they were still attached, dabbed at his right lobe, and looked at his hand to check for blood. Never mind that he probably had no more hair left than Joan's Randy, who was at navy boot camp.

"You have your girlfriend come with you next time, eh?" Olivia said. "I give her a nice permanent wave, with the discount."

Just then Gerrit might have said just about anything to escape into the fresh air of the city where he could stand behind a city bus and breathe deeply.

"You bet," he told her. "I'll tell my wife." *Not if I want to stay married.*

One of the other gals tossed over a question, cloaked well in Spanish, *"¿Tiene esposa?"* or something like that, and Gerrit was thinking that, yeah, his dome was plenty *esposed, gracias.* The women in the shop snickered, while Olivia deflected the chitchat with a frown and a swipe of her hand.

"Twenty-six-fifty," she announced.

For five minutes of buzz-saw chopping? "I mentioned the discount coupon?"

"Twenty-eight-fifty without discount."

He sighed and raided his wallet for enough bills. Either he would talk Joan into cutting his hair from now on, or he was going to learn how to cut it himself. How hard could it be?

"Come back soon."

When Olivia smiled, she revealed a row of crooked, whitewashed teeth. Gerrit guessed that she'd figured out how to use those new, improved whitening strips. Finally she stepped aside enough to let him make his way out.

Maybe he could talk Bill into moving to the city too.

⁓

Fifteen minutes later Gerrit nearly climbed a light post on Dearborn Street when a car horn rattled his thoughts of home.

"Holy guacamole!" He spun to see who had nearly run him over, but the silver Honda just swept him out of the intersection, and its driver waved him off like a swarm of flies on a cow's derrière. He could see he was going to have to learn some new street-crossing etiquette if he was to survive in this city.

"Where I come from, cows have the right of way," he told the driver, who by then was parting a Red Sea puddle halfway down the block.

At least Gerrit had come prepared in his favorite forest green Lands' End Squall Parka—the kind that beaded water like a duck's back and came with extra-comfy fleece lining inside. It had been a birthday present from Warney and company a couple of years back. Only thing he never needed in it was the cell-phone pocket.

That's another thing he didn't get: Who were all these folks talking to all the time, walking down the street with cell phones glued to their ears? Even in this drizzle, it was motormouth overdrive. So he pulled up his hood a little more snugly and made for the safety of the sidewalk. If he didn't get to where he was going pretty soon, the lady at personnel would write him off.

And he couldn't allow that to happen.

He fingered the business card in his pants pocket just to remind himself that this was all for real—this city, this jungle, this job, this interview at corporate headquarters. Thursday, September 19, 10:00 a.m. in Patricia Hunsaker's office, 12245 Rush Street, downtown.

He'd be there, Lord willing—if the wind didn't blow him away and if he could find the place. A light blue–striped police cruiser weaved through traffic, its siren piercing his eardrums. If he weren't deaf before—

Hold on. This way? He continued down Dearborn, the way the guy at the Chinese deli had told him to go. Six blocks south, then right on Walton, then past a Catholic boys' school, and two more blocks to…Clark Street? He gazed at the buildings rising around him, and they all started looking the same. In Van Dalen he'd always just look to see where the mountain was. Now, even if there had been a mountain—*Shoot!*

He checked his watch again and groaned. He would have been officially late three minutes ago, and now the rain was pelting down harder than ever. Nothing like a little cloud dump. They didn't have anything like this back home. As he checked for a break in the traffic, he looked straight across the street at a man in a wheelchair bumping against the curb. The older African American fella backed up for another run and nearly dumped himself into the gutter.

Without thinking, Gerrit sprinted in front of a Brinks armored car—with a very loud horn—and reached the wheelchair-bound man just as he crashed into the curb once more. The old guy's paper sack on his lap had begun to split open, threatening to spill a plastic plate and fork, a half-empty can of pork and beans, and a small toothbrush.

"Need some help here?" Gerrit knew the answer as he gripped the chair handles to gently turn the man around and drag him up under an awning at Virgil's Dry Cleaners. Better than being out in the pouring rain.

"Thanks, man." The old guy could barely whisper. Gerrit would have left it at that, but something in the man's voice stopped him. The wheelchair-bound man wore only a ripped pair of old pants and a threadbare T-shirt, even in this cold rain. And the guy was soaked to the skin.

"You look a little wet there," Gerrit observed. *Obviously.*

The man didn't answer, just tried to roll his wheels. But his grip slipped and he slumped forward.

"Wait a minute." Gerrit wouldn't, couldn't, just walk away. He unzipped his parka, yanked it off, and held it out to the man. "Why don't you take this?"

The gray-haired old man slowly looked up at Gerrit and studied his face. For a moment Gerrit wasn't sure he was getting through.

"That's your coat," the man finally whispered back, his voice raspy and coarse. "No sense in us both gettin' wet."

"No, it's okay." Now Gerrit was sure. "Take it."

"What will you wear?"

"I've got plenty of other clothes at home." And he did.

The old man slowly held out his hands and accepted the coat, running a rough hand across the soft fleece lining as if he'd never before felt such a thing. "Thass a nice coat," he repeated over and over. He tried the two-way, heavy-duty zipper and checked out the pockets with the Velcro flaps. Slowly he slipped an arm into one sleeve, then the other, and as he did, a smile stretched across the wrinkles in his dark face. Then he held out his hand to shake Gerrit's and asked, "What's your name?"

Gerrit had to lean forward to make sure he heard the guy, whose name turned out to be Avery Wilson. He figured the guy probably hadn't heard a lot of good Dutch names before.

"You're a good man, Gerrit Apple Core. But why'd you do this?"

"You just looked like you could use a coat, that's all."

That obviously wasn't a good enough answer for Avery Wilson. And for a moment Gerrit felt guilty for not responding with the classic Four Spiritual Laws line, "God loves you and has a wonderful plan for your life." Wasn't that why Gerrit had pulled off his coat? Sort of. Maybe. He wasn't sure. All he knew was that he couldn't just walk away.

Avery Wilson was boring a hole in Gerrit with the look in his eyes.

"But I didn't ask you for nothin'."

"I guess you didn't."

Gerrit shivered, but not from the driving rain and wind that seemed to turn him inside out. In an odd sort of way, he was glad of it—the cold—if only so that he could understand what the old man had been feeling, just a little. But the shivering—no, it was definitely not from the bone-chilling cold, but from something else entirely.

He knew without a doubt that he had just tiptoed closer to God's Spirit than he'd ever before dared. But now he was dangerously close to completely missing his interview, and he still didn't know where he was going exactly. If he stood out in the rain very long, he was going to end up looking like Avery Wilson. Much longer, and he was going to need the old man's wheelchair, too.

Chapter 17

We didn't all come over on the same ship,
but we're all in the same boat.
—BERNARD M. BARUCH

"So how do you like the Bösendorfer?" Latisha poked her head in at Joan's office door a little while after Porter Chambliss had left.

Joan shook her head and put up her hands. "I have no idea where this came from. No idea."

"Yeah, pretty nice. Nobody else I know gets this kind of star treatment." When Latisha smiled, Joan had to admire her wonderfully straight teeth. "Porter seems to come up with funding—well, actually nobody's quite sure where he finds the money. I hear he's good friends with a couple of big donors, but if you ask me, I think he's been robbing banks."

"Latisha!"

"Well?" Latisha grinned and shrugged her shoulders. "How else? All I can say is that there's definitely more going on than the salary he gets here. Have you seen the car he drives?"

Joan shook her head as Latisha went on.

"Doesn't matter. But the piano—well, that's something else. You deserve it, Joanie."

"Hmm, but that's just it. I don't. I'm sure there are other professors who—"

"No you don't. Uh-uh. Don't you go puttin' yourself down, 'cause you've paid your dues, girl. But I will tell you one thing." She paused and looked to the side ever so subtly. No one else out in the hallway would be close enough to hear. "You have a friend or two on the board, that's for sure. And in case you haven't noticed, Dr. Chambliss is a real fan of yours."

What was Joan supposed to say to that? Her friend leaned in closer.

"So that's why I'd be a little careful of him if I were you. He's—"

Unfortunately, Joan had a pretty good idea what her friend was trying to tell her. Dr. Chambliss was recently divorced. No ring. *And probably looking.*

"Thanks," said Joan, and she meant it. "I get it."

Having a real ally here on staff was going to make all the difference in the world. And no, she didn't mean Porter Chambliss.

Latisha turned to go, then spun back around. "Hey, what about your husband? Didn't you say he was applying for a job here in the city?"

"As a matter of fact," Joan said, checking her watch, "I think his interview was at…well, it's probably already over by now."

A taxi splashed by, and Gerrit had a very un-Dutch thought of flagging it down. Why pay somebody else to drive you a few blocks when you could walk to an important job interview perfectly fine yourself?

"Hey, taxi!" he raised his hand and shouted. Well, that's how he'd seen it done in the movies. You raise your hand and whistle, and the taxi stops instantly.

Almost. Another Yellow Cab followed on the heels of the first one, and a minute later Gerrit was finally speeding around the block to his destination.

"You sure you know where this place is?" Gerrit asked the cabby once more, just to be sure. Of course, he wasn't even sure the driver had understood him the first time, since Gerrit didn't speak any Hindu or Arabic or whatever, and the man in the turban only seemed to have about two English phrases in his command.

"Yes, sure." The cabbie nodded vigorously, though by now they had probably gone around the block three times. But a minute later they'd pulled up in front of 12245 Rush Street.

"Well, how about that." Gerrit glanced at the meter and gulped. "Fifteen bucks to go two blocks and a lot of round and round, huh?"

The cabbie smiled and nodded as he held out his hand for the bills. "Sure, yes."

"Well, you have a great day." Gerrit shook his head and looked down at his watch one more time before he stepped out into the steady downpour. "I'm only a half hour late."

But when he got up to the reception desk in the first-floor lobby, he decided not to mention it. Maybe thirty minutes late was fashionable around here. So he checked his tie one more time and wondered if it was still as straight as Joan had made it for him this morning. *Oh well.* He looked at the nameplate on the desk and gave it his best shot.

"Yeah, Amee. Gerrit Appeldoorn here to see Patricia Hunsaker." He tried not to sound as if he was out of breath. "I've got an appointment."

The young receptionist with the headset studied him for a minute, as if trying to decide whether she should call security. Sure, he might have looked a little wet. Okay, a lot, even soaking. But whose business was that? *Hey, it's raining buckets out there, okay?*

"I'm afraid Ms. Hunsaker doesn't work here anymore," Amee the Receptionist took a sip from her Emu Springs water bottle and touched a few keys on her phone as she spoke. Yeah, multitasking. Back home at the dealership, they talked about that at staff meetings a lot. Gerrit managed to chew gum and walk at the same time himself. But—

"She never told me that." For proof he pulled out the business card with the appointment time he'd scribbled on the back. The card looked more like a used spit wad by this time, so he shoved it back into his pocket. "Since when is she not working here?"

She held up a finger as she punched a few more glowing buttons on her console and answered the phone with a sweetened robotic "Good morning. Elco Agricultural Machinery Incorporated. How may I direct your call?"

In his day she would have been yanking and plugging those big wires they once used on switchboards. 'Course that dated him a little too much, so he wasn't about to mention it. He had enough trouble trying to figure out if she was listening to him or somebody from Tokyo. And somebody had really done a number on the poor girl's lips, with some kind of highlighter pen and a pile of shiny lipstick that probably would have gone to better use waterproofing a rusty tractor fender. Poor kid. He tried not to wince or make her feel bad about the makeup hack job.

But she never answered his question, so he tried another tack, raising his voice just a skosh for good measure. Just in case she was wondering if he was upset about this or not.

"So you're telling me that I don't even *have* an appointment?"

She answered one more call before responding. "I'm afraid you're going to have to contact the personnel office and set up another time to come in." She held out another business card for him to take. "Just call the number on the card, and they'll be happy to help you."

"Sorry, I don't think so." Gerrit didn't take the card. "You don't know what I went through to get here. Isn't there somebody else here who can help me? I'm an employee, you know. Or I was."

The receptionist frowned and twirled the card between her long, red-painted claws with little sparklies on them. Somebody needed to give this gal the word about toning things down. Finally she sighed and put down the card, but by this time she was obviously not a happy camper.

"Let me see if the person who replaced Ms. Hunsaker has a moment to see you. Why don't you sit down over there."

It wasn't a question but a take-it-or-leave-it statement. Not exactly what he'd had in mind, but it was better than a poke in the eye with a sharp stick. So he sat down in a funny little purple chair that twirled and stared at the framed *Life* magazine ads of antique green tractors on the wall. He tried his best to keep from wondering what he was doing in a place like this and why he wasn't out riding one of those tractors in a field full of real dirt, not the grimy fake stuff that covered everything in this city. He didn't even pick up one of the magazines, 'cause *Cosmo* and the *New Yorker* might as well have been written in Sanskrit.

For a minute he almost headed for the door. Almost. Hey, if the lady couldn't even keep her appointment, maybe he didn't want the crazy job here in this crazy city. But he bit his tongue and stared at the tractor photos, thought of the way Joan had bounced and smiled when they drove the rental truck into the city. He liked the feeling of seeing that more than he didn't like sitting here in this lobby.

Lord, this is where You want me right now, isn't it? He prayed quietly without closing his eyes and folding his hands, which didn't always feel right, but it was all he could manage just now. And he didn't need God to answer again, really. The Lord had already done enough answering for now, and they both knew that.

Sure, yes. On the other hand, he didn't much mind the thought of Avery Wilson rolling around town dry and warm in his forest green parka. As long as Warney didn't find out. Matter of fact, Gerrit entertained the thought of getting together some of his other things, maybe a sweater or two and some jeans, putting them all in a bag and going out and finding Avery Wilson again. He might like that.

"I said, Mr. Appeldorf?" The receptionist broke into his plans, and he looked up. No telling how long he'd been sitting there, thinking and praying and staring at the old tractor photos. Fifteen or twenty minutes, maybe more. Gave him a chance to dry out a little. And he really wasn't in the mood to correct Amee the Receptionist on how to pronounce his name. "Janet Templeton will see you now."

Janet Templeton, whoever she is. But this was good, and he thanked Amee as she told him where to go on the twenty-seventh floor. A couple of minutes later, he was sitting in front of a big desk in Janet Templeton's office—and talk about a nosebleed view. He wanted to warn her not to roll her chair too far backward or she might go right through that window and...whoa! She looked up from a folder and smiled at him.

"Looks as if you got caught out there in the rain...er...Mr.—"

He ignored the comment about his being all wet, deciding instead just to introduce himself and explain what Patricia Hunsaker had told him before he and Joan had moved east. This gal looked like she might be sensible about it. She wore one of those sensible business suits as if she worked for Donald Trump himself. Early forties, he guessed, with just a touch of gray that she hadn't tried to hide. That was a good sign. Old enough to know what was going on, but not old enough to be put out to pasture. He decided to be straight with her. No messing around.

"Ms. Hunsaker said the sales-manager job was mine. Only needed to get here and start."

Ms. Templeton cleared her throat, chewed her lip, and started shuffling through the folder. *Not* a good sign. "Mr. Appledorf...uh..."

"That's Appeldoorn." He could only let it slide so long.

"I'm sorry, Mr. Appeldorn." She took off her fancy glasses and looked straight at him. "First of all, I think Amee told you that Ms. Hunsaker is no longer with us."

"Sure, I heard that. But we had an understanding, and—"

"I understand that, but we have a problem with that kind of arrangement. I have no way of knowing what she told you, but—"

"Sure you do. I just told you." Gerrit tried to keep the heat out of his voice, but the steam was out of the kettle, and it was starting to whistle.

"I'm not sure how to say this any more clearly. It's simply not our policy to make hiring decisions without taking applicants through the proper protocol."

"Proper protocol? Like a handshake deal doesn't do it anymore, right? I mean, that's all I got."

"I'm just trying to explain to you, Mr.…ah…Gerrit. In order for you to be considered for any potential openings, you'll need to go through the application process, a screening, and an interview. It's all standard. Once that's done, and assuming you qualify, we can put your name in the pool—"

"Whoa, whoa, wait a minute." Gerrit held up his hand. "I didn't move all the way across the country in a broken-down U-Haul to go jumping into any pool. I'm already wet enough as it is. Is there a job here or not?"

She sighed and shook her head. "Currently, no. I'm sorry. All our regional sales positions are filled. But as I said, you're welcome to go through the application process."

"No job."

"Not at the moment. I suggest you check back in a few months. You can pick up all the forms you'll need at the front desk." She slipped her chair back and stood, an oh-so-subtle signal for him to hit the road. He thought about just turning and heading straight for the door, directlike, just to make a point. But he reminded himself she couldn't help it. From where she sat up here on the twenty-seventh floor—from way up here in the clouds—just about everybody must look small to her.

He pinned a tight little smile on his face and shook her hand, pretending to thank her for the little grenade she'd just lobbed into his life. *Ka-Boom! Thank you very kindly, ma'am.* He didn't really need the work when it came right down to it, and maybe she could tell. After all, the music school was paying Joan plenty for the both of them—and more. They had a nice apartment, arranged by the school, and plenty of food in the cupboards. So he could just go for more long walks here in this city, get himself lost, and give his coats to homeless guys who made him feel like he had something to offer. And who knew whether he did or didn't?

He jabbed the elevator button harder than he needed to and discovered that the little button that was supposed to close the elevator doors a little sooner didn't. Of course, he wasn't in such a hurry, was he? He had another hour or so before he was supposed to meet Joan for lunch at the little café in the building where she worked, over on Michigan Avenue, wherever that was. And maybe he'd just pick up those job application papers on the way out, the way Ms. Templeton had suggested.

Or maybe not.

Chapter 18

*There are two means of refuge from the
misery of life—music and cats.*
—ALBERT SCHWEITZER

"I am *not* going to let Joan see me like this." Gerrit kept his arms crossed as he paced the sidewalk in the little strip of park across the street from the Fine Arts Building. It was windy, but at least the sun had come back out. But Gerrit wasn't used to the weather changing its mind so quickly. Didn't do that back home. When it rained, it rained, and usually all day. Here, a little rain, a little sun, a little wind.

He checked his watch again. Five minutes to noon. Time to cross the street, maybe, but no way was he going to show up early and sit in that coffee shop all by himself. He had already seen the folks walking in and out of that place on his first walk-by fifteen minutes earlier, and he knew right off that it wasn't the kind of place where you could just go in and order a cup of coffee—not without telling the barista that you wanted a double mocha grande with a shot of whatever. That "weren't" coffee out of a pot. The stuff they served in that place was probably better to look at than it was to drink—or eat. Besides all that, he didn't see any pickup trucks parked out front. A coffee shop wasn't a coffee shop without at least a couple of trucks.

But this little park was sort of okay, as city parks went, sandwiched here between the lakeshore railroad tracks and Michigan Avenue. Grass, a couple of trees, benches to rest on, and a raggedy-looking guy with a plastic garbage sack at his feet who looked up as Gerrit walked closer. But Gerrit beat the man to the punch.

"Let's not go there." Gerrit held up his hand as he walked by. "I don't think my wife would appreciate me walking into the coffee shop without a shirt on."

The man with the plastic bag started to open his mouth, changed his mind, and finally just watched Gerrit march on.

"Maybe next time," Gerrit added over his shoulder. As he crossed the street, he kept his eye on the windows of the Artist's Café, looking for any sign of Joan. Sure enough, he caught a glimpse of her waiting for a seat, looking at her watch the same way he had. Gerrit held up for just a moment to see what the tall fellow standing next to Joan, his back to Gerrit, was doing so close to her. Looked like Chambliss.

"Pardon me," he whispered and pushed open the door. But by then the guy had said his good-byes and headed out the far door into the lobby.

"There you are!" Joan's face lit up when she caught sight of her husband. "Right on time."

"Yeah. That's me. On time." Gerrit reminded himself once more not to let the morning gloom follow him into this café. 'Course, he could hardly hear Joan with all the laughing and talking going on. A clown in a tux stood up on his chair over in the corner and started to sing some opera hoo-ha before his friends laughed and pulled him back down. They must have dared him to do it.

"Goodness, what happened to you?" No surprise that Joan noticed the haircut first thing.

"You like it?" He turned his head from side to side for effect. "It's the Continental."

"More like the Continental Buzz. Oh, honey." She reached over and rubbed what was left on his poor scalp. "They didn't leave much. Who did this to you?"

"Olivia." As if Joan would recognize the name. "She does all the big names. You know, Yul Brynner, Michael Jordan, Robert Duvall."

"But they're all—" Then she laughed. "I get it. But what about the interview?"

"I'll let you know after I order."

"Are you hungry?"

"For some good *hutspot.*" He thought he didn't whisper it loudly enough for anyone to take him seriously. Hey, they had just about every other ethnic food in this city. Why not some good old-fashioned Dutch stew? No?

Their waitress gave him a funny look as she led them through a maze of little round tables piled with dishes that had a lot of little green sprigs of nothing and steaming cups of coffee that was not coffee. Joan had his number even before they had a chance to check the daily special.

"What's wrong?" Her dark eyebrows furrowed, and she peered over the top of her menu to study him.

"Who was that?" He could lob a question back just as easily, if it came down to that.

She looked around for a second before lowering her shoulders and giving him that sideways doggie stare that usually melted him. "You mean Porter? Dr. Chambliss?"

"Sorry I missed him." Gerrit tried to keep from frowning.

She opened her mouth in mock surprise. "Don't tell me you're—"

"No, no, no." He interrupted her with a raised hand. "Nothing to do with you. Nothing at all. I just don't like the way he had his hands all over you. Leaning in, like he was whispering some kind of secret in your ear. Or is that just a big-city thing?"

She frowned and glanced down at her menu before meeting his eyes. "He does tend to step into my space a little more than I'd like. But we're just going to have to get used to that kind of thing here, dear. People do a lot more cheek kissing in the city than they do back in Van Dalen."

"Yeah, I noticed. But I'm not talking about cheek kissing with this guy."

Gerrit wondered what he *was* talking about, exactly?

Joan reached across the table and gently took her husband's big hand. "We have to give these people a chance, Gerrit. Just because they're different from all your buddies at Karol's Koffee Kup, or just because their names don't start with a 'vander,' doesn't mean they're not nice people."

Gerrit looked around at the tables occupied mainly by artists, musicians, and people with multiple body piercings. He could tell the musicians by the instrument cases piled around their chairs—a cello over here, a couple of violins over there. The artists, he guessed, were the kids with the extra earrings and the hair coloring that didn't occur in nature.

"I know." He sighed, realizing that this was not a battle he was going to win, and he wasn't even sure he wanted to win it. "I'm doing my best. I'm just not comfortable with that guy. And everywhere I look reminds me we're a long way from home."

"Are we?"

Ouch. He avoided her eyes, realizing what he'd just said. He couldn't look away for long, though, and when he peeked back over the rim of the menu, she was waiting for him. *Lord, how did I deserve this woman?* He didn't mind lobbing the question to heaven, since he was pretty sure that all the noise down here was not going to make a fig of difference to the Almighty. And Gerrit really didn't need an answer either. Just sitting with Joan in this Artist's Café like some kind of musician's spouse was enough for him today. He remembered once again where his home really was.

Right here with Joan.

"Tell you what." He closed his menu and set it down on the table. "I have no idea what the difference is between"—he peeked again at the menu—"pistachio *chèvre quenelle* and tomato *harissa* glaze. Not the foggiest, and I'm not about to look stupid by asking the waitress. So you just pick what you think we'll both like, and I'll come along for the ride. I'm game, whatever it is. Deal?"

He decided it was worth it just to see her smile—a lot like the way she had smiled on their honeymoon—even if it meant ordering one of those things he couldn't even pronounce. She folded her own menu and placed it on top of his as the waitress approached them.

"We'll both have…" She paused and pursed her lips. "No, actually, do you have any chili dogs?"

So maybe it wasn't the cheapest chili dog he'd ever eaten, but it might have been the best—even if about a dozen folks stopped by the table to say hi to the new piano professor and he got a couple of good stares.

What, I got "hick" written across my forehead? he wondered. But each time he stood and shook hands as if he were running for office or at least making a go at being friendly. He would keep doing it, too, for as long as it took. And no matter how much he might remind people of Jed Clampett, he could always jerk his thumb at the sophisticated, dark-haired music professor and say, "I'm with her."

Making an effort had to count for something, didn't it? Well, at the moment it was all he had. That and the bedrock knowledge that God had brought him to this city for a reason. Supporting Joan, sure. But God wasn't passing out any other explanations. Not that He needed to, but it would have been nice.

Another music teacher with the shortest hair he'd ever seen on a woman came over to check out Joan and her farm boy.

"We've heard all about you!" The woman pumped his hand. *Wow!* Her hair was even shorter than his, and it made him look twice at her just to make sure, though he kept his eyes on the level. Yep, her voice gave her away. "Can you really teach us how to milk a cow?"

He hadn't heard that one before. *Is she serious?* But she kept a straight face.

"Uh…I'd be needing an animal to demonstrate on. Haven't seen one around here yet."

Well, they thought that was funnier than it was in real life. The hard part was getting past the feeling that they weren't exactly laughing *with* him. But Joan looked over with a smile and a nod. It was time for her to get back to work. She had a staff meeting at one, and look at the time!

"Thanks," he whispered in her ear as they extricated themselves and headed for the door. He leaned over to steal a quick kiss, which wasn't standard procedure for him in public, in plain sight of other folks, but today he was willing to make an exception. Somehow he'd managed to gloss over things when the conversation had steered itself to his job interview. "Still up in the air," he'd told her. "Paperwork to do yet. Always new folks to deal with, and that slows things down."

All true, but he didn't show her the folded-up job application still stuffed in his shirt pocket. And he didn't pass along the details about his meeting with the ever-helpful Ms. Templeton. Joan had enough things on her mind: a new job to learn, new people to meet, and new students to teach. They would talk about his troubles later, after she'd had a chance to settle in. For now he wasn't going to come to her whining and complaining that the folks at Elco Agricultural Machinery weren't being nice to him. Not yet, anyway. He stepped out of the building back into the wind, where fits of sunshine fought their way off the lake, and he paused for a moment to stare down a taxi driver.

"No way, fella." He shook his head just a little as he changed his mind about the taxi. The guy couldn't hear him, but it didn't matter. He'd had enough taxi rides for one day, thank you. As he stood there, he couldn't help looking back over his shoulder at Joan's new world. Once more out on the street, out of Joan's reach, he felt the shiver of aloneness catch up with him. If he had stayed there much longer, he might have turned and run back to her arms, the only place in this city where he now felt at home.

Instead, Gerrit made a left turn down Michigan Avenue and walked toward the famous old Orchestra Hall, where the tallest buildings sprouted from the lakeshore and a pair of elephant-sized stone lions guarded the steps to the Art Museum. A gaggle of Japanese tourists was taking turns snapping pictures of each other standing in front of the statues. One of them looked up at Gerrit with his camera outstretched.

"You want a snapshot?" Gerrit took the camera. "Sure. Now everybody stand there and say, 'Taxi drivers rip you off.' "

Maybe the puzzled looks weren't quite what the tourists had in mind for their souvenir photographs, but Gerrit snapped a couple more shots just to be sure he got a decent one. Then he smiled, bowed, and returned the camera.

"There you go." The tourists repeated their accented thank-yous and smiled before Gerrit hurried off.

Maybe he would get ambitious and make Joan dinner, surprise her when she came home from work. Shoot, he could cook some. It sure wouldn't be pistachio *chèvre quenelle* or whatever that urban stuff was called. *Let's see…cabbage, potatoes, sausages, and plenty of mayonnaise for the spuds.* Never mind that the doctor had told him to leave off the mayo because of his heart problem. What were Dutch-style spuds without a good dollop or two of mayo? He could throw this together; he'd done it before. But first he had to find a grocery store, and figure out whether they had any Dutch Dubbel Zout licorice here in this city.

He continued up Michigan Avenue in the direction of their apartment, hoping he could outrun the gnawing loneliness in the pit of his stomach. And he couldn't help wondering if anybody else in this city of two and a half million felt anywhere close to how he felt. Businessmen in dark suits power walking to their next meeting. A mom steering her stroller though the midday sidewalk crowd. A couple of guys carrying tools covered with wallboard dust. A bellhop standing guard outside one of the ritzy hotels—the one he would have stayed at if he were a guest on *Oprah*. Were any of them lonely?

As an experiment, Gerrit tried to catch people's eyes just to see what they would do. Back in beautiful downtown Van Dalen, he couldn't have gone more than ten feet without someone saying "Ho" or "How's it going?" And the weird part was that people actually waited for an answer.

"Howdy." Gerrit sidestepped a middle-aged woman coming out of a little shop on the corner of Randolph Street. Either she wasn't in the mood for exchanging howdies, or Gerrit looked too much like her ex. In any case, she gripped her package to her chest and made a beeline for her Beemer parked on the street. The car's alarm yelped as she unlocked the front door.

So much for that experiment. For the next few minutes, Gerrit gave up trying to greet the citizens of Greater Chicago. But then someone's gaze caught his from behind a little glass window, and Gerrit couldn't help stopping to check out the puppies at the Benson Pet Shop. *How much is that doggy in the window?* Once inside, more curious stares met his as Gerrit worked his way sideways through the crowded aisles lined with cages stacked three high. He didn't mind the smell so much; sort of reminded him of the barn back home in Van Dalen. And he didn't mind the racket so much either, for the same reason.

But he couldn't just walk past the little cocker spaniel puppy, who was cowering and whimpering behind bars in the far corner of his tiny cage.

"Hey, little guy." Gerrit leaned closer and poked his finger inside the cage. "I know the feeling."

He knew all right, though he wished he didn't. And maybe it was Gerrit's low voice, or maybe the little dog just knew a friend when he saw one. But after a couple minutes of coaxing, the spaniel unglued himself from the back of the cage and crept a little closer, his entire hind end wagging. Without thinking, Gerrit undid the prison door, reached in, and scooped up his little soul mate.

"That's okay, that's okay." Gerrit scratched him behind the ears as the puppy licked his cheek. "I can understand how you wouldn't want to stay cooped up in there. But I don't think my wife would appreciate it much if I brought you home."

She wouldn't, would she? Gerrit thought about it a little longer, but he knew it wouldn't work. He'd be working somewhere eventually, she'd be working, and the poor puppy would just trade one cell for a slightly larger one. Either way, the little guy would be left all alone, and Gerrit knew *that* feeling all too well. No, it wouldn't work.

"I'm sorry," he told the puppy. "It just wouldn't—"

"Excuse me, sir!" A wide-eyed young employee rushed over to the dog's rescue. "You're not allowed to take the animals out of their cages."

"Sorry." Gerrit turned to replace the dog himself, but the young gal had already reached out to take it. "I was just putting him back."

Gerrit let the girl take over, but not before giving the puppy one final scratch behind the ears. In the process of putting him back in the cage, she nearly dropped the animal as she screeched and held him out at arm's length. A little stream dribbled onto her shoes.

"They do that when they're scared," Gerrit told her, and he couldn't stop his voice from choking up just a little. Good thing it was so funny. "But you probably already knew that."

He bit his lip and turned to go just as a Siamese cat reached out from another cage and scratched his elbow. Instead of jumping, Gerrit patted the paw, and the cat just looked him in the eyes. *Shoot! Between the spaniel and the cat.* And when the Siamese let out a long, mournful yowl, Gerrit could almost swear the little guy was talking to him.

"Sorry, pal."

"That's all right." By this time the employee was sponging off her shoe with a rag.

"I meant…oh, forget it."

Maybe, he thought, *I shouldn't have stepped in here after all.*

Chapter 19

Music can name the unnamable
and communicate the unknowable.
—LEONARD BERNSTEIN

*J*oan glanced nervously at her watch and checked her assignment book to make sure she had her schedule right. Tuesday meant that she had Performance Basics at eleven o'clock and Advanced Performance master class at ten past one. But before all that, she'd be tutoring at least three advanced students. She ran her finger down the list:

"Jennifer Greene, Mariano Duncan, and...Zhao Wei."

Or is that Wei Zhao? Though she hesitated to admit it, she could never remember the difference between Chinese first and last names. Either way, he would be showing up any minute. And sure enough, someone rapped on the door of her office just then, almost too softly to hear.

"Come in." Joan closed her appointment book and cocked her head to make sure she had really heard someone knocking. A moment later a young dark-haired Chinese man poked his head in.

"You're Zhao Wei?" She waved for him to enter, and his face lit up. He looked like a teenager to her, but she guessed he was probably in his midtwenties. "Please come in."

"Mrs. Apple...App—" He screwed up his face and referred back to a scrap of paper in his hand as if he'd been rehearsing and now could not quite deliver his lines. In the process he bumped the little bust of J. S. Bach, nearly knocking it off its perch of honor on the table next to the piano. Joan dove for it.

"Oh no!" Zhao Wei tried to grab it as well, but he wasn't quick enough. Joan caught little Johann before he hit the ground and returned him to his perch.

"That's okay," Joan assured the young man. "He's a very special little statue. Has sentimental value. No harm done."

"I am so sorry." Zhao had turned a shade of pink.

"Really. Don't worry about it. Please, just call me Joan."

Joan drew up a chair next to the ebony piano bench and extended her hand. She usually preferred keeping things more formal with students, but in this case she thought it might work better to be friendly.

"Mrs. Joan." He finally smiled and bobbed a little with his head as he shook her hand. "I am Zhao. Pleased to be your student."

At least it sounded like that's what he said. As she explained who she was and what they would be trying to accomplish in their tutoring time, he seemed to understand most of what she said—at least judging by his body language and his attempts to answer her. The challenge was making out what *he* said, and she strained to tune her ears to his accent, to catch clues of words and fragments of phrases that would signal his meaning. And if she couldn't understand, she resorted to Zhao's tried-and-true tactic: smile and nod.

Joan passed him the syllabus, which detailed the guidelines for their tutoring practicum class, deadlines, planned recitals, improvement matrices—all of which he probably could not read.

She finally decided to cut her teacher-pupil lecture short. "But that's enough chatting. Let me hear what you can do."

She pointed to the keyboard, then to a pile of sheet music she'd brought out for her students to try. Now here was a language they could both understand. A little Bach…maybe some Prokofiev and Shostakovich …and, of course, one of her favorites, Debussy's *First Arabesque*.

But he must not have understood her completely, because he nodded and launched right into Rachmaninoff's Piano Concerto no. 3 in D Minor, an arrangement made famous in the movie *Shine*. *Well, all right.* Not what she'd asked for, but a supremely difficult piece to be sure. But apparently not too difficult for Zhao Wei. He attacked the music with a precision and spirit that nearly knocked Joan out of her seat. Barely a dozen measures in, and she could safely say that rarely had she ever seen such raw talent. At that moment Zhao might have been blind to the world, as he closed his eyes and swayed, his fingers alive to the intricate rhythms and counterpoints Rachmaninoff had created. As Zhao coaxed a magnificent sound out of Joan's Bösendorfer, a bead of sweat trickled down his temple, disappearing into the thick black mane over his ears.

Yet when Joan looked more closely, she noticed something odd about Zhao's fingering, a couple of quirky habits that any responsible piano teacher would long ago have caught and corrected. Then there was the way he sat far too close to the piano as well as the pumping action of his arms.

Very odd. It almost reminded her of Gerrit when he'd first started taking lessons from her, and the thought crossed her mind that he and Zhao might have quite a bit in common. Perhaps she should introduce him to Gerrit. Both men could probably use a friend in this city. Perhaps she'd introduce them later.

As Zhao continued, Joan noticed that his pedal work didn't quite match the verve of his keyboarding. In fact—and she would have to find a way to tell him this gently—it was a wonder he played so marvelously despite his collection of bad habits.

But on he played, and the music captivated her with a heart and soul that any pianist would die for. She had discovered a diamond to be sure— a diamond that could still use a bit of polish. *But, oh, what a sound!*

Presently Zhao reached the end of the last measure and then seemed to awaken. He took a deep breath, opened his eyes, and rested his hands in his lap as the final chord echoed through Joan's office. How much had the performance taken out of him? There certainly was no mistaking the joy on his face. This young man apparently loved his music as much as it loved him.

"Where did you learn to play like that?" She could hardly get the words out. "It's remarkable."

"I play well?" He sounded almost like one of her beginning students back in Van Dalen. Not his playing, of course. Just his question.

"More than well." Her mind had already raced to their first recital, to the stir this prodigy would surely make. "But you must tell me where you learned."

Though he hesitated, she thought he understood the question.

"Your teacher?" She tried again. "In China?"

"I play for a teacher in Beijing. Mr. Xin Lian."

She didn't know whether that was *play, played,* or *had played.* Apparently he didn't know either.

"Ah, I see. He taught you." She would have to look up this Mr. Xin Lian. Maybe someone here on staff knew of him.

Zhao shook his head. "Mr. Xin Lian had many students. I went to him, and he say I need instruction here in Chicago, United States. Mr. Xin Lian sponsor me, but he does not teach me."

Does not, did not, or *had not.* Either way, gratefully that made some sense. But it still didn't answer her question. She wasn't sure how else to ask. "Then who?"

"My father played *erhu.* It is Chinese violin."

She nodded. "A beautiful instrument. Did you learn to play it?"

"Music, I learned. But I love piano even more than *erhu.* My father…"

He looked away and pressed his lips together. They had hit a sensitive spot, and Joan was beginning to see what drove this young musician.

"I don't mean to be nosy…" she told him.

He looked back at her with curiosity and brought a hand to his nose. "What is…?"

"I'm sorry. Nosy means to be too curious, asking questions that are not mine to ask."

"Oh." He nodded and flashed a white-toothed smile—pleasant, though he clearly needed braces. "I do not mind questions."

Well, then. Nosy or not, she still wanted to know where this talent had sprung from. "So your father didn't teach you piano, I assume?"

Zhao kept his eyes focused on the keyboard as he told his story. "My father...at first he did not approve. He think very Chinese."

"I don't understand."

He paused before going on, as if measuring how far he should go in betraying family secrets. "Piano is Western, he say. Not as good as traditional Chinese instruments. So I teach myself from listening to music over and over. When I am little boy."

This was getting stranger and stranger. And it was becoming obvious that she might need to work with the young student on his verb tenses as well as the finer points of his piano technique. *But a self-taught virtuoso?*

"That's how you got started with the piano?"

"And I see video of Vladimir Horowitz. I play it many, many times."

Oh my. Stranger still. Zhao reached down into his backpack and pulled out a videocassette that looked as if it had been through a rock tumbler. The battered label was lettered in precise little Chinese characters, except for the "Vladimir Horowitz" part. Obviously Zhao had put that tape through its paces more than a time or two. Perhaps in secret?

"Let me understand what you're saying. You learned to play the piano by listening to recordings?"

"Recordings, yes. Stephen Hough, Nikolaus Lahusen, Sviatoslav Richter—many times. Many, many times."

He struggled to pronounce other English words, but the names of some of the world's finest pianists rolled off his tongue as if they were old friends and family. And in a way, apparently, they were.

"I've heard of this kind of thing before, but I've never seen it." Joan suddenly felt as if she should have been recording this session, for a documentary perhaps. And though she had a feeling she knew what would happen when she asked him to sight-read, she pulled out the music anyway, starting with Bach.

"Can you play this for me?"

He hesitated for a moment as he studied the cover carefully.

"B-a-a-ch." He sounded out the letters like a small child learning to read his first chapter book. That brought another flash of a smile, and he nodded. "Yes, Bach. I can play some Bach."

"This Bach." She tapped the sheet music with her finger. "Variation 26 of the *Aria mit...*" She pronounced the German title carefully. "We know it, of course, as one of the Goldberg variations. Can you read it?"

Joan had no intention of embarrassing the young man, just finding out what he could do. And she would have preferred not having a visit from Dr. Chambliss just then. He knocked on the door but didn't wait for her to say, "Come in."

"Just seeing how things are going!" He nodded at Joan's student at the piano. "How's Mr. Wei doing? You know, he comes highly recommended."

Joan nodded. *How could he not?*

Dr. Chambliss turned to Zhao. "Playing for Mrs. Appeldoorn, are you?"

Zhao nodded nervously, and Joan tried to say something about "maybe another time." But he squinted at the sheet music, knit his fingers for a moment, spread the music out in front of him, and launched into one of Bach's more difficult pieces.

How could it not bring a smile to the administrator's face? But from where Joan sat, she was the only one who noticed that Zhao did not turn the pages at quite the right time. Almost, but not quite. And though he interpreted the music as well as any student she had ever seen—better, perhaps—she was certain of one thing: Zhao Wei could not read music.

Incredibly, he had much of the piece memorized. And what he didn't have memorized, he filled in with a kind of dexterity that made Joan cover her smile with a hand. This young man could even compose on the fly. Fortunately, Dr. Chambliss wasn't staying for an entire concert, and after several measures he waved them on with a smile and a nod and drifted back into the hallway. Zhao was sweating again, but Joan guessed it was for a different reason. When the door had closed, she motioned for him to stop.

"Very good, Zhao. Very good. We'll be able to work on a few things together from now on."

He nodded and smiled, though he probably didn't know just how much work they really had to do.

"But tell me more about your family."

Zhao took a deep breath and checked over his shoulder. His fingers still trembled a bit at the keyboard. Had he heard her?

"You mentioned your father?"

"Yes, family!" At that he pulled out his thick wallet and showed Joan photograph after photograph of his father and mother, a sister and an aunt, his grandfather and grandmother. His father, a stern-looking older version of Zhao, posed in front of a beautiful two-stringed *erhu,* the long-necked Chinese violin.

"You must miss them." As soon as she'd said it, Joan wanted to bite her tongue. What had made her say such a thing? She saw the emotion well up in his eyes.

"Once more, I'm sorry." She lowered her voice. "It's just that so much of music comes from the heart. It always helps me to know a little bit about my students."

"I understand."

Did he? She could say nothing else, and she would not embarrass her new student more than she already had. He put his pictures carefully back in his wallet, pausing for a moment over the photo of his father. Then he glanced up once more at the door, as if Porter Chambliss would suddenly pop back in.

"Dr. Chambliss liked your music very much, Zhao. I thought it was quite creative myself."

"I think perhaps he send me home if..."

Though he didn't finish his thought, she could guess the rest. And she knew that he was trusting her, a stranger, with his secret.

"Nobody's sending you home, Zhao. I've already heard enough to convince me that you belong here at Gaylord. Play another piece for me. Anything you like."

He smiled at her suggestion and relaxed his shoulders.

"But I'll tell you what." She showed him with her own hands how the wrist hung limp and her fingers flitted like butterflies over the piano keys. "Let's see what we can do with your approach to the keyboard."

Chapter 20

I used to own an ant farm but had to give it up.
I couldn't find tractors small enough to fit it.
—STEVEN WRIGHT

So much for global warming." Gerrit turned up the collar of his thin Seattle Mariners Windbreaker, but it was no match for the icy fingers of the wind rushing at him from the lake. The mid-October blast had turned the sky to a dull pewter and had flash-frozen golden autumn leaves to their branches before they even had a chance to litter the streets. Even puddles of sleet had turned solid under his feet, and he stepped gingerly as he walked toward Lincoln Park.

Winter already—and record cold? Well, at least it matched his mood. Who was in a hurry anyway? No job. Nothing to do. He rubbed his cheeks, trying to keep from icing over and wondering what he was doing out here rather than sitting safely inside his warm apartment and watching the latest *Oprah*. Today she was doing some more of those makeovers. Come to think of it, maybe they should do one on his attitude.

Sorry, Lord. Seemed that every time he talked to God lately, he was apologizing. Just like when he talked to Joan. *Sorry, sorry, sorry.* And he was. He looked around the city park and realized that he hadn't been this far north before. Joan had told him there was a zoo up here someplace. Maybe he could go watch the penguins freeze their tails off.

He crunched over frozen blades of grass, doing his best not to keep replaying the words of the phone call over and over in his mind the way he'd been doing nonstop for the past three days.

"It appears we've filled that position as well, Mr. Appeldoorn."

In other words, nice try, but no cigar.

"Your qualifications are quite unique."

In other words, you don't fit anywhere.

"With your permission, we'd like to keep your name on file in case something comes up."

In other words, don't hold your breath, old man.

After nearly stepping on an abandoned Frisbee, he picked it up and flung it with a mighty grunt as far as he could. It didn't do wonders for his shoulder, but he watched as the saucer soared past a statue of Hans Christian Andersen and landed in the middle of a frozen rose garden. He decided to follow the Frisbee to a pond closer to the lakeshore. Looked like the zoo was just over there.

"So what's going on here, Lord?" He decided to ask once again, though the cold gray underside of heaven wasn't giving up any answers lately. Not a one. "How 'bout a little clue for an old guy who doesn't know where he's supposed to be and what he's supposed to do anymore? Just a clue. Where do I belong?"

He wasn't used to asking *that* question. Where he grew up, folks didn't have to ask. They knew. Dad worked a farm, and so did you. Dad built houses, and you helped. Your family lived in Van Dalen, and nobody even dreamed about moving away. So what was he doing wandering around a frozen park in big-city Chicago, Illinois?

"I know I told her my home was with her, Lord. You know I meant every word of it. But I was thinking You'd work things out a little better."

Careful there, buddy. He knew who he was talking to. Still, it made him feel better—a little—to list his grievances with the Almighty. He wasn't going to dump it all on Joan. She was having a whale of a time with her new job, working with musical geniuses and coming home all bouncy and rosy-cheeked. Like the job had been made for her, or the other way around.

Him? He looked down at his hand, and it was shaking. The constant noise of sirens made him feel like he was living inside a prison. He'd stopped running by the pet shop because it made him feel even more depressed. This park was probably the best place for him, especially since nobody was there to see him talking to God like one of those homeless guys. So he walked around a little garden area by the pond, where someone had set up a little trail with big rocks that had been chiseled with portions of a Shakespeare quote, Burma Shave–style.

"Shall I compare thee to a summer's day?" Gerrit put on a little bit of an English accent as he read the first stone. "Thou art more lovely and more temperate: Rough winds do shake the darling buds of May, and summer's lease hath all too short a…"

He picked a burger wrapper off the last word.

"…date."

Verily, that wast lovely, he supposed, though he had to think for a minute to catch the meaning. *Hmm.* And then the part about how "thy eternal summer shall not fade… Nor shall Death brag thou wander'st in his shade."

That old Bill Shakespeare was a pretty confident guy when it came to death and dying. Gerrit read the sonnet aloud all the way through to the end, not thinking anyone would hear or notice. One other person was out with her dog by the pond, and she must have been as whacked as he was. Dogs in the city had to get out just as much as they always did, he supposed, cold or no cold. Only this dog wasn't listening to his master much. The black furry mutt was heading across thin ice straight for a small flock of geese that had taken shelter in the only unfrozen little pocket of water, right in the middle of the pond.

"Barkley!" The girl with a nose ring and an empty leash hollered at her dog, who wasn't listening. "Get back here!"

A lot of good her shouting was doing, 'cause old Barkley had ideas of his own about a goose salad. Only the geese knew how to fly, and the dog didn't. That would make a difference when the gangly mutt started sliding and then cracking through the ice in the middle of the pond. With a panicked honking and a *whoosh* of wings, the flock took to the air just as Barkley went through the ice. That only made the girl shout even more, but at first Gerrit didn't think too much of it. Barkley got himself into this mess; he ought to be able to get himself out. But with all her waving and yelling, the girl might need CPR pretty soon.

When Gerrit noticed after only a few minutes that Barkley wasn't thrashing around at the edge of the ice anymore, he had a pretty good idea that (a) this dog wasn't getting out of the pond on his own, (b) his owner had no idea what to do, and (c) if somebody didn't come to the rescue pretty quick, they weren't going to be able to fish Barkley out of there before next spring. So Gerrit tested the ice at the edge of the pond; it immediately started to spiderweb under his weight. Despite the extreme cold, the ice hadn't had much time to thicken up. But Gerrit thought he could see the bottom of the pond, which meant it wasn't too deep. Just to be sure, he found a stick and poked it down through.

How deep can a city pond be?

He found out for sure a moment later when he slid out as far as he could, within about six feet of the exhausted dog.

"Hey, be careful out there!" the owner advised as Gerrit broke through the ice and found himself standing in waist-high pond water. About what he'd figured, except the mud at the bottom of the pond pulled at his shoes a bit. But now he was committed, and he ignored the water's needle-prickly, numbing cold as he plowed through the ice to the rescue.

"Come here, mutt." He managed through chattering teeth. The dog was about out of gas, barely thrashing at the water, so it really wasn't much effort to grab his collar and steer him back to the edge of the pond. Gerrit lost a shoe in the process, which was not so good.

"Barkley!" The owner hoisted her dog onto shore as Gerrit followed.

Shoot. He had liked those shoes. And hopping around the city on one foot was not going to work too well, especially not in this weather.

"I can't believe it." The girl hugged her shivering dog like she was never going to let him go again. "Why did you do that?"

"Your dog looked like he could use a hand is all." Gerrit shrugged. "Anybody would've done the same thing back home."

"Oh. Where's that?"

He had to think for a minute, and the question reminded him that he still wasn't quite sure of the answer. Or was he?

"Actually," Gerrit pointed a thumb back toward the city, "I'm just a quarter mile back that way."

The girl removed the bandanna from her head to towel off her dog. It didn't do the pooch a whole lot of good, but it was better than nothing. Just then Gerrit himself could have used a bandana—or two.

"Anyway, that was so cool." She turned to leave. "Thanks."

"Anytime." Gerrit shrugged. "Used to have a dog who got herself in trouble like that a time or two."

"Back home, you mean."

Another pause. "Uh-huh. Sometimes they just need a hand."

Right now the only one who needed a hand was Gerrit. As the girl said good-bye and walked away, he looked down at his dripping pants and muddy feet—running shoe on the left and what used to be a white sock on the right. He couldn't stay out here. But instead of turning for home, he looked past the pond to a familiar sight—only not-so-familiar here in Chicago.

A dairy barn? What in the world?

Admittedly, this was no time for an outing to the zoo. If he was smart, he'd simply hurry back to Lake Shore Towers. No argument there. But the barn was much closer than his apartment, and if this barn was anything like the one back home, he'd be able to clean up inside there a little easier than slogging through the lobby and elevator at the Towers and tracking mud across their white-carpeted apartment. And the barn ought to be warmer than out here.

He headed for the barn at a slow trot. Actually, it was more than just one barn, which made things even more interesting. One big red barn stood to the south near the pond, and another white barn faced it across a courtyard. An old-fashioned windmill stood guard in the center by some benches and was spinning without a reason. It looked a bit like a farm, sort of the same way a museum looks like real life, but he didn't stop to read the Farm-in-the-Zoo sign or look at the map that showed where the sheep and the goats were kept. He just hurried along ignoring the *squish-flop, squish-flop* sound he was making and the frostbite he was no doubt developing in his frozen sock-clad foot. He could have run but thought he probably already looked strange enough.

Why hadn't anybody told him about this place before? Didn't Joan know about it? Now, even in this city, he could smell the cows. Even over the ear-splitting sound of a passing siren, he could hear their low shuffling and moos, the most wonderful noise in the world. The sign in front said Dairy Barn.

He pushed open the big door and just stood there, letting his eyes get used to the dim light and the wonderful noise.

"My, oh my." Gerrit grinned at the sight of three Guernseys in stalls over to the right, munching contentedly on their feed and waiting their turn to be milked. Over on the left a half-dozen goats lay around on their hay bed behind a pipe railing. And up ahead, behind glass, Gerrit discovered the source of the racket.

"Oh, come on." A young guy struggled to bring a large cow into position for milking. The cow could probably tell that the guy had never done anything like this before. She planted her hooves and grunted—nothing that a good slap on the hind end wouldn't move. But the milker didn't have a clue. He looked like he was trying to discuss the matter with her, maybe take a vote on what they should do and when. Gerrit had to chuckle at the sight.

"Oh!" The young guy jerked up his head as if Gerrit had just caught him playing with matches. "I didn't hear you come in. Are you here for the milking demonstration?"

Why not? Gerrit peeled off his remaining shoe and socks and grabbed a pair of rubber boots parked by the entry.

"Actually,"—Gerrit held up his hand—"you just wait right there. I'm here to give you a hand."

Gerrit believed every word, and he hoped the guy would too. He cruised around to the employee entrance on the left, pushed his way through, and joined the struggling milker.

"I'll show you how this thing works," he told the young man, whose shoulders sagged in relief.

"Am I glad you're here," the guy told him, after introducing himself as Boyce. "I haven't been trained for this part of the zoo yet. All I've been doing is feeding reptiles, but everybody called in sick today."

"No problem." Gerrit introduced himself, untangled the milk feed lines, and had the cow in place a moment later. "We'll get this figured out."

"Wow!" Boyce stepped back to watch. "I've never seen anybody get the milk going so fast before."

"Been doing this sort of thing since I was a kid." Gerrit already had the vacuum fired up and creamy milk coursing through the barn's clear piping to the stainless-steel holding tank. "It's not rocket science."

"Well, all I can say is it's a good thing you were working today." Boyce nodded at the family with two small kids in winter coats, noses pressed up against the glass. "Otherwise I might be looking a little silly in here."

Gerrit grinned and winked at the nearest little kid as he dropped his voice to a whisper. "I hate to tell you this, but I don't really work here."

"You're pretty funny, Gerrit." Boyce laughed and handed Gerrit a wireless microphone headset. "How about you voice the demo today?"

"Uh…" Gerrit had tried to tell him. Now this little family was looking as if they expected a show.

Boyce clicked on the sound.

"Well, here we are. Welcome to…" Gerrit turned aside to whisper "What's this place called?" Which didn't do much to brighten Boyce's expression.

"Right." Gerrit nodded his thanks and rubbed his hands together. "This is the milking barn at the Lincoln Park Zoo, and you're going to be glad you stepped in out of the cold, folks."

A half hour later all the milking was done, but Gerrit was still spinning yarns about milking by hand and strange cow personalities. He threw in a couple of udder jokes for the small crowd that had gathered and answered a handful of questions before parents thanked him and turned their strollers toward the door.

"Come on back for the next show," Gerrit called after them. "We do this twice a day, whether we want to or not!"

The smile hadn't left his face from the moment he'd slipped his cold feet into the boots. But then he noticed a gray-haired woman in a brown doctor's smock standing in the corner, arms crossed. As soon as the last person left, she marched past the fancy black-and-white tiled milking platform to where Gerrit was cleaning up.

"I think I'd better go," he whispered to Boyce. He could probably slip out the other exit before—

"Excuse me!" The woman with the traffic-cop expression didn't waste any time catching up to him. "Who are you?"

Gerrit pulled up straight and turned around slowly. *Busted.* So there was nothing for it but to smile and put out his hand. "Gerrit Appeldoorn. How do you do?"

She never uncrossed her arms but looked him over as if he were a telemarketer interrupting her supper and she was on the Do Not Call list. *Oh, right.* Those guys weren't legal anymore.

"I ought to call the police." She skewered Boyce with her laser glare before he could back away to the other side of the milking stall. "Boyce, tell me how this person got in here. He's obviously not wearing an employee jacket. I don't believe he's even a docent." Her laser eyes shifted back to Gerrit. "Is that correct?"

"I thought he just forgot his jacket at home." *Give Boyce credit for trying.* But his lame excuse rolled off the boss-woman's back.

"Look, I apologize if I caused any trouble." Gerrit held up his hands in surrender. "It's not the kid's fault. I just thought he looked like he could use some help. And then these folks started coming in, and your girls obviously needed milking, so one thing led to another."

The boss-woman let Gerrit explain, but she never uncrossed her arms.

"You heard him, didn't you, Ms. Bryant?" *Give Boyce extra credit for bravery.* "He was totally great, and he knew everything about the cows, and the kids even thought his jokes were…" His voice trailed off as she held up her hand for him to shut up. "…funny."

And now she began firing questions like "I assume you're from Wisconsin, Mr.…what was it again?"

"Uh…Appeldoorn. Actually, no. Washington State."

"I see. So what brings you to Chicago?"

He explained about Joan's job and the move and about his job at Elco that hadn't materialized. He hadn't wanted to say much about that part, but he couldn't duck the incoming questions fast enough. Finally Ms. Bryant uncrossed her arms, which might have been a good sign—or a sign that she was ready to hit him.

"Normally we're not in this situation, Mr. Appeldoorn. We have a number of highly skilled people rotating through from other zookeeper positions."

And you're telling me this because?

"But we're short-handed right now, as you see. Two people out sick, long-term. One's having a baby. One just quit. No, two."

"We're short-handed," Boyce repeated, and she frowned at him.

"I believe I just said that, Boyce." She turned back to Gerrit with an eyebrow raised. "If you're interested, Mr. Appeldoorn, our administrative offices are just over on Clark Street. I can't promise anything, but I can let them know you'll be turning in an application."

Wait a minute. From calling the police to "How would you like to work here?" in less than five minutes? Gerrit wasn't quite sure what he'd just heard.

"Unless you're not interested, of course." She crossed her arms again. *Interesting woman. Could have been a wrestling coach.*

But as he looked around the milking barn, he figured that maybe God had just answered his "Where do I belong?" question.

"Tell me where that office is again?"

Chapter 21

Never go to bed mad.
Stay up and fight.
—PHYLLIS DILLER

You told them you wouldn't work this afternoon?" Joan looked at her husband sideways as they walked together down LaSalle on the way to church. She wanted to be sure she heard him right.

"It's Sunday, remember," he told her, as if that explained everything. Considering where this man was born and raised, though, it did.

"And what did they think of that?"

"Looked at me like they thought I was nuts."

"But you can understand that, can't you?"

"Understand it?"

"Well, the zoo's open on weekends because that's when families can come. And you always milked on Sundays back in—"

"Back in Van Dalen," he interrupted, "all we did on Sundays was what we absolutely had to. Nothing more. Sabbaths are for resting."

Joan decided not to bring up the fact that Sabbaths were Saturdays, not Sundays, according to the way the Bible looked at it. But then she and her husband didn't always agree on exactly what the Bible said.

"But you'll go to a restaurant on Sunday," she reminded him. "You're making those people work."

Whoops. This time it was his turn to frown, and it didn't look good on his clean-shaven Sunday-morning face.

"I thought you liked the way we did things in Van Dalen." He must have decided not to argue the point about going to restaurants. "You said you liked not mowing the lawns on Sunday. And the fact that everything was closed."

"I know I said that. But can you imagine everything stopping here in the city just because it's Sunday?"

"Don't see how that would be a problem."

"This is Chicago, honey. Not a small farming town."

Rule Number One about maintaining marital bliss: never belittle your husband's roots.

Gerrit's frown turned darker still. "And we're going to change our standards 'cause of where we live?"

"No, we're not. I'm just saying that if you're going to work at a place that serves the public on weekends, you might just be prepared to work on the weekends."

"Oh." He held his forehead. "I can't believe I married a relativist."

"I am *not* a relativist. I just think there's a case for some grace here. What about Hebrews?"

"Lot of 'em still keep their Sabbath last time I checked."

"No, no." She opened her Bible, not knowing whether she could find the right verse. And sure enough, she couldn't even walk and find the book of Hebrews at the same time.

"I know it's in here somewhere."

"That's comforting. What are you talking about?"

"The verse in Hebrews where it says the old covenant is obsolete and going away."

"You might try Hebrews eight." He paused while she fumbled for the reference. "First and Second Timothy, Titus, Philemon, Hebrews…"

Some people might think farmers didn't know their Bible. They'd never met her husband.

"So you know the verse I'm talking about."

"Sure I know it. I just don't think it says what you think it says."

"Brother." She closed her Bible without locating the verse in question. Of course, Joan knew she was arguing with a staunch Calvinist. He had no choice but to say what he did.

"Did you remember that the Lord said he hadn't come to abolish the Law but to fulfill it?"

"So you keep kosher?" She hadn't meant to snap back so quickly, but he had to see how wrong he was about the ceremonial law. "God changed His law with the new covenant, Gerrit. But you sound like Peter arguing with God about what he was supposed to eat and not eat. That vision with the big tablecloth?"

"I suppose you're going to tell me you had a few visions of your own."

"Not lately." This was getting a little nasty.

"Well, some things God don't change."

"Doesn't. And other things change He does." She could Yoda-speak with the best of them. Only problem was, she knew Gerrit hadn't seen the *Star Wars* movies with the wise little backward-speaking creature, so her sarcasm was lost on him, which was probably just as well. She was done arguing anyway, and apparently so was he.

They walked the next block in awkward silence.

Finally she had to ask. "You never told me what they said when you told them you wouldn't work on Sunday."

A ghost of a smile played at his lips. He seemed to love winning his arguments, and in this case the last to speak was the winner. Or the one who stayed quiet the longest. But that might be a guy thing, too.

"They said fine."

"Fine? Just like that? Fine?"

"Just like that. Fine. I'm just stopping by to help with the milking this afternoon."

"*What?*" She stopped short in the middle of the sidewalk. "After all that, and now you tell me you're going in to work this afternoon? Whatever happened to the fourth commandment?"

He held up his hands and gave her an expression like "Don't you know?"

"It's the same as what I told you before. The Lord said it was okay to untie your ox and lead it to water on the Sabbath. Or pull it out of a well."

"I didn't know we were talking about oxen."

"Same thing. And I'm not doing the show, just milking the cows. Just like back home. You ought to know that by now."

She winced at his last comment. By then they'd almost reached the corner of LaSalle and North Clark Street, and the large brick church loomed just ahead.

"I don't know if you're being consistent or just obstinate," she told him and instantly wished she'd zipped her lips. A woman walking by them gave her a quick eyebrows-up look, like a librarian shushing unruly kids. Gerrit seemed to ignore the comment and just looked up at the sign: "Simpson Memorial Church. All are welcome."

Well, that was a good thing. Joan hoped that welcome would include this newlywed couple who stood arguing outside its doors. The couple who could not agree on even the simplest of theological conundrums. *Never mind.* They walked up the stairs together, caught up in the Sunday rush of people herding up a wide set of stairs and through arched entries.

"I wonder if we're going to see Latisha here," she told Gerrit over the growing hubbub of people in the lobby.

"Latisha? That somebody I'm supposed to know?"

"Oh, come on. You remember me talking about my friend from the school. We worked together in New York years ago. I'm pretty sure she attends here too."

Maybe she attended the other service, though even if she were at this service, Joan would have a tough time finding her among all the people. In fact, by contrast, Latisha might be easier to locate in this crowd if she were white.

The building itself looked as if it was built sometime in the early 1900s in a hearty stone-and-brick Craftsman style that opened its arms to visitors in a high-ceilinged foyer. Beyond that lay the massive horseshoe-shaped main sanctuary, crowned by a full-sized balcony that reached nearly from side to side. Joan guessed that the entire sanctuary seated perhaps thirty-five hundred.

"Welcome." An older gentleman smiled broadly and handed them a bulletin. Joan had been here once or twice for a cello concert years ago, which was probably why she'd thought to suggest they try this church. She had been surprised that Gerrit had agreed to come here in the first place rather than insisting they find a good Reformed church he could feel more comfortable in.

"It's not like the church you're used to," she'd warned him two weeks ago, and that had been true for any number of reasons. But he'd echoed her words back at her when they left the church that first time.

"Not like what *you're* used to either."

True both ways. And maybe that's what brought them back. This was not like the traditions either had held before they married. But this morning Gerrit belted out the songs—hymns and choruses alike. He leaned forward during the sermon, even jotted a few notes in the margin of his bulletin. Pastor Mike Clifton was not exactly the kind of speaker whose sermons one could nap through, but it was just like Gerrit to pretend they'd not been arguing, as if nothing bothered him the way it did her.

Stubborn Dutchman.

And today they even ran into someone Gerrit knew from the zoo.

"Hey, it's Farmer Gerrit!" A college-aged girl came up to them after the service. "Am I glad to find you!"

"Oh?" He looked to Joan as if he were trying to recall the girl's name, which is probably why he didn't mention it when he introduced Joan.

"Carmen Ayala." She had a very nice smile as well as something urgent to ask. "And I sure am glad I ran into you here. Are you working this afternoon?"

"Not exactly. Just—" Gerrit began, but Carmen cut back in with a smile.

"Perfect! My best friend from Cincinnati just showed up to visit, and I was hoping...I mean, is there any way you can work for me this afternoon? I know it's totally short notice, but a couple of Cub Scout groups are coming this afternoon, and I figure you're better with little kids anyway. And besides, I'd really really really appreciate it."

Gerrit opened his mouth and started to speak, then he must have changed his mind. Joan held her tongue as he glanced over at her, but she didn't say anything.

"Sure, Carmen." He finally sighed and nodded. "What time do you start?"

"One thirty!" Carmen almost squealed as she gave him a quick hug. "I owe you one."

"Or two," he whispered, but Carmen likely would not have known exactly what he meant. Maybe this qualified as an ox in the well too? This time Joan didn't dare ask.

"And that's it for our milking demonstration." Gerrit coiled up a hose and looked out at the sea of little Cub Scout faces. He was getting used to all the questions from these city kids. Even enjoyed them, in fact. After a couple of weeks, he could also tell when one of the little boys was about to throw him a silly question. He caught the little nudge from the kid's buddies—the dare. *Here it comes.*

"Excuse me." The little guy didn't wait to be called on. "How many teats does a cow have?"

Of course that got the reaction he wanted, a room full of giggles and a red-faced den mother. But really, she shouldn't have acted so shocked. This was pretty tame compared to some of the questions he'd fielded from the public-school kids during the week. Junior highers were the worst, or maybe sixth graders. To them, bovine reproductive habits were the big joke of the day. So was that the best the little guy could come up with? Gerrit was ready for him and raised his hand for quiet.

"Why don't you come in here and count 'em for us? And then you can tell the rest of your group."

Gerrit crossed his arms and stood back. He wasn't going to act shocked. This was a dairy farm, after all, even if it was in the middle of the city. Dairy farms had dairy cows. And dairy cows had teats. Even on Sunday afternoons they had teats—four per cow, last time he checked. And what was so shocking about that? Every kid in Van Dalen knew the answer to that question, plus a lot more, like how to turn a bull into a steer. *Shall we discuss that one, kids?*

Gerrit waited as the boy grinned and came through the door to the glassed-in milking room. *Ha!* This kid didn't know what he'd gotten himself into, but Gerrit already had one of the girls prepped and ready for a test squeeze. These city cows didn't give quite as much milk as the cows back in Van Dalen did, but they knew the routine well enough. And so did Gerrit.

"How about since you're back here, you give it a try?"

"Uh…" The Cub Scout froze, but Gerrit squeezed out a steady little stream of milk, sprinkling his poor victim right on the edge of his running shoe. The boy yelped and jumped a little, and the audience giggled even more.

"Come on." Gerrit held out a hand. He didn't want to embarrass the kid *too* much. "It won't hurt you."

"I thought I was just gonna count, uh—"

"Okay, so take a closer look."

The boy did, as Gerrit continued his demonstration and let his mind wander for a moment. He replayed the argument he'd had with Joan and wondered what he could have said differently to keep from hurting her. It seemed that for her, sometimes the commandments seemed optional, as if she could pick and choose. That could not have been what the Lord had in mind when he'd chiseled the commands in stone. Jesus Christ—the same yesterday, today, and forever. Wasn't that the God he knew?

"Mister?" His humble Cub Scout volunteer looked at him expectantly, as if he had another question—perhaps about cow poop this time.

"Oh, sorry." Gerrit switched back to the present. "Thinking about something else. Guess I missed the question."

Part of the reason was that his wife had shown up at the barn door and was leaning against the railing, pretending to read the sign about goat varieties. Talk about timing. But he was able to answer the rest of the questions, innocently enough, before the den mothers thanked him and the pack finally moved on to check out the tractor barn. *That's what they really came for, isn't it?* Eventually the crowd thinned out enough for Gerrit to sidle over to where Joan stood waiting for him.

"Listen, I'm—" he started the same time she did, and he looked up to see her eyes brimming with tears.

Ladies first, he motioned with his hand. She shook her head—*No, you go ahead.* But he insisted and she went ahead.

"I'm the one who's sorry, Gerrit." She looked away, and he could see her lip quivering.

Uh-oh. "No, I get stubborn," he told her in a low voice, trying to avoid the waterworks. "I just plow ahead, and I…I shouldn't do that."

"You *are* pretty good at plowing," she admitted, only he sort of wished she hadn't. "But it was my fault, mostly."

"What was?" His face must have asked the obvious question too.

"I wanted you to compromise what you believed. And when you did, I thought I'd won."

He sighed and looked around. He hoped the Lord might allow him a little slack this time for working on Sunday—even if his wife didn't quite get it, and even if he wasn't sure how to make her understand.

"Maybe we need to practice this arguing thing a little more," he told her, "until we get better."

Finally she smiled; a weak smile was better than no smile at all.

"I don't like that kind of practice," she told him. "How about if we just don't do it at all?"

Hmm. He wondered how that might work, but not for long. Screaming brought him back from his pondering.

"What?" He turned around just in time to see one of the Nubian goats butting a little girl aside like an NFL blocker and then heading straight for the half-open barn door. The little boy who had opened the pen had also been knocked to the side.

"Get the door!" Gerrit shouted to the mom who had just stepped inside the barn and had left the door open behind her. But she only jumped backward and pulled her stroller to the side as the goat slipped outside to freedom.

Shoot. His boss wasn't going to be pleased. But he had to let everyone else know what had happened, get a few more hands to round up the runaway. As he trotted to the door, he pulled out his walkie-talkie and radioed for help.

"We got ourselves a Code Yellow right outside the dairy barn," he yelled, then pulled his voice back. "Need a few hands to help rustle him up."

Argument or not, Joan matched Gerrit step for step.

Chapter 22

We do not know what we ought to pray for, but the Spirit
himself intercedes for us with groans that words cannot express.
—The Apostle Paul to the Romans

*G*errit woke with a start, confused, wondering if he had left any farm chores undone. He didn't think he had forgotten anything, but something definitely had happened to wake him. Almost as if someone had shaken his shoulder. The plowing? All the girls milked? *Something* was very wrong, but what? For a moment he wondered why the siren sounded so close, as if Larry Spoelstra had a fire to chase.

And then he remembered where he really was. Two thousand one hundred sixty-three point nine four miles from the farm in Van Dalen where he'd grown up, according to the Internet map thingie his granddaughter Mallory had explained how to use. Though he'd been pretty proud of himself at the time for finally figuring out how to put that piece of technology to work, it didn't matter much now. Truth was, he'd rather be waking up twenty-one hundred miles to the west, as long as Joan was there with him. He reached over with his toe just to be sure this bad dream hadn't turned worse. She sighed and turned in her sleep, which was good. Two people didn't both need to be awake at… He checked the clock radio. *Oh, brother.*

Two-thirty.

Wide awake, he clasped his hands behind his neck and stared up at the ceiling of the little box of an apartment they shared.

Why do people choose to live in these things, exactly? Boxes piled on boxes piled on boxes; box buildings reaching to the clouds. No wonder so many people were grouchy and didn't have time to talk. Different mail carrier every day, never the same person, double locks on everything—and for sure, nobody ever left car keys in the ignition here!

And all these sirens, as if they were working hard to erase what hearing a person had left at the end of the day. Another siren wailed down on Lake Shore Drive, and this time Gerrit even saw a flash of red reflecting off the ceiling, even this high up.

What am I doing here?

Oh, but he could answer that question. *She* was what he was doing here. And *she* slept through everything, including the sirens and the jets overhead from O'Hare and Midway, the constant background roar, mostly traffic, but a lot of other buzzy sounds too. And not pleasant. Not the way he defined pleasant. The buzz and clank of the building, as if it were a living thing, got to him too. The guy down at the front desk, Morris something, told him it was just the heating system and that he should ignore it.

Fine. But just how was he supposed to do that? The Lord only knew how much he missed the quiet nights in Van Dalen, when he still lived on the farm and the loudest sounds were the wind rustling the row of maple trees out on the front drive or the low moos of the cows in line for their first milking. Maybe you'd hear one of Marty Middelkoop's raspberry pickers in July or a tractor off in the distance during August haying. And goose music in September, or the soft patter of October rain on the roof. Even Mallory's sweet giggling out in the yard when she and Missy played fetch with a Frisbee. He remembered how the farm spoke to him with every slam of the back-porch screen door.

"Just stop it," he scolded himself softly, because he knew he'd chosen to leave those sounds behind him. Now he imagined that Joan's soft up-and-down breathing was his winter rain and rustling wind and sweet giggling. After all, she'd brought another kind of music to his heart. He closed his eyes and imagined the feel of her hand nestled in his, and that would be enough.

Still she heard none of it, none of the wailing sirens that kept him awake and reminded him of how far away he was from Van Dalen. She didn't hear the clank of the heating system or the water rushing through pipes overhead when someone flushed the toilet. She probably didn't even hear his snoring, if he ever got to sleep, and at least that was good.

Gerrit checked the glowing red numbers on their alarm clock to see how much sleep he was losing. Three fifteen. In an hour and a half the alarm would spring to life again—not too early, just too soon after this all-nighter. It still sounded like rush hour down on the street, eight floors below. Besides his wife, didn't anyone ever sleep in this city?

Certainly not him. And as he lay awake, his mind wandered to his kids. To Patti and her husband, Eric, busy with their kids and their church in Montana. He would have to call her again soon. It wouldn't do much good to call Bruce and Julianne, though. Bruce was always out on patrol with the Coast Guard, and Julianne was always—gone. Just like his oldest son, Gene, who was always out flying, leaving his wife, Nancy, at home with the kids. And then, of course, Warney and his wife, Liz, trying to keep up with their new jobs in Olympia. At least Warney sounded happy, schmoozing with all those politicians, trying to get laws passed for farmers. *Good for him.* Gerrit was glad Warney finally liked his job, since he obviously hadn't taken much to working the family farm. But that was ancient history now. And Mallory? Maybe they could come visit over the Thanksgiving break.

But probably not.

And of course Joan's son, Randy, was almost more of a son to him than Warney, though Gerrit would sure as sin never admit that to anyone. Certainly not to Randy, probably not to Joan, and maybe not even to himself. The kid had a good heart, even if he came across as a bit of a goofball sometimes. Emotional and a little naive. Up and down. Hard to predict. But hard not to like.

And now, sure as he was breathing, Gerrit knew the kid was in trouble—more than just he's-having-a-tough-time-at-boot-camp trouble.

"What are you doing awake?" Joan asked him without moving, and he jerked almost as much as he had with the siren. He thought of not moving, not answering, but she turned over to look him straight in the face; he could tell by the warm breath. So he slipped an arm around her shoulder and drew her closer.

"What made you think I was awake?" As he waited for her answer, he grazed his cheek against hers, and it was warm in just the right way. From here he could breathe in a soft whisper of her scent, a slight echo of orange blossom she'd dabbed there yesterday morning. *No hurry.*

But she paused a moment at his question, as if confused.

"I don't know," she finally answered. "I was dreaming, I think. And I just knew you weren't sleeping."

Well, that was a little spooky. But he was learning that side of Joan, her touch of the mystical. Not in a New Agey sort of way. Just not what he'd been used to back at First Church in Van Dalen. Back home if it wasn't written up first in the bulletin, announced from the pulpit, or read from the pew Bible, well, it probably wasn't from the Lord. Back home they had the Lord figured out pretty well, and back home Gerrit could have told anybody that He wasn't into night whispering. Just that once, in the book of First Samuel, chapter three, beginning at verse one: "In those days the word of the LORD was rare; there were not many visions."

There weren't many visions today either. Joan, on the other hand, had a little different way of looking at things. Not bad, understand, and not *The Twilight Zone,* or he might not have married her. Just different—different from the way he'd always seen the world. 'Cause here he was laying in his bed—laying, lying, whatever—waiting for the next time God would call his name. And he could hardly believe he was even entertaining these kinds of thoughts. Maybe he wasn't really one hundred percent awake after all.

"Remember your dream?" he asked, his nose rubbing against hers.

Another pause, and she snuggled a little closer, which he didn't mind at all.

"Only pits and pieces." She giggled softly before correcting herself. "Bits and pieces. Although I think Randy was in it. I wish we could call him; find out if he's okay."

"Hmm. Don't think they're letting recruits carry around their cell phones."

"But you never told me what woke you." So she still wanted to know. "Was it the sirens again?"

Now it was his turn to pause and think. *Hang on a sec. Strange.*

"I *thought* it was sirens." Then he tried to explain the feeling of waking, the almost-feeling of a hand on his shoulder, but he didn't do a very good job of it. Some of the language just wasn't in his vocabulary. "But when I woke up, there was something else."

No use getting weird about it. Funny thing was, Joan seemed to know exactly what he was trying to say even before he said it. *Well, that figures.*

"I know." She whispered back. "I think the same thing happened to me. So…"

"I don't mean it was like a Samuel experience or anything like that. It was just a little…weird. Maybe it was just a dream too."

"Maybe."

Of course she would know the Old Testament story of Samuel, the priest's assistant who heard God calling him in the night. Woke him up until he said, "Speak, Lord, your servant is listening." Well, Gerrit wasn't going that far with this thing, but even now he could almost still feel the hand on his shoulder. And it wasn't his wife's.

"I'm not used to this stuff," he whispered. "But we should probably pray for him."

Gerrit didn't even think about explaining who the "him" was. She knew.

So what else could they do but pray for the kid? Even though this was definitely not the way things were done back home at First Church, it was very okay. They took turns, and they both lifted up the kid to his God, asking stuff for him that had hardly come to mind except when they opened their mouths to say it. Now that was definitely not the way they did things at First Church. But they kept praying for Randy, and Gerrit even had a hard time believing how they could keep going like this. Still, it was good. It was good. And a few minutes later he checked the clock once again.

Almost four.

Funny how a guy's take on life could change, big time, when he was horizontal and whispering stuff to his wife. Even so, the thought occurred to him that when the sun came up and the buses started running and the *real* daytime noise started pounding on his eardrums, this time together might fade like the dreams he couldn't remember. Like winter fog burning off the fallow fields. *Poof!* Gone. Or maybe the alarm would jangle it out of his memory, and hitting the snooze button more than likely would not bring it back. *Maybe, maybe not.*

But once again he knew he had found his only home in Joan's arms. And for now until breakfast time, well, that's all a guy could ask for.

Chapter 23

No man should be allowed to be president
who does not understand hogs.
—HARRY S. TRUMAN

G errit undid and redid his tie for the fourth time. *A guy just gets a little out of practice, that's all.* He wasn't about to go marching into Joan's staff party looking like the country bumpkin they all thought he was. *No sir.*

"No one said you actually had to wear a tie." Joan was just trying to make him feel better. She could just pull on a potato sack and still look like… The thought brought a smile to his face.

"What are you smiling at?" She spritzed her hair and glanced at him in reflection. Her dark red gown looked pretty good backward or forward. Reflection or not, the dress hugged his wife's form in all the right places.

She pulled the tie straight for him, and he let her. *There.*

"Nothing." He slipped on his favorite jacket, the one with the suede elbows that probably went out of style twenty years ago, but he didn't give a fig.

"Thou shalt not lie, Gerrit Appeldoorn."

Uh-oh. He choked on his own spit and tried to keep from turning just a little pink. Sure enough, she already knew him way too well. That could be a little dangerous sometimes.

"I was just trying to think." *Good time to change the subject.* "Maybe you should just go to this thing without me. I think I might have a stomachache."

"You do not."

"Okay, then. But really, it's going to be pretty awkward."

"Only if you start talking politics. That's one thing you have to promise me you won't do, okay?"

He held up his hands, as in *I give up.* "Why would I talk politics?"

"I just want to be sure."

"I promise I won't be the one to bring it up. But listen—really—who am I going to know at this thing?"

"Gerrit!" She turned away from the mirror to face him. "That's just the point. You've seen some of the staff, but they all want to meet you."

"Yeah, right."

"Besides, I promised everyone you would be there. It'll be good for you to meet some more of the people I work with. And you don't want to embarrass me by not showing, do you?"

She took his tie and pulled him a little closer. And yep, that's all it took.

"So are you ready to go?" he asked. *Never mind the lipstick.* A moment later she dabbed his lips with a tissue as they headed for the door. Yeah, they were as ready as they'd ever be. And he didn't miss when he aimed a kiss her direction.

Not at all like the clowns at the party. Holy smokes, he'd never seen so many air kisses in his life. Or so many beautiful people, for that matter, elbow to elbow in the Gaylord Conservatory of Music reception hall on the fourth floor of the Fine Arts Building.

"Follow me," Joan whispered in his ear.

No problem there. Gerrit wasn't about to wander off on his own in this particular crowd. Already he was getting the stares, and he was pretty sure it wasn't because of his white cowboy hat. Actually, it was more than that. He wasn't deaf, after all. When someone said, "There's her farmer boy," he could hear it just fine, even from a couple of guys over across the room a little ways. A guy just didn't miss those kinds of comments.

And maybe Joan heard it, too, judging by the way she kept squeezing his hand.

"They don't mean anything by it," she whispered. She'd heard. "You just show them what a nice guy you are."

Well, that probably would have been a little easier to do if he hadn't run the hors-d'oeuvre server over just then, sending a plateful of little squids-on-crackers flying all over the floor. A wonder they hadn't pelted a lady who was standing there in her fancy strapless dress. She moved away in a hurry, even in those silly stilettos.

"Wow, I am *so* sorry."

Gerrit knelt down and helped pick up the mess. He was pretty sure they didn't operate on the five-second rule here. Too bad all this food would go to waste. He heard a snicker behind him and recognized the tone. Or maybe he was being just a little too sensitive about all this. He really shouldn't worry about a room full of city people staring at him and laughing. Hey, this kind of thing happens every day to klutzes and country fools. By that time his face had to have turned as red as Joan's dress, so now they went together even better, right? She gathered him off the floor like one of the squid appetizers and pushed him off through the crowd to the side of the room.

"Just let it go," she coached him, but he'd already fumbled behind the line of scrimmage. If he didn't have the stomachache before, now would be the time.

And speaking of time, he glanced at his watch. *Goodness, where did the time go?* But as usual, Joan read his mind before he even got his tongue in gear. Is that what happened to people after they'd been married a few months?

"You are not bailing out on me yet, mister," she whispered into his ear. "We've only been here five minutes."

He looked over at her and gave her his best "Who me?" expression.

Just then, Dr. Chambliss found them, and Gerrit knew he would have to shake the lizard's hand. Too bad his own hand was feeling extra sweaty at the moment.

"Joan!" Porter's air kiss was more on target than Gerrit would have liked. And, yes, Porter noticed Joan's red dress.

He looked over at Gerrit with what seemed to be a challenge in his eye. "You look great, Joan! Glad you brought your farmer with you this time. Good to see you again, Gary," he said, extending his hand.

Gerrit didn't correct him. He just put all his strength into seeing if he could make the guy's eyes bulge.

"Sorry I forgot my cows," Gerrit grinned and squeezed. "Won't happen again."

"Er…right." Porter extracted his hand from Gerrit's grip and flexed his fingers just a little. Even if no one else would have noticed, it made Gerrit's day. "I think I'll go find some more of those appetizers—if they have any left."

Another dig. And this time Joan even caught the barb in her boss's parting shot.

"What is it with you two?" She brought her voice back to a whisper again. "Were you actually joking, or—?"

"Can't say I appreciate the way he aimed his eyes," Gerrit snapped back, and this time the flush he felt in his face wasn't from knocking over any squid plate. Weird thing was, Joan wasn't acting like she appreciated him being protective, which made no sense to him in a place like this. No sense at all.

"He was just being polite," she countered, and probably she was just saying that to give Porter the benefit of the doubt, but it didn't feel good to Gerrit.

"Whoa, girl. If that was just being polite, I'm…" But just then he couldn't think of a witty way to finish up, except to mention that the man's suit looked *way* too expensive.

"You have a problem with a man being well dressed?"

"He can wear pink pajamas for all I care." Gerrit felt his cheeks steaming. She was actually defending Chambliss now? "Just makes me wonder what kind of salary they're paying the man that he can afford that kind of suit. Not that I know anything about suits, but—"

"Now you sound like Latisha." She frowned and didn't say anything else. Maybe that was just as well, since two of Joan's teacher friends were wading toward them through the sea of people. Maybe now was a good time to lighten up.

"Bogies at two o'clock," he told her.

"Why don't you give them some of your famous Dutch charm?" she answered in a whisper.

"You mean, like share some of my Dubbel Zouts?" He reached into his pocket for the Dutch salted licorice treats that turned most people's mouths inside out, but Joan must have cleaned out his pants pockets. Besides, she rolled her eyes just enough for him to notice as she introduced her friend Latisha and another woman whose name Gerrit couldn't recall.

"It's a pleasure to finally meet you, Gerrit." The minute Latisha returned his handshake, he knew why Joan called her a friend. "I've heard so much about you."

When Gerrit hesitated, she flashed him a warm smile.

"Oh, don't worry," she told him. "Really, it's all good."

Funny how quickly you can tell when another person is straight shooting, no nonsense. Gerrit knew right off why Joan was so pleased to have reconnected with this tall African American woman. Unfortunately, after a few moments of small talk, Joan and Latisha excused themselves to run to the ladies' room, leaving Gerrit standing by himself by the punch bowl.

Great. He remembered feeling like this once before, when Jimmy Van Tessel from the PTA had talked him into volunteering for the dunk tank at the fair. He'd sat up there dripping on an unseasonably cold August evening, waiting for someone to come along and dunk him again.

"Hey, we'll even warm up the water for you." Jimmy had promised him. If they had, maybe they'd warmed it up from ice cubes to thirty-five degrees. He'd vowed never to volunteer for dunk tanks ever again. Only here he was, standing by the punch bowl, shivering like a fool, two thousand one hundred sixty-three point nine four miles from—

Stop it, fool. Another teacher approached from the side, spilling a little punch on Gerrit's boots. *Whoa, there.* The other guy didn't even seem to notice, but it was awfully early in the evening for that kind of thing. At least the guy looked friendly and mostly nonthreatening, which is more than Gerrit could say for the other sharks who were circling the punch bowl and eyeing him as if he were some kind of tuna sandwich.

Fine. Gerrit looked down at his boots and decided on the spot. *They want famous Dutch charm? I'll give 'em famous Dutch charm.*

"Barad Overstreet." The gray-haired professor shifted his glass to his left hand before shaking Gerrit's and lost a little more punch in the process. *Oh, man. What's in that stuff, anyway?* By this time, Gerrit had a pretty good guess. "You must be Joan's guy. We've heard a lot about you."

What was it all these people had been hearing about him?

"Gerrit Appeldoorn." Gerrit smiled as widely as he could and pumped the guy's hand.

"Apple…" He made Gerrit repeat it, then shook his head. "What kind of a name is that?"

So Gerrit had to explain about his Dutch grandparents, about the farm, about moving to Chicago from Van Dalen.

"No kidding?" The guy slowed down his speech and raised his volume several notches. "So how do you like America?"

That was a great joke, and Gerrit had to smile politely, but Professor Overstreet wasn't through with him yet. After a little more high-volume back and forth, he made it clear that he taught voice here at the school, and that he wanted Gerrit to meet his buddies over in the corner of the hall.

"Hey, gentlemen." As he led the way, he lowered his voice but certainly not enough to prevent Gerrit from hearing. "You want to get a farmer's opinion on the election? This should be good."

Gerrit paused, remembering Joan's strict warning not to talk politics. But he had only promised not to be the first to raise the subject. Where was she anyway? And besides, who else was offering to strike up a conversation just now?

It was either this or he could stand there and decorate the punch bowl. He followed Barad—*Brad*—to a huddle of professors in the corner by a big painting of a half-dressed lady. As it turned out, each of the profs had consumed at least as much punch as their friend Brad. And as it turned out, they really didn't want to talk politics. They just wanted to grind him into the ground with their half-baked notions. Brad's buddy Thomas Winslow was probably the worst.

"Come on." He said that a lot, and Gerrit couldn't tell if it was him or the punch talking. "You're not saying that people really believe that stuff anymore? I mean, besides a bunch of priests—"

"Hold it right there." Gerrit interrupted, raising his hand. He could take half-drunk idiots trying to make him look foolish, but not this kind of cow manure. "I don't know too many priests. Still, I happen to agree with them about protecting little people who aren't born yet."

"Well, there's a hot button from the Heartland." Professor Overstreet laughed. "So are all farmers as right wing as you?"

Right wing? Gerrit had no idea how all his comments had added up to that cockeyed result, but this discussion was definitely going from bad to worse. And the reason he was standing here arguing with these jokers was…?

"All right, gentlemen." Gerrit did his very best to measure his words, not that they'd remember any of this in the morning. "I don't think we're going to agree on this, and you probably never really wanted to know my opinion anyway. So I think I'll jump ship."

Gerrit backed away, this time expertly avoiding another appetizer-toting woman in a white apron. *Unbelievable.* He'd had just about all he could take of these people, so maybe now would be a good time for a breath of fresh air. Grabbing a Ritz cracker with some nauseating-looking cream topping and little green sprinkles, he bailed out the exit door and headed for the elevator. No, make that the stairway. That way he wouldn't have to deal with the elevator-operator guy, who seemed nice enough but whose accent he had a tough time deciphering. Taking the stairs, he wouldn't have to deal with anyone else in this crazy place. A couple of minutes later, he burst through the street doors, not looking back, and gulped in the cool air off the lake. As he was resting at the curb with his hands on his knees, a yellow car pulled up to meet him.

"Cahb, seehr?"

Gerrit started to wave the guy off, then changed his mind. *Shoot, why not?* He could be there and back before Joan even realized he'd left. Wasn't it just a couple miles north along the lakeshore?

"Yeah." Gerrit yanked open the back door and slipped inside. "Lincoln Park Zoo. The dairy barn."

⌒

"I'm so sorry." Joan told Zhao Wei, who was helping himself to yet another curried meatball on a toothpick. "I was hoping you could meet my husband."

"He is ill?" Zhao had polished off at least a dozen.

Joan pressed her lips together. Brad Overstreet hadn't been able to tell her much, except that her farmer boy had left in a huff, and the men's room was just down the hall. But Gerrit wasn't in there. She'd asked one of the young servers on his way out. Even the elevator operator hadn't seen him, or didn't think so.

"No, I don't think he's ill." *She* might be now, but not Gerrit. And she had a pretty good idea what had happened to him. So she took her student by the shoulder and guided him to the group of professors gathered around Dr. Chambliss.

"I'm very sorry," she told Zhao, "but I must leave. Will you be all right here?"

He downed another meatball and nodded. Yes, he assured her, he would be fine, and the food was very good.

"Then I'll see you at your lesson Monday." She patted him once more on the shoulder and ducked out, clutching her fancy purse. She could have kicked herself with those horribly uncomfortable pointed high-heel shoes. And at just that moment, one of the heels snapped off.

"I can't believe it," she mumbled as she hobbled out the door. She stripped them off and trotted in her nylons as fast as she could toward the elevator. Never mind that the couple strolling down the hallway stared at her.

"Family emergency," she told them, slipping into the elevator ahead of them. Well, it was.

Once on Michigan Avenue, she flagged down the nearest taxi and told the driver where to go. Fifteen minutes later she was wincing her way down the gravel path toward Gerrit's dairy barn, praying she was right. If not, he'd be back home, surely.

She kept up a purposeful pace—the way women are supposed to do after dark in the city—and headed past the ponds straight for the employee entrance at the back of the barn. She tried to ignore the sharp little pebbles digging into her feet and knew she'd pay for it later. Her nylons had already torn through before she'd even gotten out of the Fine Arts

Building. But the barn would be warmer—that is, if it turned out to be open. She reached for the door handle, and it turned.

Good. Except she had no idea how to turn on the lights. So she stood just inside the door, waiting for her eyes to grow accustomed to the gloom. Over on the far side of the barn, she could make out the faint green lights of one of the milking machines behind the glass. A timer of some kind was clicking off the hours.

But no Gerrit.

A shuffling sound on the far side of the barn made her jump, but that would only be one of the several cows her husband spent so much time with. And by this time she could make out their dark forms, hunkered down in the hay of their stalls, and she could smell their pungent breath. It was all so different from the city outside.

She remembered when she began falling in love with that man, in a place just like this, back in Van Dalen. He'd showed her how to milk his "girls," and he'd laughed when she had stepped right in a…oh, never mind. And he'd played Beethoven for his girls on that ridiculous old record player of his. Something about increasing milk production with happy cows. Only that seemed like such a long time ago, certainly a very long way from this city. And the man she had fallen in love with wasn't here. She turned to go.

From somewhere behind the cows, she heard the low but unmistakable melody from Beethoven's *Pastorale,* Symphony no. 6, the one they'd listened to over and over when she'd tried to teach Gerrit basic piano. He did know how to whistle. Of course, she had to stop.

"You still know the tune." She spoke barely above a whisper, figuring he'd hear it just fine.

"I had a good teacher once."

By this time she could make out the difference between the cows and the goats and the husband, and she could almost zero in on his voice. "I thought I might find you here."

He didn't answer right away.

"It was either home or the farm," she tried again. "I was betting the farm." Her chilled stocking feet told her it was a good thing she'd bet right.

"This is no farm," he finally replied, his voice flat and detached in a way she hardly recognized. This was her Gerrit?

"What did you say?"

"I said, this is no farm. This is a museum, and it's all pretend. And we're all on display here."

Joan wasn't following, and his morose tone of voice frightened her. Better to change the subject, even back to the one she would rather avoid.

"I didn't mean to abandon you to the wolves." She offered what she hoped might be an olive branch.

"Didn't you?" he snapped. "Wolves probably handle their liquor a little better than those clowns."

She sighed. This hadn't turned out the way she'd thought it would. Not even close.

"I'm sorry, Gerrit. I should have stayed with you."

"You got that right."

One of the cows mooed softly, and she wished she could see his face better to know how much hurt lay behind his words. By the sound of it, though...

She shivered. "I thought you could handle yourself."

"Nothing to do with that. Just wasn't my kind of crowd, that's all."

"I know you didn't want to go in the first place."

"Yeah, can't think of too many places I've felt more at home."

This time she winced at the bite of sarcasm, even from across the barn. And she might have run over through the darkness to find him, but her feet just wouldn't move.

"I wanted to introduce you to Zhao," she finally told him. "You two would have a lot in common."

"You actually invited your whiz-kid student to that thing?"

Now it was her fault, was it? How was she supposed to know? But she nodded, even though he probably couldn't see her. Maybe it was just as well.

"He was polishing off the appetizer trays all by himself. But I would never have invited him—not if I'd known it would be like that. I…"

Her voice trailed off with another shiver, and she swallowed hard fighting off the tears.

"Maybe you should have found out first."

"You know what I should have done? I should have stayed home, rented an old Cary Grant movie, made some popcorn, and curled up with my husband on the couch. That's what I should have done."

There. If he wouldn't take *that* peace offering, she had nothing else to offer. She waited for him to say something, but his delayed responses were starting to drive her crazy. Was that a guy thing or a Gerrit thing?

"Did you hear what I said?" She knew he had.

Finally he cleared his throat. "Maybe you're right." His voice had softened, and the faint blue glow of his wristwatch night-light told her he was checking the time. It also gave away his position—a dark silhouette against the black-and-white markings of a large Holstein. She stayed there in the dark, teeth chattering, shoulders shivering, feet aching, waiting for him to say something, anything. She saw him take a few steps toward her, then hesitate in the middle of the barn.

She couldn't make herself meet him halfway. Not this time. She had already come looking for him, after all. Shouldn't that be enough? Now he should be the one to come all the way across, apologize for acting like a child, and wrap his warm arms around her.

Daddy used to hold her that way years and years ago when she skinned her knee or when someone in the neighborhood made her cry. Funny how she remembered that now. And she imagined how she would lose herself in Gerrit's big hug, forgetting all about being a music professor and burying her face in his chest so he wouldn't hear her quiet sob. Maybe it didn't really matter now if he did, so she let the unseen tears run down her cheek. None of it mattered, really. Not the silly party and not the empty conversations. Why didn't this stubborn Dutchman see that? Her advanced degree didn't matter, and neither did the social protocol at Gaylord. Certainly not her shredded nylons or the broken heel she'd left behind in the school hallway.

So what really did matter?

As if trying to answer her silent question, he held his head in his hands, the big rough farmer hands that she loved so much, that had never yet gone soft. Then he headed for the door and held it open for her the way a valet might, or someone who expected a tip for his services.

"I should get you home," he told her, his voice dull.

As he turned to go, she crossed her arms tightly.

Unforgiven.

Chapter 24

The computer can't tell you the emotional story. It can give you
the exact mathematical design, but what's missing is the eyebrows.
—FRANK ZAPPA

Hey grandpa whats up?????

Never mind that the kid didn't know how to use a capital letter or any sort of punctuation—unless it came at the end of the sentence! Gerrit was certain Miss Hoogaboom, the English teacher for several generations of students at Van Dalen High School, would turn over in her grave if she could see the way kids were typing these days.

IM-ing, he reminded himself. This was a totally different animal than typing, and Gerrit wasn't sure he was following all the rules—if there were any. But if it meant being able to keep in touch with his granddaughter, he would do what it took and take what he could get. Besides, Warney was impressed too.

Staying pretty busy the past couple of weeks. He hunted and pecked the letters as quickly as he could with two fingers. Mallory's response flew up on his screen before he could finish the rest.

still working on your new website???? I think that's 2 cool!!!!!

Gerrit bit his lip and shook his head as he labored over the keyboard, trying to keep up.

"Why use one exclamation point when you can use five or six?" he mumbled, but he would keep those kinds of editorial comments to himself.

They tell me it's almost online.

So *www.citymilker.com* wasn't officially just *his* Web site. And he sure didn't understand all the hoopla about putting a cam web—make that Web cam—above the milking stations. But the zoo administration was making a big deal about it, and that was fine by him. As long as he got to work in the barn, he wasn't complaining.

cool, gpa—what duz gma joan say about it????

He paused to come up with a good reply. What *did* Joan say about it? What did she even know about it other than what he told her over dinner, briefly, before she dashed off to evening rehearsals? Busy, gotta go. But she had to feel the gap that had come between them—a wall, maybe—ever since that night in the barn, after that stupid reception they never should have gone to. And yes, it was his fault, mostly, not hers. Only he could never figure out a good way to tell her so. And then she would come home tired with that look in her eyes that he wished would just go away.

still there, gpa????

Still here. Barely. He sighed and decided a good side step would work best.

She misses you a lot, he typed, and it hurt his fingers to hit the keys so hard before he hit Send. *Oh, wait a minute.* He added: *And so do I.*

Well, it was all true. He glanced at his watch, then at the sticky note on his computer screen.

Uh-oh.

Fifteen minutes before he had to meet with this Zhao character for the first time. He typed a quick *Gotta go! See ya! Love, Grandpa* and dashed out the door. Too bad punching the elevator button ten times didn't seem to hurry things up at all.

Five minutes later he was wheeling his new bike out of the storage room and making his way down Clark Street.

"Always late," he huffed.

The good part about the bike was passing one of the taxis he'd promised himself he'd never take and giving the immigrant guy a smile and a wave. Usually the drivers just acted surprised that anyone noticed. Once in a while they waved back, but not always. The not-so-good part was when it started to rain—a cold, nearly frozen sleet that came in sideways off the lake. Could have been snow, they said, but not yet.

"Brother," he mumbled to himself. Bikes were not made for this. But he'd gotten this far, and just a few minutes later, he was parking his bike in the delivery alley next to Gaylord, double-checking the chain lock, and smoothing his wet hair before stepping inside the building. So he looked like a drowned rat.

"This isn't a beauty contest, is it?" he asked the Russian elevator man.

Viktor looked at him with raised eyebrows.

"If is, then I can tell you, Meester Applesauce, you don't need to worry about winning."

Mr. Applesauce. He hadn't heard *that* one since the third grade.

"That's what I thought." Gerrit nodded and stepped out on the fourth floor, where he was to meet Zhao Wei in the conference room.

"Mr. Appeldoorn?" Leslie Phillips, Latisha's young assistant from the admin office, approached him, looking puzzled.

"Sorry I'm a little late." But that wasn't the problem.

"Are you okay?" she wanted to know.

He stopped to look at his reflection in a glass door. "Yeah, I guess it's a little rainy outside."

"I see. Well, your wife asked me to tell you that she would have been here, but she had a meeting with the headmaster."

He frowned. Dr. Chambliss. Right. Why was he not surprised? But that didn't matter now. Zhao smiled and nodded when Leslie introduced them in the conference room. He didn't seem to mind what Gerrit looked like.

"Now, Joan has explained to you everything about the purpose of this orientation program?" Leslie looked at Gerrit, a pen poised over her clipboard.

"She told me." Though he couldn't for the life of him remember the name of the program. Not that it mattered.

"You're free to go anywhere in the city so that Mr. Wei has an opportunity to practice his conversational English. Like most Chinese students, he's taken English in school, but it's much easier to pass a written exam than it is to actually speak and understand our language. Isn't that correct, Mr. Wei?"

Zhao smiled and nodded when she said his name. Gerrit wasn't sure that Zhao had understood the question.

"In any case," Leslie continued, "the idea is to enjoy yourselves and learn at the same time. Our program affords its participants a unique opportunity for cross-cultural learning experiences within the larger context of the urban environment. The spoken-language component is of benefit to both parties."

This time both Gerrit and Zhao stared at her blankly, but that didn't seem to slow her down.

"I'll provide you both with a supply of blank evaluation forms, which you should fill out every week for the rest of the semester and into the next, since it's already late in the year. Or would you prefer responding online?"

"I'm getting a Web site," Gerrit informed her, "but if it's on paper, that's even better."

Gerrit took her forms, as did Zhao Wei. And after giving a few more guidelines that only she seemed to understand, Leslie left them alone to smile and nod at each other. Well, the bobble-head routine was going to get old in a hurry.

Gerrit was the first to break the awkward silence. "Uh…my wife tells me you play a mean piano."

"Mean piano?" Zhao's dark eyebrows scrunched together.

Whoops. "Sorry. Let me say that another way. I hear you're really good."

After another pause, Zhao must have narrowed down the meaning. "Piano, yes." Zhao finally nodded and smiled. "I play piano."

Great. Now they had that fact established.

"You play too?" asked Zhao.

Gerrit held up his hands and shook his head. "No, no. I mean, not what you'd call playing. Joan, she taught me some of the basics before we got married. Haven't been able to practice much lately, though."

"Your wife, she is very good teacher."

"I always thought so, but…"

But it hit him just then how much he almost envied this young man for the time he could spend every day just sitting beside Joan, the way Gerrit used to be able to do back home in Van Dalen. But he knew it could never be that way again, so what good did it do to think back on it and moan and groan? And what good did it do for him to pretend to try to help this guy and yet feel bent out of shape about the whole arrangement?

Zhao nodded and smiled again, and again Gerrit had no idea whether Zhao had understood a word. For sure, he didn't understand what was racing through Gerrit's mind—and that was a good thing. So they both just stood there for a minute.

Well, this is going good. Gerrit searched his brain to think of a friendly thing to say. What had he been thinking when he said he would help this guy practice his English? His stomach growled, which in this case gave him an idea.

"We should get a bite to eat. You want to get something to eat?" Gerrit made a shoveling motion with his hand, as if he were stuffing a super-sized order of fries into his mouth—with extra mayo on the side, Dutch-style. *Hey, a little sign language can't hurt.*

"Eat, yes, sure." Zhao followed him out to Michigan Avenue. Now they were talking. At least the sleet had stopped for a while, but Gerrit still pulled up the collar of his damp jacket.

"So what kind of food do you like?" Gerrit remembered the stories Joan had already told him about this guy's enormous appetite. Funny thing was, Zhao Wei looked as skinny as a light pole.

"Many kind of American food are all good. Maybe except steak."

"You're kidding. Medium-rare sirloin, sizzling on the plate, little bit of barbecue sauce on the side? Oh, man. You don't have beef in China?"

"In China we eat everything with four legs except table, and everything with wings except airplane." He pointed up at a building ledge, where some pigeons were roosting. "Favorite is pigeon. You should try? There are so many here in Chicago."

Gerrit swallowed hard, and the image of the sizzling steak vanished from his mind, replaced by…uh…well, maybe another time.

"Thanks for not mentioning dog meat." By this time Gerrit's stomach had turned.

"Dog! Oh yes, also very good. We serve it in stews and soups. Tastes like—"

"Don't say it."

"No?" Zhao smiled. "Is much better than bloody meat."

"Bloody. Right. When you put it that way…"

"I learn to eat American cheese, however."

Will learn or *have learned?* Cheese was okay with Gerrit, either way. He could teach Zhao how to eat it, or they could talk about eating it. But it was going to take awhile to tune in to this guy's accent—not to mention his taste in food.

"So how about this?" Gerrit pointed to a little storefront café around the corner on East Van Buren. A large painting on the window told them—in any language—what they could expect to find inside. "You like hot dogs?"

Zhao's face lit up, and Gerrit realized what he'd just said.

"No, I mean..." Gerrit did his best to backtrack. "You know these aren't real dogs, don't you?"

As it turned out, Zhao had never tasted real American hot dogs before, kosher or otherwise. *Honest to goodness?* So Gerrit's official job now was to change all that—and talk about it besides. And no, it wasn't real dog meat. So he ordered two, loaded with all the chopped onions, sliced tomatoes, and sour pickle slices each Chicago dog could possibly carry. Zhao attacked his with relish. Literally.

"I never had one of these either," Gerrit explained, leveraging another bite into his mouth. "Not until a couple of months ago."

"You are American?" Zhao raised his eyebrows in surprise. "I thought all Americans eat hot dogs for breakfast."

"No, no. That's links, and they're different."

"Links?"

Gerrit would have to get used to the parrotlike nature of their conversations. "I'm as American as they come." Gerrit washed his mouthful down with a swig of Coke. "But hey, back home in Van Dalen, they don't come like this. We have hot dogs there, but Chicago's a whole new world for me, too."

Zhao didn't quite seem to understand that until Gerrit told him a little more about Van Dalen, about coming to the city, not knowing what to expect, all that. The other man nodded at everything Gerrit said.

"Then we are much the same. Have much in common," said Zhao.

Maybe they did. And for the next few hours, they made their way north along the waterfront, stopping often to talk, trying to figure each other out. Or Gerrit tried to figure Zhao out, and Zhao made Gerrit repeat or explain everything several times. Oh well. Gerrit should have expected this would come with the assignment. And he really didn't mind explaining.

"Chicago is also very different city for me," Zhao explained as they approached the Hans Christian Andersen statue in the park by the zoo. "Not so big, like Beijing."

"Not so—" Gerrit laughed. "Did you say not so *big?*"

"Oh yes. Beijing much bigger. But the neighborhoods, people more friendly. Families talking on the street. Young peoples playing, not gangs. Many more markets, many more peoples. Here I see more of the old peoples sitting alone, lonely."

That part made far too much sense. "You mean you don't have any lonely folks in China?"

Gerrit hadn't meant to touch a nerve. It was just sort of one of those things that slipped out, without thinking. He probably should have kept his mouth shut about the lonely thing.

"Sorry." Gerrit thought he'd better backtrack. "You don't have to answer all my dumb questions."

It occurred to him as they looked out over Lake Michigan that he still hadn't quite developed his sense of direction here in the city.

"You know, where I come from, when we look out across the big water like this, we're looking west. That's where the sun always sets—over the water. When I was a kid and we'd go for picnics on the beach, everybody used to make this *tsss* sound when the sun made it to the horizon and then touched down into the ocean. You know?"

Zhao smiled and nodded. Of course, he did a lot of that. So Gerrit went on with his story.

"I used to wonder how long it would take to build a raft and sail all the way across to China, kind of like Thor Heyerdahl. You know, the Kon Tiki Norwegian guy who used to build these things and sail all over the oceans to prove his points? Don't recall what the points were, exactly, but I think he pretty much proved 'em. Anyway, this place is all backwards. When we're looking toward the water, it's east. That's Michigan just over there, out of sight. Not China, for sure. And this ocean isn't salty. Fact is, it's not even an ocean."

Zhao looked off across the slate gray water as if he hadn't heard a word, as if his thoughts were far away. So they said nothing for a few minutes, only watched the gulls diving and chasing each other as an older woman tossed scraps of bread into the wind.

"This is bread?" Zhao finally broke the silence as he pointed at the feeding frenzy.

Gerrit nodded. *Sure it was.*

"In China we do not feed good food to birds," Zhao continued. "It is for people."

Which made sense, and Gerrit nodded in agreement. When you didn't have a lot of rice to go around, well, it'd be women and children first.

"Come on, Zhao." Gerrit finally straightened up and headed toward the zoo. "Let me show you where I go when I get…well, let me introduce you to my girls."

Chapter 25

Life is tough enough without having
someone kick you from the inside.
—RITA RUDNER

As soon as Joan heard the door buzzer, she knew something was wrong. Either that, or Gerrit had forgotten his keys again.

"Is that you, Gerrit?" She leaned into the intercom as she glanced at the counter for his key ring.

"Hello? Mrs. Appeldoorn? Joan? It's Terri Westervelt. Randy told me your address, and I called the school, but they said you'd already gone home for the day, and I was hoping…" Terri's voice crackled and popped before it dropped out entirely.

Joan had heard enough, and she buzzed Randy's girlfriend up. Or rather, his fiancée.

"Terri! What in the world brings you to Chicago?" Joan embraced the tiny young woman when she appeared at her front door, then took her by the hand and drew her inside. And it didn't take a woman's intuition to understand why she was here. "Did you see Randy already?"

Joan knew the answer to her question, but that was only a start. When Terri's eyes filled with tears, Joan had a pretty good sense that this was not going to be just a pleasant visit.

"They don't let them see anyone yet," she explained in a tiny voice. "Not until they graduate from boot camp."

Next week, then. Terri sank into Gerrit's favorite chair, looking as if she might never climb out. "Is your husband…?"

The hesitation in her voice revealed more than the unfinished question.

"I think he might have taken a friend to the zoo. Wanted to show him where he worked. He won't be back for a while." She reached across and grabbed Terri's hand. "Goodness, dear, we had no idea you were coming all this way for the graduation. You're a little early. Do you need a place to stay?"

By this time Terri only stared at the floor. She never lifted her eyes to speak. "Mrs. Appeldoorn, you should know something. I'm pregnant."

Joan never let go of Terri's hands and tried not to act as disappointed as she felt. It didn't help that her suspicions had been right.

"Well, I hate to tell you this, dear, but you're showing more than a little bit. In fact, I had a pretty good idea of what was going on when I saw you standing at the door. Were you hoping to keep it a secret?"

"Not exactly." Terri shook her head and shrugged. "I know for most people it's totally not a big deal anymore."

"For most people. Which doesn't change the fact that you know the difference between…"

Joan decided against finishing her comment. The raw hurt showed in Terri's eyes when she looked up.

"I'm sorry," Joan told her, still holding her hands. "I know you didn't come here for a lecture."

"No, it's all right. I do know the difference between what's right and what's not. We always had these talks in youth group, and I had all the Bible verses memorized, the ones that talked about…you know."

Joan knew. She nodded as Terri went on, this time with a sad smile.

"Funny thing is, I even got one of those old True Love Waits bracelets from my girlfriend, and even though I didn't wear it, I was really going to. But…"

Again her voice trailed off, and again Joan let her explain.

"But I guess, as you can see…"

In this case, true love didn't quite wait. Or maybe that was the point. How true was it then?

"Randy knows?"

"Oh, he knows. I wrote him as soon as I was sure. But that's the problem."

So being pregnant and unmarried isn't the problem? This was the part Joan really didn't want to hear. "You're planning to get married?" Maybe not in a church now, and maybe not in a white dress, but married nonetheless. They could get through this. They could.

But Terri broke down sobbing. Joan could only kneel by the girl's side and offer her shoulder, waiting for the torrent of tears to pass.

"Surely you're not thinking of—"

"Oh no." Terri shook her head violently and cleared her throat. "Of course I'm going to keep the baby. There was never any question. Not even my mom would say that. But Randy—he hasn't written me in weeks. I'm afraid he's having second thoughts about everything. I can't phone him, and he doesn't have e-mail. And now my mother said she won't talk to me unless I agree to give the baby up for adoption. That's why I came to see you."

"Oh dear." Joan put her arms around the girl and held on tight. It was a good thing her son wasn't anywhere close by just then because Joan was ready to knock some sense into that boy's head—and she might have used any blunt object at hand. But since that wasn't an option, Joan kept holding on to Terri while the girl emptied her heart and her tears, saying how much she wanted this baby, how much she had wanted to be a mom someday—just not so soon. Finally, Joan went to find some tissue, and they both stood in the little kitchen.

"I don't mean to just dump on you, Mrs. Appeldoorn, but—"

"Please call me Joan. And don't you worry; you can tell me anything you like."

"It's just that I want you to know that I love your son very much, and I want him to be the daddy to our little girl—or boy—if that's what he wants. I just don't want him to feel like I trapped him into this."

"Hold on a minute." Joan gripped the girl by the shoulders and looked straight into her eyes. "Whatever happened between you two, my son was not trapped into anything. That much I can tell you for sure. And as soon as we can get that kid pried away from his drill sergeant or whoever is keeping him locked behind the gates of that navy base, we're all going to sit down together and have a good talk about all this. You understand? We're going to get this straightened out. In the meantime, you're more than welcome to stay here with us."

"But I don't want to be any trouble."

"Oh, stop it!" Joan eased off and patted the mother of her grandchild on the shoulder. She even tried her best to smile. "I hope you don't mind my saying so, but we're pretty much past that point."

Which was right when Gerrit came marching through the front door with his "Honey, I'm home" whistle. And while he probably hadn't been expecting slippers and the newspaper, he couldn't have been expecting Terri. Especially not Terri standing in the kitchen, obviously pregnant and with mascara running down her cheeks.

"You're home early, dear!" Joan tried to sound a lot cheerier than the situation called for.

"Zhao had a school meeting to go to." A dark shadow crossed his face, just what Terri was probably afraid of the most. "So we cut things a little short. But—"

He held up a small black suitcase. "Somebody left this outside the door."

"Oh," squeaked Terri. "That's mine. I'm sorry."

Joan looked from Terri to Gerrit.

"Look who's come to visit us," she told her husband.

Gerrit stood rooted near the doorway, his jaw still scraping the carpet. Not that Joan blamed him. At least Terri had warmed Joan up with a few details first, which had probably made it easier for her to adjust to the situation. But this scene had hit Gerrit face first with no warning.

"Uh…hey, Terri." He appeared to be making a valiant effort to recover, but he was never very good at that sort of thing. Gerrit Appeldoorn was many things, but subtle was not one of them. And neither was Terri's appearance. Finally Gerrit cleared his throat.

"Someone going to tell me what's going on here?"

A couple of hours later, Terri's tears still hadn't dried, and Gerrit hadn't softened as much as Joan would have liked. But she would work on him a little more as they finished the dishes.

"I just don't know what kind of message we're sending here," he hissed, and Joan jabbed a sudsy pot his direction for rinsing. Sometimes this man could be such a… How about *pharisee?*

"Lower your voice, please." She motioned with her eyes to where Terri had parked herself out in the living room and was leafing through last month's *Christianity Today.* "What kind of message were you thinking about?"

"I just mean, you open your arms to this kind of stuff, and it's like, 'Hey, no problem. You can be married or not. No big deal.' Don't you see that?"

"We are *not* opening our arms to this kind of *stuff,* Gerrit. We're opening our arms to the mother of our grandchild when she needs us."

"I know that, but—"

"You know how her mother is pressuring her."

"I'm not so sure her mother isn't right."

"What?"

"No, I don't mean *that* kind of pressure. You don't think—?"

"If we're talking about abortion, no. That's not what we're saying."

"Good. So I'm still saying we should let them work it out."

"But how can you *say* that? Terri's mother won't even *talk* to her own daughter unless everything goes exactly the way she wants it. Would you just slam the door in Terri's face, the way everyone else has?"

"I didn't hear her say that anybody has slammed any doors, least of all us."

"You heard what she told us."

He rinsed his pot, but not very well. One side was still covered in bubbles, and he shrugged when she grabbed it back.

"That's just one side of the story," he whispered.

Joan pressed her lips together to keep the steam from escaping. Could Terri hear any of this?

"Gerrit! Right now this girl needs love and understanding more than anything else. I thought you would understand that. How about a little grace?"

"Grace is for people who repent. How do we know she has?"

"Exactly! How can you know her heart? You should be looking for ways to build bridges to this girl instead of blowing all this Pharisee smoke at the issue."

"Pharisee smoke! Now you just wait a minute!" His voice climbed a couple of decibels too high, and Joan warned him again with her raised eyebrows. So he lowered the volume again and went on. "I'm not saying she can't stay here. We've got an extra bedroom. I'm just saying we need to be careful of the message we're sending."

"Well, then, speaking of messages, maybe we'd better have one ready for the father of this baby as soon as we see him."

She shoved the pot back at Gerrit, right in his face.

"That part," he told her as he ducked, "I believe we agree on."

Fine. And with that she dried her hands in her apron before ripping it off and throwing it on their little kitchen counter. She was done. He could finish up the dishes himself.

"Where are you going?" he asked.

She didn't answer. Right now she was thinking that the world would be much more pleasant without men, particularly the ones she was related to. Instead, she hurried past Terri, who was reading on the couch, and headed for the bedroom, locking the door behind her.

And no one was going to stop her from having a good cry.

Chapter 26

It's the friends you can call up at four a.m. that matter.
—MARLENE DIETRICH

L isten, honey, you've just got to keep it in perspective. God's still in control here."

Latisha had a way of calming the waters, which was probably why Joan found herself once more in her friend's domain, looking for advice. The phone would probably ring again in a moment or someone would stop by with a question, but Joan had to talk to someone.

"I know what you're saying, Latisha. It's just that Gerrit and I—"

"Now wait a minute. So this isn't really about Randy getting his girl-friend pregnant, is it? This is about Joan and Gerrit learning how to deal with a family crisis."

"You're making it sound like no big deal. Like it's all okay." Gerrit had said that very thing to Joan, and here she was leveling the same accusation at her friend.

Latisha gazed steadily at Joan and twirled one of her cornrows. "You know me better than that, girl. Of course it's not all okay. Did you know that I was four months pregnant with Liselle when I got married?"

Joan shook her head.

"Of course you didn't. I'm not proud of the stupid things I've done."

"But then..." Joan narrowed her eyes, trying to remember if Latisha had ever told her about Liselle's father.

"Yeah, he married me, but he was already looking for other honeys at our wedding reception. Ran off with some hairdresser a year later."

"I'm sorry."

Latisha laughed. "Honey, that was a long time ago. You see me crying over it now? Listen, that's not why I was telling you about this. I was telling you because you need to make sure you and Gerrit are straight together on this, right? Because you and Gerrit... Well, just don't let anything get in between you. Hear what I'm sayin', girl?"

"I hear." Boy, did she hear. And of course the phone rang just then, though Latisha let it ring while she pointed at Joan.

"Serve him a good dinner tonight, girl. I know the past week with your guest has been tough, but men always soften up once they've got a bellyful of good food. Then you make sure... Well, I'll leave the rest to you."

She winked at Joan as she finally picked up the phone.

"Good morning. Gaylord Conservatory of Music. Latisha speaking."

Sure, it was a little crowded that evening with four people circling their small dining-room table. Make that five. Terri had gingerly scooted her chair back a little in the place just opposite Gerrit. But Gerrit was finding out that Joan sure knew how to put on a good dinner, and more than once he'd tried to tell her that her home-baked lasagna was as good as—or better than—any he'd ever had in an Italian restaurant.

How else could he apologize for his grumpy behavior over the past week?

No, it wasn't exactly the intimate dinner for two she'd promised him earlier in the day. But when Randy called that afternoon to tell her he had a couple days' leave—and recruits rarely did—well, maybe God had something better in mind.

"Don't mind if I do." Randy ladled another serving of steaming lasagna onto his plate.

"You act as if the navy hasn't fed you for the past eight weeks." Joan surveyed her son's plate, but anyone could tell she wasn't upset about it. Gerrit knew she'd love it if Randy took thirds and fourths. *Eat, eat.*

"Not like this." Randy should have closed his mouth before he answered, but it probably wasn't Gerrit's place to say. Then whose place was it? He wasn't blood related to either of these kids. And they still hadn't had "the talk." He glanced over at Joan, who avoided his gaze. *Not yet?*

Maybe after dessert, which was a celebration chocolate cake with white frosting and blue lettering that read *Anchors Aweigh, Randy!* Yeah, what this fella needed was to *lower* his anchor, not weigh it. Or whatever they did when they got to harbor.

"You be careful not to spill anything on those nice white pants," Joan told her son, and so far he hadn't. Meanwhile Gerrit fidgeted with his fork, looking for a good segue into the conversation. What were they waiting for? He'd thought Joan might say something.

"I'm really sorry you guys couldn't get in to see my graduation ceremony." Randy still hadn't finished chewing his lasagna. "You know I tried to get you on the guest list, but they were really tight this time for some reason."

Gerrit knew cows who chewed their cud with better manners.

"But still," Randy went on, "we can watch the video after dinner." Yeah, and he probably borrowed the money from his mother to buy it.

"It was a really cool ceremony," added Terri.

Terri would know. Not that Gerrit cared that she had been the only one allowed in—and she wasn't even family yet. Hey, it was just as well that they watch a video. Finally he caught Joan's attention, but she only shook her head, a subtle gesture to wait.

Wait? While they were waiting, this baby had already grown another couple of inches. He noticed Terri had eaten more than her share of dinner as well.

"That was very good, Mrs. Appel—er, Joan." Terri finally put down her fork and dabbed at the corner of her mouth with a napkin. "I don't think I can eat another bite."

"Not even some cake?" Joan had turned into a diet buster with her lasagna and salad and garlic bread and chocolate cake and coffee and—

"Actually, I wonder if now's a good time to discuss something." Gerrit pushed his chair back and carefully folded his napkin next to his plate. After sampling a bit of the cake frosting with his finger, well, he figured the "Anchors Aweigh" cake would have to wait. Joan sounded like she was choking, but Randy and Terri turned to look at him.

He had a good speech all prepared. He touched his shirt pocket to make sure it was still there. He'd carefully pecked out the speech on his word processor, just in case he needed it. He'd talked about doing the right thing and about pleasing God in all our decisions. He'd even thrown in a couple of good Bible verses for backup so they couldn't argue the point with the Almighty. He'd also talked about following God's law and protecting each other's reputations. About picking up after making a mistake and about asking forgiveness. And now that he thought about it, maybe he should have added that line about the freedom of second chances. Just the kind of stuff he wished for in his own so-called life but now always seemed to elude him.

It would have been a fine speech, and his intentions were pretty good, if he said so himself. But Randy raised his hand and interrupted before Gerrit could even get the first word out.

Shoot.

"Look, I know what you're going to say, Gerrit, and I don't mean to interrupt. But Terri and I have something to tell you."

"Why don't you let Gerrit have his say first?" Joan piped up, and Gerrit could have reached over and kissed her on the spot. Or on the lips. But Randy shook his head. *Put a guy in a white uniform and look how he acts.*

"Trust me, Mom, Gerrit. I think you'll want to know this first. And then I promise, if you want to bawl us out after that, bring it on."

Was that some kind of navy challenge? Gerrit opened his mouth, but Joan squeezed his knee under the table. That could mean a number of things, but he decided that this time it meant to shut up. So he just listened.

Okay, sailor boy. I'll give you two minutes, and then...

"Well." Randy stood up for effect, and the glow on his face didn't convince Gerrit that a lot of groveling and apologizing was in the pipeline. "The *Reader's Digest* version is that Terri and I are married now."

Gerrit's fork clattered to his empty plate, and for a long moment they listened to a siren pass by outside on Lake Shore Drive. A shy smile crept across Terri's face, matching Randy's.

"You've got to be kidding" turned out to be the only words Gerrit could manage at the moment, while Joan seemed to be holding her face in place.

"We decided it was the only right thing to do." Randy's explanation came faster now, as if he wanted to dump the entire load of Very Good Reasons on them as quickly as he could manage. "I know we blew it before, and I have been acting like a jerk. Basically, I think I was in shock, trying to figure things out. But this afternoon, as soon as they let me off base, we drove to the Cook County Courthouse, filled out all the papers, and made it official."

Joan and Gerrit traded "What now?" looks, but Joan was the first to recover and start hugging the newlyweds. Gerrit finally caught enough breath to stand up and offer Randy his hand, but instead he was pulled into a group hug. *Oh well.*

"We're happy for you," Joan told her son and Terri, and she looked at Gerrit for backup.

Okay. He decided his speech probably would need some modification at this point. They still knew he wouldn't just rubber-stamp what they'd done before getting married. But considering the hole they'd slipped into, maybe this wasn't the worst thing that could happen. But wait a minute—

"I didn't notice any ring." Gerrit stepped back and checked.

"That was Terri's idea." Randy smirked as he reached into the pocket of his sailor uniform.

"See, we didn't *have* to have rings to be legally married." Terri sounded a bit more upbeat than she had the day she'd appeared on the Appeldoorn's doorstep.

"And we both felt bad about not having any family there for the ceremony," Randy added, looking at his mother. "I know you would have wanted a church wedding, Mom, but that just wasn't going to happen. Instead—"

"Instead," Terri began, "we decided to save the ring part of the ceremony for tonight, while we were here with you."

"You can do that?" Somehow it didn't seem right to Gerrit. Like it wasn't following the wedding script, not even a justice-of-the-peace-type wedding script. But Randy flipped open the little ring box and held up a small, plain diamond ring.

"Like I said, we're already married, Gerrit. My wife just hasn't had a chance to put on her ring yet."

"All the way through the meal"—Gerrit shook his head—"and you didn't say a word about it until now."

By now Randy was smiling full force, and his mom was losing it. *Whatever these kids are going to do, they'd better get on with it.* And they did. Gerrit and Joan looked on while Randy and Terri took turns placing a ring on the other's finger. They looked at each other, and an electric current seemed to pass through the room. Even Gerrit felt it, and that's when he realized that his own wife was gripping his hand hard enough to cut off the circulation. That could mean a number of things, but he decided that this time it was probably a good sign. He held on and just watched the private little ceremony there in the kitchen.

"You may now kiss the bride, I guess," Gerrit mumbled. What else could he say? Joan let go of his hand for a moment to clap quietly just before another group hug. And this time Gerrit didn't offer to shake anyone's hand. He just held on to shoulders and pulled together the little family that had just grown by one. *Make that two.*

"We're so sorry it happened this way," Randy whispered as the huddle broke, tears glistening on his face.

"Me, too." Gerrit looked at his son-in-law and ran his hand over the boy's crew cut. *Join the club, sailor.* "But from now on we don't look back, all right? We just keep hanging on to the Lord, looking forward."

He guessed that was the short version of his speech anyway, and he looked at Joan to make sure she knew he meant it. 'Course, she could probably take it to mean several different things, but that was okay by him.

"Is that what we're doing?" Joan barely whispered the question. "Not looking back?"

Gerrit knew it wasn't meant for the other couple. Of course, Terri didn't catch the hidden meaning.

"We think Randy might be assigned to San Diego for more training." She bubbled, holding the ring up so the tiny diamond glittered in the kitchen light.

"Then you'll stay with us while he's training?" asked Joan.

Terri shook her head. "We only have two more nights of leave, and then Randy has to go back to the base. If he gets shipped out, I'm going with him."

"Two nights." It occurred to Gerrit that their little two-bedroom apartment might be…well…a tight fit for two couples.

At that Terri turned beet red and Randy laughed.

"Don't worry, Gerrit." He must have read the look on Gerrit's face.

"I've been saving up, and we're staying at the all-suites Omni Hotel in the heart of Chicago's Magnificent Mile!"

$\backsim$

Two days later Joan pulled out another stack of quarters to feed the Sears industrial-sized washer. And, no, she didn't mind doing Randy's shirts before he shipped out. It was just the white uniforms she was a little scared of.

What if I turn them pink? she wondered as she carefully sorted Gerrit's white undershirts and blue jeans as well as her own work blouses. With all the grass stains and hayseed in the pockets of Gerrit's clothes, she imagined it was almost like doing the wash back on the farm in Van Dalen. Now *that* she could do without. She was just about to toss Gerrit's shirt in with the rest of the colors but stopped when she felt a crinkly bulge in his pocket.

What's this? she wondered, unfolding the sheet of wrinkled paper. It was a speech, apparently aimed at Randy and Terri. A manifesto on what the couple had done wrong, and what they needed to do to get right with each other and with the Almighty. Had Gerrit really intended to say all this?

Actually, most of it was crossed out, and barely legible notes had been scribbled in the margins.

"I see you found it."

When she turned around, Gerrit was standing in the laundry-room entry holding another basket of wash. There was nothing she could do except nod and hold it out to him.

"Were you really going to—?" she managed, and he shook his head.

"That was just the first draft." He reached over, took it, and crumpled it before sending it sailing across the room right into a trash can.

"I know you meant well." She never took her eyes off him. "But if you wanted to tell them something, why didn't you talk to me about it?"

He shrugged and put the laundry basket down beside hers. "Didn't want you to think I was sticking my nose in where it didn't belong."

"But you didn't think I would find out anyway?" She heard warning signals going off in her head, the way they usually did when another disagreement was coming on—or a monster headache. Maybe they were the same thing. "I'm your wife now, remember? Not just someone who shares your bed. That means—"

"Look," he told her, his voice infuriatingly soft. "I didn't come down here to argue."

She looked at the nearly empty laundry basket. "Then what *did* you come down here to do?"

"Uh…"

He stopped at the sound of footsteps pounding down the basement stairs and heading their way. A moment later Randy poked his head in at the door.

"Find your suit, old man?"

One good thing about Gerrit: His face usually gave him away, just as it did this time. He probably looked the same way when he was a little boy and his mother had caught him with his hand in the cookie jar.

"Suit?" Joan crossed her arms and looked them both over.

"Oh! I didn't see you there, Mom."

Well, too late now. "I was here the whole time. What suit do you mean?"

"Oh, you know." Randy hemmed and hawed in his oh-so-obvious search for an excuse. *Strange.* "People wear suits. Like coats and ties?"

The two men still looked at each other like co-conspirators, and someone obviously needed to come clean. Gerrit sheepishly reached into one of the baskets and extracted his faded aqua swimsuit with the Hawaiian fish motif.

"No," he mumbled. "Like this kind of suit. Couldn't find it in the drawers since we moved."

"Oh." She relaxed—a little. "Why didn't you tell me? I just threw it in. Had some old grass stains on the seat. Did you two find a pool?"

Not that *she* would even think of going swimming this time of year. No one could pay her to go swimming in this kind of chill. Not even in a heated pool. But oh well.

"Well"—Gerrit started for the door—"not exactly, but we'll be back."

"Wait a minute." She held on to the grass-stained suit in a small-scale tug of war. "What does 'not exactly' mean?"

Again the co-conspirator look. These men were hiding something.

"It's just a community swim," Randy explained. "Kind of an annual thing some kid down at the Bible college started a few years back. It's a big deal now."

That still sounded crazy, unless…

"We're not talking about the *official* Polar Bear Swim in Lake Michigan." That was the local event all the papers talked about where a bunch of insane people jumped into the ice water, just for…why?

"It was his idea," they both said, pointing at each other. Obviously, this was some kind of inexplicably male thing that Joan was doomed never to understand. By this time her husband had snatched his suit and was following Randy out the door.

"Your heart, Gerrit." If no one else was going to say it, she would.

He held up his hand and kept going. "Doctor says mild exercise is okay. Just not anything strenuous."

"And you don't call jumping into a freezing lake in November strenuous? How cold do you think that is?"

"I'm sure they'll have people there with defibrillators and stuff." Randy wasn't helping matters at all. "It's a safe event."

"Defib… What?"

"He's kidding." Gerrit wasn't giving up the macho act. "It's just a dip and then I'm out. Nothing to it."

"Gerrit Appeldoorn," she called as they trotted down the hall, "I'll never forgive you if you leave me a widow!"

"I'll take care of him, Mom."

Just then she could have strangled both of them for this stupid, childish, macho display, and that would have settled the matter more quickly. Instead, she sighed and returned to her load of wash, throwing Gerrit's white socks in with the colors. She took back everything she'd said before about him being sweet. Bullheaded and foolish was more like it, and that went for the younger one, too.

Men.

~

Less than an hour later, Gerrit stood shivering on the lakeshore, wondering why he couldn't seem to catch his breath. Well, he'd just jumped into a freezing Lake Michigan, right? That would explain it. He chuckled and watched as Randy and a hundred other insane people splashed around in the dark, knee-deep water for a few glorious seconds.

"Whoo!" Randy bounded up on the gravel shore, and Gerrit threw him a towel. "Now that's a manly man thing to do, huh?"

Gerrit flexed his muscles in agreement, trying his best to look like a pro wrestler and forcing himself not to grimace as he did. No need to worry anyone. But Randy noticed, even in the shadows of dusk.

"Hey, you all right? Because Mom would flip if—"

"Don't even go there." Gerrit stopped that conversation before it began. He'd already dug into the pocket of his wadded-up trousers where he kept a small bottle of nitroglycerin pills the doctor had prescribed after his last heart attack. He did his best to sound like a man in control, not a man gasping for breath. "Let's just get back to the apartment before we freeze our fannies off."

"No argument from me." Randy's teeth were chattering as he rubbed a towel over his buzz of dark hair.

While Randy pulled on a pair of shoes, Gerrit managed to slip a pill under his tongue. Not because of anything serious, understand.

But just in case.

Chapter 27

The Statue of Liberty is no longer saying,
"Give me your poor, your tired, your huddled masses."
She's got a baseball bat and yelling, "You want a piece of me?"
—ROBIN WILLIAMS

*I*ronic?" Gerrit fished his chopsticks out of the mushu chicken again as he searched for a good way to explain the word. "Ironic is like… uh…things getting twisted around, and the last person in the world you'd expect to…"

No, this wasn't coming out right. Zhao sat across from him, smiling and bobbing his head as he expertly scooped up rice with his own chopsticks.

"You know what I mean?" Gerrit was just about to ask for a fork.

"I don't think so." At least Zhao was learning to be a little more up-front, American-style, and not always so polite. "I read this word, and I think it has to do with metal. I do not understand."

"Oh, right! *Iron*-ic. No, no. It's nothing to do with iron." Gerrit looked around at the crowded little restaurant in Chicago's crowded little Chinatown, fully aware that his was the only white face in the crowd. And then he thought of it.

"I know." Gerrit pointed one of his sticks. Hey, they were good for making a point, even if he couldn't pick up much food with them. "Ironic is *me*, the farm boy, trying to teach *you* about life in the big city. *That's* ironic."

The light came on in his friend's eyes. "Oh! Or perhaps me trying to teach you English?"

"That's it! Ironic is making friends with a person who understands you but who hardly speaks your language." Gerrit returned to his chopsticks, carefully gripping one and then the other before he stabbed an odd-looking piece of...whatever it was. He was going to get this if it was the last thing he did.

"I think I understand ironic now." Zhao was quiet for a moment. "But there is so much more."

"Like what?"

A slow, shy smile spread across the Chinese man's face. "You know we Chinese students are good in reading and writing, but many struggle to listen and speak. I think the most difficult part is pronunciation."

Well, Gerrit wasn't going to argue that point.

Zhao pointed at a bowl. "Here in this restaurant I might order *hoong dul sah,* which is sweetened red-bean soup we eat in wintertime. But if I say I would like some soap with my lunch, the waitress thinks I am crazy!"

Gerrit laughed. "Is that all?"

"No, not all. When I was walking with another student in Chinatown and a lady was looking for her son, she grabbed us and asked if we've seen him. I tell her, 'Yeah, I saw him just passed away.' The lady nearly fainted."

"Ha! I guess you meant 'just walking by.' Well, that was close."

"Yes, but not close enough. When I first came, people ask me, 'What's up?' I always look up and say 'ceiling' or maybe 'roof' or 'sky.'"

"And you weren't joking."

"Now it is a joke." He scooped up more rice and looked at Gerrit sideways. "Only I still don't know how to make myself melt to the American life."

"Is that what you want to do?"

Zhao didn't answer at first, only stared down at his food. It occurred to Gerrit that he might have crossed the line into a place the Chinese man didn't want to go, but Zhao wasn't finished.

"I think surely the different culture is the most difficult thing to get fit in." Now he seemed to wrestle with a jumble of words, though Gerrit could decipher their meaning. "How to choose the safe topic and how to know limits of personal privacy."

Gerrit nodded. "I understand. Sometimes personal privacy is over-rated."

"Overrated?"

Whoops. Gotta watch those fancy vocabulary words. "I mean, sometimes Americans think personal privacy is more important than it really is, or more important than it should be. People can't talk about things like politics anymore, or their faith, without getting all bent out of shape."

Zhao nodded as if chewing on the words, not just the steamed rice.

"I mean upset." Gerrit made another mental note to watch what he said. "What's the hardest thing to get used to? I mean, about living here in Chicago?"

"The most difficult thing?" Zhao chose his words carefully, more slowly this time, as if he was treading carefully in a minefield of ideas that might explode with any step. "Most difficult thing to get used to is that Americans…don't seem to have close relationships."

Gerrit swallowed hard, knowing that Zhao had nailed something very close to the heart.

"I see lonely older people sit looking out their windows," Zhao continued, nodding toward the outside. "But at school, it's just 'Hey, what's up?' and slap on back, but then they just pass away—I mean, they run away. Not many like you, who sit and listen."

Gerrit knew a window had opened, and he prayed silently for words to tell this man what he believed—that the worst loneliness came from not knowing God, that Jesus reached across the gap. The Sunday-school answers had always made so much sense when he was sitting in Sunday school, but here in this Chinese restaurant, across the table from Zhao, Gerrit wasn't sure he could honestly say that he himself wasn't lonely too.

That wasn't because his theology wasn't good, was it? No…

Come on, he coached himself, *Tell him the Four Spiritual Laws, that...*

He must not have been paying attention to what he was putting in his mouth just then, or maybe he'd inhaled a bit of rice, but something sent him into a coughing fit.

"You all right?" Zhao stood up and started to pound him on the back, which was nice of him but didn't make much difference. Meanwhile, Gerrit tried to nod and hold his hand up to tell them that yes, he was fine, just like he'd been fine the other night during their dip in the lake. Only this was different.

"Just..."—he couldn't get the words out quickly enough as he gasped for air—"just went down the wrong pipe."

That's really all it was, so there was no need to call 911. They even got the attention of the restaurant owner, who probably came over to perform the Heimlich maneuver on him. But Gerrit waved them all off and even guzzled a little cup of tea to prove he was okay.

In the meantime he felt that small window of opportunity slam shut on his fingers. All he could do was wipe the tears from his eyes and try to act normal. Zhao looked as if he was doing the same, shifting back to a safe conversation topic.

"You like this?" asked Zhao, pointing at a bowl they shared. *Is this a trick question?* Gerrit chewed some more and swallowed carefully this time so as not to choke. Up to now everything had tasted like a dish he might have tried before at one of those Asian buffet lines. Pretty safe. But this?

"Sure, I think so." He chewed some more. Gray, chewy, salty. Then his stomach suddenly jerked as if it might need to rebel. "Or maybe not."

"Thousand-year-old eggs." Zhao took another bite of his own, and his eyes nearly rolled back into his head with pleasure. "A delicacy."

"How old did you say?" Gerrit would have spit it out if people hadn't already been looking at them. *Hey, the show was over awhile ago, folks.* "It's not really—"

"No, no, not really thousand. Just duck egg, salt…a few days old only. Not thousand years."

"Good to know." Gerrit finally forced it down, wondering if he might be eating anything else that had been prepared during the previous millennium.

Zhao laughed as if he'd just pulled the classic Chinese insider joke. After all, this was sort of home turf for him, which, when Gerrit thought about it, was kind of…

Ironic.

Too bad they hadn't found a Dutch restaurant around here yet. Or someplace that sold Dubbel Zouts, that horrifically salty Dutch candy. Gerrit washed the egg thing down with a sip of hot tea fresh from the teapot, burned his tongue, and checked his watch. Six thirty already?

"Whoa." Gerrit tapped his watch for emphasis. "Don't we have to get you to the auction in a few minutes?"

Yes, they did. So as Zhao bantered Chinese instructions with the waitress and collected the rest of their dinner in little cardboard to-go containers, Gerrit stuffed his fortune cookie into his pocket, paid the tab, and collected his cow by the door.

"I think they will like it," Zhao told him, holding the door. But Gerrit still wasn't too sure.

"I dunno." He wrestled the half-sized Dairy Farmers of Wisconsin display cow and tried not to run into anyone as they hurried down West 22nd to the El station. "They already think I'm an odd duck."

"A duck?" Zhao wondered. "That sounds like another of your American slangs."

"It is. But at least I'm not a thousand-year-old duck egg."

They laughed together, and it felt good. *Easy for him.* Zhao's auction item wasn't so odd—just a live piano accompaniment, up to three songs at any special event or birthday party. People would be sure to bid that one up, especially after they heard his little CD of sample songs, which was also on the auction block. Yeah, Zhao wasn't the one with the cardboard cow who was gonna make a fool of himself.

"This is about the dumbest idea I've ever had," Gerrit mumbled.

"No, no. You're a farmer, and farmers have cows. I think it is a very good joke."

"See, that's the thing. It's not supposed to be a joke. Just a way to raise money for the school."

Well, they would see about that. Forty-five minutes later, Gerrit hung back as Zhao hurried into the building. He unfolded his cow and propped her up to one side of the concert hall's ornate double-entry doors, inside the lobby and out of the weather. It stood next to the display of items and suggested opening bids: piano-student performances, season tickets for the Chicago Symphony Orchestra, a piano tuning, a private wine-and-cheese event, dinner for two at the fancy (and very pricey) Fogo de Chão Brazilian barbecue restaurant, and a couple dozen other items—the kind Joan would never ask him to pick up at the grocery store on the way home.

"Milking lessons and one tractor ride for up to three kids." He read over his own handwriting to make sure he hadn't spelled anything wrong. Looked okay. He still wasn't sure why he was doing this, though. And his supervisor at the zoo? Well, what she didn't know couldn't hurt her, right?

"*There* you are!" Joan saw him and hurried over. She was wearing one of her fancy, long black gowns, definitely not your ordinary we're-just-practicing-tonight blue jeans. "I saw Zhao and started wondering. You took good care of him for me, didn't you?"

"Sure." Gerrit sidled up to steal a kiss while no one was watching. "I think his sprained fingers will heal in no time."

"You always joke when you get nervous." She returned his kiss but looked around the way she did when she didn't want to be embarrassed in public. "You're sure you want to do this?"

"Okay, so here's the thing." He'd better explain it to her right the first time. "All your professor friends think I'm some kind of hick, right?"

"No, they don't."

He sighed. "Come on."

"But, Gerrit, I wasn't thinking you would actually agree to do this. I mean, this is so…not you."

True. It wasn't, but it was too late now. So he held his ground.

"What about the tractor ride?" she asked. "Did you clear the insurance questions with your supervisor?"

"Don't think we need to worry about that, Joan. I do know how to drive a tractor."

By the way she rolled her eyes, he knew she didn't much care for that answer. But she wasn't going to get one she liked anytime soon.

"That's not what I meant, but…all right, then. I have to check on a few of my kids, and T. J. hasn't shown up yet. Do you think you can work the soundboard by yourself this time?"

"No problem." He waved her off. "You go do what you gotta do. Don't worry about me. I'll make sure all the mikes are working."

Which might not have been such a big deal if it hadn't been for the rumbling in his stomach, which was growing worse by the minute. Fortunately, no one could hear him over the orchestra kids playing a spunky little tune by Aaron Copland—something about a rodeo. He liked the melody just fine and normally would have bobbed to the music, but he figured he'd better not make any unnecessary movements just now.

The rumbling grew worse when the crowd gathered in the lobby and Porter Chambliss started to auction off one of the dinners. Gerrit had to admit that Dr. Chambliss was a fair enough auctioneer. Nothing like Will de Weerdt back home, understand, but he got the job done in his own way. He did manage to pull the bidding for the Chicago Symphony Orchestra season tickets up past five thousand dollars, which was good.

And box seats, no less! And when the bidding topped seventy-five hundred (probably double the actual value), Dr. Chambliss beamed and told the crowd that this was going to help next year's scholarship program more than they could imagine.

Gerrit's stomach was still rumbling, which was not good. A few people in the crowd glanced over at him and frowned. *Hey, sorry.* Finally it was time to auction off the cardboard cow.

"And now we've got a very special item here." Dr. Chambliss warmed up as if he was going to tell them all a great joke. "You all know Joan Horton, here. One of the finest pianists and loveliest ladies I've ever had the privilege of knowing."

Even from ten feet away, Gerrit could see his wife's cheeks flush. But he had to clap along with the rest of the crowd, even if the guy wasn't using her married name. Maybe it was just an artistic thing. *Or maybe the guy needs his clock cleaned.*

"Well," the headmaster chuckled as he spoke, "turns out her new man has a way with cows, and he's willing to pass along a little bit of that country know-how to the highest bidder. Give your kids a day on the farm, and a little udder squeezing besides. What am I bid for a behind-the-scenes tractor ride and a personalized milking lesson?"

Now I know this was a mistake. Gerrit slumped behind the soundboard, wishing desperately that he hadn't let Joan volunteer him. But he couldn't blame her. Only himself. As the bidding began (at only fifty dollars?), he leaned over and whispered to Zhao.

"I think your hundred-year-old egg is going to make another appearance."

Bidding or no bidding, Gerrit had no choice but to make a run for the rest room.

"Well," said the auctioneer, "looks like our farmer isn't used to being auctioned off like this."

Which brought a laugh from the crowd, but it didn't matter anymore. Right now only one thing mattered to Gerrit.

~

"This isn't the way home." Joan paused and looked up at the street sign. But Gerrit took her hand and continued in the wrong direction.

"Trust me. Tonight it's the right way."

She looked at him questioningly but followed. It was the least she could do for the $172 farmer. No telling when the winning bidder, their own Dr. Chambliss, would collect on the tractor ride, though. He had told them it would be for his two grandkids, which was fine with her.

"All right," she told him. "But I still think you would have brought a little more at the auction if you'd stayed around for the rest of the bidding."

"If I'd stayed around for the rest of the bidding, you don't want to know what would have happened."

She really didn't. Right now it was enough that the school had exceeded its goal for the scholarship fund.

"I'm sorry the Chinese food didn't sit well with you. Poor Zhao felt terrible about that."

"Not as terrible as me."

"But you're okay now?"

"Let's just say, easy come, easy go. And from now on I'm going to stay away from those old eggs."

And that was all he would say about Chinese food tonight. He led her down Schiller Street and around the corner to Sedgwick. She still didn't have any idea where they were heading.

"Are you going to tell me where we're going?"

"I don't think so."

"Not even a clue?"

"Nope." He marched on, and after a few minutes, they finally crossed the street and stopped in front of a small shop, open late for holiday shoppers. He held the door open for her to go inside.

"Benson Pet Shop?" She hesitated. "Is this what you wanted me to see?"

The young guy behind the counter grinned when they stepped in. "Hey, Mr. Appeldoorn. Here to pick up—?"

But Gerrit held up a hand and didn't let the guy finish.

"Oh yeah." The clerk zipped his lips and nodded. "Just let me know when you're ready."

Ready for what? Joan followed as Gerrit guided her past hamsters, rats, and fish tanks.

"Why do I get the idea that some kind of conspiracy is going on here?" she asked.

Gerrit kept a hand on her arm as they climbed the stairs up to the cats and dogs on the second floor.

"Because there *is* some kind of conspiracy going on here." He looked as if he was working hard to stifle a grin. "Is that a bad thing?"

"You tell me." But she wasn't digging her heels in—yet. Not until she saw the hand-lettered sign taped to the bars of the cage.

"I'm going home with…"—her voice trailed off as she read—*with Joan Apple-dorn!*

"Shoot." Gerrit pointed at the sign. "Spelled our name wrong."

True, but she just couldn't get her eyes off the blue-eyed occupant of the stacked cage.

"He's the smartest little city cat you're ever going to meet." Gerrit unlatched the door and reached in to pick up a meowing young Siamese. "Every time I come by here, he reaches out and hooks my shirt with his claws."

He handed over the kitty, who was now in full purr. Joan didn't ask how many times Gerrit had been by here, and he didn't volunteer the information.

"You like him?" he asked, and she cleared her throat before answering. *Gerrit! Dear, sweet Gerrit...*

"Oh, he's gorgeous, Gerrit. You know how I love Siamese. But, honestly. I thought you really didn't care for cats unless they catch mice out in the barn."

"Well, maybe we can put this little guy to work so he earns his keep." He shrugged.

"So you're sure about this?"

"Sure I'm sure. I mean, I felt bad for these other guys." He looked over at the pens with the puppies, but only for a second. "But it just wouldn't be right to keep them cooped up in an apartment with no woods to run in."

"Lots of people keep dogs in the city, you know." She thought she should mention it, just for the record.

"Oh, I know. I've stepped in it. But seeing as how you like cats so much, I figured this fella here would take to city life a little easier."

Enough said. And by this time the little gray and black ball of fur had already curled into Joan's arms as if he knew exactly where he belonged. Well, of course.

"So he's just like the one you had when you were a kid?" Gerrit asked.

"The markings are a little different, but not much. He is a lot like Amadeus."

"Good." His smile widened into a grin. "That's the idea."

By this time the store clerk arrived with a small pet carrier in hand.

"So you're taking Copland home with you today, are you?" The clerk opened the carrier door.

"Oh, is that his name?" asked Joan. "He already has a name?"

Apparently he did. And Gerrit helped the young clerk hold the door open while Joan pried Copland off her sweater and gently deposited him in his box.

"That was just my idea the other day when I paid for him," Gerrit told her. "It's not like he's used to being called that or anything. You can change it if you want."

"Copland is perfect." She poked a finger into the cage and let the cat lick her fingertip. "I can't think of a better name."

Of course they couldn't leave without making sure Copland had everything he needed. Joan heard Gerrit mumbling something about how barn cats got along just fine without kitty litter. This, however, was no barn cat. "You'll want the high-protein mix," the clerk told them a couple of minutes later as he handed across the first of several plastic shopping bags. High protein was good. "And here's the chew toys, the collar, and the kitty litter. You know how that works now, right?"

"She does." Gerrit pointed his thumb at his wife. " 'Cept I'm the one who's going to be doing most of the cat-sitting."

"Well, enjoy." By now the clerk was smiling broadly. "Here's the name of a good vet for when Copland needs his next round of shots."

"Shots?" Gerrit got a grip on all the shopping bags. "Who said anything about shots? This little guy's gonna need more maintenance than a dairy cow."

"Which reminds me." Joan looked at him seriously. "You're not thinking of taking him anywhere close to that barn, are you?"

"Great idea! We're always trying to clear out some of them rats that get into the feed."

The clerk rolled his eyes and clamped his hands over his ears. "I am not hearing this. Please tell me you're not serious."

Gerrit seemed to actually consider the idea for a minute as he looked from Joan to the clerk. By this time Copland had reached through the bars of his cage and had snagged the cuff of Gerrit's trousers.

"No, just kidding." Gerrit sighed. "He's pretty much just going to live in our apartment, poor little guy. Like me. But, hey, it's a lot better than what he's been used to, being lonely in this cage and all. And the view's not bad either."

Lonely, Joan thought. *Is that how my husband feels?*

She couldn't help wondering as they carried Copland the cat out of Benson's Pet Shop. Out on the sidewalk Copland let out a long, low yowl and waved his claws at a pair of passing legs.

"I know what you mean, buddy," Gerrit whispered to the cat.

"Did you say something?"

"No, nothing." He shook his head and got a better grip on the handle. "Nothing at all."

But she had heard him plainly.

Chapter 28

There is only one satisfying way to boot a computer.
—J. H. GOLDFUSS

*G*errit adjusted the phone on his shoulder and did his best to jot down what his granddaughter had just told him. *Slow down, slow down.*

"Okay, maybe we should just go through this one more time," he told her. "Pull down which menu and right-click where?"

This learning how to be a computer geek wasn't as easy as Mallory let on, but he had definitely made some progress since he'd first gotten his computer. He'd even done more of that instant-message stuff the other night, chatting with Mallory over on the West Coast. Piece of cake.

"It's not that complicated, Grandpa. All you do is follow the directions when they pop up on the browser. Online buying is supposed to be easy."

"Easy, right. Where have I heard that before?"

Where he came from, pop-ups were good eating. He had to admit, though, the girl had a lot more patience with an old man than her parents did. More patience, too, than the tech-support guy in Calcutta who had tried to help him when the machine froze up last month. Nothing against the Calcuttans, of course, but when he finally hung up, he still wasn't sure what language they'd been speaking.

"Okay," he told her, finally on the right page and clicking through to where he needed to be. "You say hackers can't steal my credit-card number?"

"No worries, Grandpa."

Easy for her to say. She wasn't the one hanging out all her personal and financial information like the week's wash for the whole world to see. But the kid knew about these kinds of things, and she was one of the brightest young ladies on the planet.

"So, okay. I want one copy of this *JESUS* DVD in Mandarin Chinese. So I click on…"

He paused a minute, waiting.

Another minute passed.

"What's happening, Grandpa?"

"The hackers are copying down my credit-card number as we speak, that's what's happening."

"But you haven't entered it yet, have you?"

"Oh. Good point. Still, nothing's happening. All I see is the hourglass of doom."

And a minute later, still the hourglass.

Mallory sighed. "I think you're going to have to force-quit the browser, Grandpa."

"Force-quit. That doesn't sound good."

"Maybe I'm just going to have to help you do it when we co—"

From the sound of it, she must have bitten her tongue.

"Mal? You still there?"

"Still here."

"The last word just cut out."

"I was just saying, it would sure be easier to help you if I could come visit."

But that's not quite what she'd said. There's a difference between "when" and "if," you know. *Whatever.*

"You bet it would be easier, Mal. So get your folks to send you out to Chicago as a Christmas present. I hear they decorate up pretty nice around here for the holidays."

"That would be cool, Grandpa."

They laughed a fat-chance, it'll-never-happen kind of laugh, the way they did when they talked about sailing around the world someday or taking the train and backpacking across Europe the way Rick Steves did on his TV shows. But when it came down to it, they hadn't come any closer than the Calcutta techie to solving his problem. If nothing else, though, at least he'd proven to himself that he had the nerve to order things online. He could do this. *Maybe.*

"All you've got to do," she finally told him, "is restart and go through all the steps again. Can you remember what to do?"

He glanced over at his scribbled notes.

"Hey, you're talking to one of the world's most technologically advanced farmers."

They laughed again. So okay, he could do this, and as soon as he got back from giving Dr. Chambliss's grandkids that fund-raiser tractor ride, he'd get his hands on that video…er…DVD. Whatever. He'd blown his chance with Zhao before; he wasn't going to blow it again.

Joan leaned up against the dairy barn and smiled at the scene. Gerrit had perched the two Chambliss grandkids up on the tractor with him, and little Molly and Ashton both gripped one side of the wheel as they careened around the pond by the zoo's farm. On the far side they scattered a loudly honking flock of Canada geese, and even over the racket of the birds, Joan could hear the young children screeching with delight.

Of course, Gerrit smiled and joked with them. He was great with the kids. And he had no idea what they had been through. Maybe she didn't, either—not really. She only knew what Latisha had told her about Porter's son, the children's father. About drug charges and arrests, rumors of a painful history of drug abuse. Joan was almost glad she hadn't been around last year when the news reports first broke. These kids, these innocent kids, should never have to live through such a nightmare—and neither should their mother.

How old were they? Five or six? Seven, maybe? She couldn't help tearing up at the thought of such little ones having to live through the sins of their parents. But now all anyone could see were two sweet, lively young kids bundled up against the winter chill. As they came chugging through the park, she turned back inside the barn. She'd be waiting there with a thermos of hot chocolate and a plate of cookies, and Dr. Chambliss would get his $172 worth of a special day for his grandkids, milking lesson included.

Too bad he wasn't even here to enjoy it with them.

The next morning Porter didn't mention anything to Joan about the tractor ride or the zoo outing, so she launched right into her first tutorial of the day with Zhao Wei. But she couldn't help thinking about the two Chambliss grandkids.

"Mrs. Appeldoorn?" The question yanked Joan out of her daydream. But the lights looked so pretty out on Michigan Avenue, especially now against a backdrop of gently falling snow. In the distance the slate gray lake brooded and the sun never could quite make its appearance.

"Yes, beautiful," she answered. Did she mean Zhao's piano playing or the view? Perhaps both. And perhaps it was all a matter of personal taste—yes, it had to be—but nothing matched the city skyline, the lights, the lake. Not even Gerrit's mountains, though she probably wouldn't say that to his face. She might also not tell him that for the first time in a very long time, she felt so much…at home. But she certainly wasn't paid to admire the view. "Continue, please."

Zhao paused at the keyboard and seemed to know what she was thinking.

"He still goes to the farm every day?"

She nodded. Zhao knew.

"Almost every morning, even if it's not his shift. Even through the snow and the wind, as if these cows depended on him. Sometimes I wonder if he might not be happier if..."

Her voice trailed off as she realized what she was saying and to whom. She turned away from the distraction of the window and back to the music. They had only a few more days to polish Zhao's piece for the midyear recital, Ravel's Symphony for the Left Hand. Polish? As if Zhao needed it. Now she had to ask.

"Zhao, has Gerrit seemed well to you lately?"

He looked back at her with a quizzical expression. "Well? I have not offered him any more thousand-year-old eggs. I am very sorry—"

"No, that's not what I meant. I was just wondering."

She ran a hand through her hair and adjusted her seat. Perhaps she shouldn't have brought it up; perhaps Gerrit just needed a little more rest. So she waved off the thought and pointed to the top of the page.

"Never mind, Zhao. Let's begin back here. You remember what these notes are for. Now, just imagine that you are the man this symphony was dedicated to. You've returned from the Great War, bruised and crippled. You've lost your right hand, and perhaps that isn't all. People have gone on with their lives, and you don't know where you fit in anymore. Can't you almost see the tears the composer left on this score? Now again, from measure twenty."

Worried that she had shared too much, she plucked out the first several notes to help him hear where she wanted him to play. Zhao paused for a moment, as if actually looking for the tracks of the composer's tears, before he straightened his back, took a deep breath, closed his eyes, and launched back into the music.

Right from the start she'd known he was a gifted pianist, or he wouldn't have been allowed to progress this far in the program at Gaylord. Despite his self-taught idiosyncrasies, he knew how to put his fingers on the right keys at the right time. Like every truly great pianist, he seemed wired for sound. She just hadn't known how much soul he would be able to add to the music, how much feeling. And that was what she was searching for, but at the same time that was what she was most afraid of. She worried that he might actually find the sorrowful heart of this music.

As he continued to play, she turned once again to the window, watching the snow swirl and eddy on the ledge outside. On her side of the ledge, just inside, a potted geranium sat forlorn and bare. It had withered after she'd tried to transplant it into a bigger pot, despite her best efforts to revive it. She guessed she must have damaged the roots in the process, and no amount of watering or sunshine or steam heat from the building's ancient radiators seemed able to bring this little geranium back to life.

And for just a moment she wondered how Gerrit's roots were doing.

Gerrit knew something was wrong the moment Zhao stepped into the restaurant for their Thursday lunch meeting. As had become their custom, they met at a little place on the corner of Cedar and State streets called the Corner Bakery.

"Over here!" Gerrit waved through the lunch crowd. From a distance he couldn't quite decipher the look on Zhao's face, but it was obviously not the usual.

Gerrit had already ordered his favorite chili in a bread bowl from the cafeteria-style front counter. And normally Zhao would chow down on an extra-large serving of chili as well. But this time Gerrit's friend only slipped into the booth and poured himself a glass of water. So, of course, something was wrong, but Zhao waited politely as Gerrit paused to pray silently over his meal.

"Amen." Zhao whispered the word when Gerrit raised his head, which was startling. What did Zhao think that meant?

"Thank you." Gerrit unfolded a napkin and waited for his friend to explain. Funny how he'd always thought that Chinese people were so inscrutable, mysterious, and hard to read. Of course, that was before he'd met Zhao Wei.

"You're not having anything to eat today?" The question was not whether, but why. But Gerrit's stomach was rumbling, so he decided to start eating while he waited for an answer.

Zhao shook his head. "I received an e-mail from my sister in Beijing," he began, and an emotion Gerrit had never seen in his friend colored his words. They'd talked about lonely before, but this wasn't lonely. "It's about my father."

"Is he okay?" Gerrit was afraid he knew the answer even before he asked.

Zhao hung his head. "He had…seizing. In hospital. Very serious."

"A seizure?"

"Yes, seizure. My sister says he has some cancer. He sleeps all the time."

"A coma?"

Zhao looked up with tears brimming in his eyes. If he didn't know the meaning of the English word, the sound of it was evil enough to recognize in any language.

"Doctors don't know how long he will live," Zhao said finally. "Two months, maybe three."

Gerrit couldn't eat any more; the news had stolen his appetite. "I'm really sorry, Zhao. You're going home, then?"

Of course he was, but a look of doubt spread across his face.

"I promised to play in the recital this weekend, and—"

"Now, hold it," Gerrit interrupted him. "The recital isn't so important. You just go home on the first flight you can get, and that's all there is to it."

But Zhao shook his head. "I promised I would play. Your wife expects it."

"No, no, no, Zhao. It's not like that at all. I know Joan would totally understand if you told her. You haven't told her?"

"She has much on her mind. I would not want to worry her."

"Oh, come on. If you don't tell her, I will. I mean, if you're leaving, she's going to find out pretty soon anyway, right?"

Zhao sighed. "I would rather play first and leave after. I want her to feel glad, not sorry."

"Sure, but she's your teacher. And people care."

Finally Zhao bowed his head slightly, nodding slowly. So all right—but there still seemed to be something else. Zhao looked at Gerrit with pleading in his eyes, the desperate look of someone with no hope.

"Then you will pray to God for my father?"

Chapter 29

Everyone is kneaded out of the same dough
but not baked in the same oven.
—YIDDISH PROVERB

*H*ere's to the newlyweds!" Warney raised his glass, and Gerrit was about to give them an "Aw shucks" when he realized who the newlyweds actually were. *Oh, right.* Terri nearly hid behind her man. But she was showing in other ways that weren't so easy to hide.

"To the newlyweds!" Everyone else in the apartment raised their glasses of sparkling cider and clinked them together. It wasn't hard to reach as they sat elbow to elbow, shoehorned between the kitchen and… Well, Gerrit's folding chair backed right up to the front door. But this was the way Joan wanted it: Everyone together in the same place, at the same time.

Warney and Liz, with Mallory in tow. Gerrit didn't say anything when Mallory quietly slipped pieces of her roast beef under the table to Copland. The little guy needed a break from his high-protein kibble once in a while, didn't he?

Next to her sat Warney's sister, Patti, her husband, Eric, and their toddlers, Josie and Noah.

Then Gerrit's next-oldest son, Bruce, in his sharp, white Coast Guard uniform, on leave for this special occasion with his wife, Julianne, and their eighteen-month-old little girl, Emily.

The oldest, Gene, was there too, but with a cell phone glued to his ear. His wife, Nancy, watched their two young ones.

Oh, and Joan's son Randy and his new wife, Terri, of course. Not to mention Shane, Alison (pregnant again), and little Erin.

Not counting Joan and Gerrit, that made nineteen, right? Or twenty…twenty-one if you counted the little ones "in the oven." Gerrit had to admit that he'd never seen the kids happier. No talk about managing the farm or about what they were going to do about the stupid milk prices or how they were going to survive another year. And no arguments about debt or whether or not they should take out another loan for the tractor they needed. They were just family, crowded around folding tables, sitting on folding chairs, in a crowded little apartment on the eighth floor of a crowded apartment building in Chicago.

Joan touched his hand under the table, giving him a look that said "I love you" and "It's okay."

Meanwhile, they all laughed at another of Randy's boot-camp jokes with his lockjaw imitation of the drill instructor. Mallory laughed the hardest at her new Uncle Randy.

And the apartment didn't look half-bad. Joan's red candles cast golden circles of light from the buffet and two window ledges, and a fragrant wreath helped make the little apartment smell like a forest.

So why did Gerrit feel like such a party pooper?

"Excuse me for a moment." He pushed back his chair and, without really knowing where he was going, turned toward the front door. "I'll be right back."

And he really meant to come right back. Maybe he could clear his head a bit up on the roof.

"I'm sorry, Father." When he prayed, his breath hung on the still evening air. A siren split the night, but he didn't jump this time. Did that mean he was finally getting used to all the racket in this city, this constant decibel attack? "I should be in there celebrating. Finally all our family is together in one place for the first time ever, just the way Joan wanted it, and I'm up here moping. What's wrong with me?"

God didn't answer right away, and honestly, Gerrit wasn't sure he really wanted to hear the answer. Still, it felt good to be able to vent a little—even if the temperature was down in the teens, almost too cold to snow. It didn't feel so bad this time without the winter wind blowing off the lake, so he turned his face to heaven and opened his mouth to catch snowflakes. He bobbed and dipped to capture them on his outstretched tongue, wishing they had a taste. Wishing...

If only God's answers would come like so many snowflakes.

Or maybe they did after all. Snowflakes melted on his tongue too quickly for him to even recognize their shape. And sometimes God's words seemed to come the same way, like a dream he couldn't quite pull out of his memory even moments after waking. He knew a snowflake had fallen on him, just like he knew he'd dreamed. But they both disappeared so quickly, too quickly. Was God talking to him like that? He tried not to swallow, tried to see if the flakes could pile up on his tongue. But the little drizzle of snow only lightened, leaving Gerrit's theory untested.

It was a dumb idea anyway. Minutes later the door squeaked open behind him, and he turned to see who had followed him up here.

Joan. Of course Joan. She stood framed in the light of the door, shivering and clutching her arms and peering out his direction. He didn't mind just staring at her shape. Did he have to say anything?

"Gerrit?" She leaned out a little farther. "Are you out here?"

For a moment he entertained the possibility of just standing there, silent. Obviously her eyes hadn't adjusted enough yet to see him standing there, the statue in the snow, tongue in the air.

"I'm here." He didn't think she would hear his whisper. But then she was the one with the sensitive musical ear, right?

She looked down and maybe she followed his footsteps in the snow over to where he was standing. And to her credit, she didn't ask any more questions. No "What are you doing up here?" and no "Everybody's wondering where you are." She simply stepped up to him, slipped her arms around his waist, and held him as close as she sometimes did in bed at night when the city noises made him shaking crazy.

He wasn't sure how she knew what not to say, or that she should stay quiet and wait for him to break the silence. But she did, and he loved her all the more for it, as their old arguments faded behind them. He squeezed her, too, as hard as he dared while still allowing her to breathe. This is how people survived in arctic blizzards, wasn't it? Those and winters in Chicago.

He buried his face in her hair and breathed her soft *I'm here,* and for now that was enough. He felt like a baby for doing it, of course, but he couldn't help it and hoped he wasn't squeezing too hard. How many times did he need her touch to remind him of what he already knew in his head but kept losing in the din of the city sounds?

"I know I've told you this before," he finally whispered. "But the only place I'm home anymore is right here in your arms."

As she looked up at him, her lips brushed his. Snowflakes fell right on his nose, and it tickled almost as much as her eyelashes. She didn't answer, just waited for him to continue.

"Problem is, when you're not wrapped around me like this, I keep forgetting what I already know. I'm sorry for being such a baby about this, Joan."

"Tell you what." She snuggled just a little closer, if that was possible. "As soon as everybody leaves tonight, I'll help you remember just a little bit more."

How could a man turn down an offer like that? He felt his heart beating in his ears, and it wasn't on account of the cold.

"So what do you say, farmer boy? Shall we go back in?"

"They're probably wondering what happened to us."

"Nah. We're still newlyweds. They understand."

"I don't think so." Gerrit was never really sure whether they understood, but he wasn't going to miss Joan's dessert of cheesecake smothered in sweet huckleberry syrup, which Joan wasted no time serving to her eager family a few minutes later.

"Pretty good stuff, huh?" Warney would probably never master the art of chewing and talking at separate times. "We picked up the jar at a roadside stand on the way up to Mount Rainier. I was afraid it was going to break inside my suitcase, but here it is."

By this time Copland had jumped up into Mallory's lap, but no one seemed to have the heart to shoo him away.

"Yeah, that's pretty good." Gerrit eyed the plate in the middle of the table, wondering who would qualify for seconds. "But I have to admit, folks here in Chicago know how to eat well too."

"Oh, come on, Dad," Warney said. "Next you're going to tell me you're a Cubs fan."

"Not yet." Gerrit grinned. "But wait till next year."

"Ack! I can't believe it!"

The men went back and forth like that during the rest of dessert, bantering on about baseball and boot camp, Coast Guard icebreakers, and Warney's work in Olympia. The women grew tired of that in a hurry and peeled off into their own conversation about, well, Gerrit wasn't quite sure, except that it probably wasn't about who threw better fastballs. They were probably comparing pregnancy notes, finding out more about Alison's and Terri's babies-on-the-way. Over on the male side, they'd just about worn down the tread of their guy talk, so Warney switched to hometown news.

"So, Dad, what do you hear from home?" Warney leaned back in his chair as far as the wall would allow.

A little stiffness where his seat met the folding chair told Gerrit they'd better retire to the living—oh, that's right. They already *were* in the living room. Gerrit thought over his answer and said, "Home?"

Funny that Warney would ask. Or maybe it wasn't so funny.

"Sure. You still get the paper, right?"

That would be the *Van Dalen Sentinel,* not the *Chicago Tribune.* Gerrit did take note, though, that he had to think about which paper Warney meant. That had to be a sign, right?

"I still get it in the mail. Read the obituaries, mostly, to find out who's died. Kind of depressing when you think about it. Used to read the letters to the editor, but how they're going to pay for the new library doesn't seem as important to me as it used to."

That's when Gerrit decided—and not a moment before. It was one of those "By golly, if I don't do this now, this is going to fester" kinds of decisions. He'd only just now realized that it had been festering and that he'd been thinking about it for weeks without really knowing. Kind of like trying to live with a hangnail and then realizing it's infected. And even though nobody else might see that this was an infection, he could see it now plain as day. *This sucker needs to be lanced.*

So he pushed back his chair and stepped over to the coffee table where he'd parked the last two or three issues of the old hometown paper. With a flourish he scooped them up and transferred them to the trash under the kitchen sink.

There. But nobody else got it except probably Joan. So, fine, he would explain it to them.

"See, it's kind of like driving your pickup while keeping your eye on the rearview mirror the whole time. That only works when you're going in reverse. Going forward, you just keep crashing into things, which is what I've been doing ever since I got here."

It was about the truest thing he'd come to know since they picked up and moved. No one answered, though. They probably didn't dare. Not even Joan. Matter of fact, Randy's and Warney's eyes were pretty big now. Were they getting it? All right, he'd spell it out—as much for himself as for them.

"I've been telling Joan that my home is here with her, but I was still keeping track of things in Van Dalen like I lived there, not here. Can't say that's been fair to her, and I'm apologizing for that right now, Joan. Matter of fact, guess it hasn't even been fair to me when you really think about it."

He tried not to look over too much at the tears running down Joan's cheeks or at her dabbing them with a cloth napkin. He'd start bawling himself, likely as not. It hurt to say it, but it was like he was giving away an old friend—and maybe he was. But he knew what he had to say, and he was going to say it.

"Doesn't mean I'm not going to keep in contact with friends and such. Maybe they'll visit here. Maybe we'll visit there. But the *Sentinel*? Had a six-month subscription that's expiring next month, and I don't think I'm gonna renew it."

"Whoa, Gerrit." Randy's eyes were still looking like full moons. "You really know how to make an announcement. Kind of like going up to the front of the church during a revival service and confessing all the junk in your life. You sure you haven't been going to Mom's church?"

Everyone laughed at that one, which loosened up the "What's he doing?" tension in the room. Joan didn't say much, only kept her hand on Gerrit's, maybe to make sure he was really there and saying all the stuff he was saying. He wouldn't blame her for wondering. He'd even taken the big steps, made it look like he meant it. Only thing she hadn't known was that he'd left his heart back home—no, back *there*—and that now he was reeling it back here. Shoot! *He* hadn't known for sure that he'd left such a big chunk of himself back in Van Dalen.

But it sure was time to set things right. And if it meant going up to the altar, the way Randy said, then that's what he'd do. He would pack this homesick act up there and leave it, since it wasn't doing him much good here in Chicago. Come to think of it, maybe he'd just done it right here, in front of the folks who loved him the most.

They talked then about the folks Gerrit worked with at the zoo, about Joan's students, and about what would be happening at the recital coming up the next day. Gerrit told them about Zhao Wei and his family and about the *JESUS* DVD he had given his Chinese friend—Chicago stuff.

Gerrit wanted to share about Zhao's father but respected his friend's wishes and bit his tongue. There were plenty of other things to discuss, and they could have talked like that all night, maybe, until Mallory stifled a yawn.

Nancy checked her watch once again. "Already ten fifteen?" She stood up and started looking for her purse. "Us old folks have to get back to the hotel before we turn into pumpkins."

"I'm not a pumpkin, Aunt Nancy." Mallory would have toughed it out, of course, but the others started to stand as well. Party over.

"Maybe not, Mal,"—Liz stretched and started to get her coat from the collection draped over a living-room chair—"but we need to get you to bed too. And your Grandma Joanie has a big day tomorrow with the recital and getting ready and everything."

Grandma Joanie. Gerrit looked over at his wife and winked. Right then she didn't look at all like a grandma—not at all.

"But she's not playing." Mallory tried one last time, though she must have known it was a losing effort.

"No, I'm not playing." Joan snuggled Mallory into a bright yellow coat after helping thread two arms through the puffy pink sleeves. "I have a worse job: worrying about everybody who is."

"Hmph. I thought we're not supposed to worry, but in all things give thanks."

Joan laughed and planted a kiss on her new granddaughter's cheek as their guests headed for the door.

"Nice try, Pastor Mallory. Remind me of that again tomorrow when I'm running around biting my nails off."

"Mom, did you hear that?" Mallory took Joan's hand for a closer look. "You don't bite your nails, do you?"

"Mallory Ann Appeldoorn." Her mother sounded a warning. "You're stalling."

"Okay, okay." This time Mallory followed her parents to the door and found herself trapped in the hugging maelstrom before everyone finally found their way out. They would all meet again the next day, Saturday, at Gaylord's performance hall between two thirty and three. Gerrit couldn't save them all seats, especially if he was helping run the soundboard.

"Watch out. Dad's getting high-tech." Warney tossed the comment over his shoulder as they headed down the hallway.

"I've always been high-tech!" Gerrit shot back, and he shut the door before Warney could argue back. All Gerrit heard in the distance was a resounding "Ha!"

He leaned against the door and set the locks, waiting for the echoes to catch up with him. As much as he enjoyed everyone's company, a person could only take so much of a big group like that. He'd have to rest up for another dose tomorrow. Except—

He groaned at the sight of dirty dishes and glasses, coffee cups and silverware, all piled up by their little kitchen sink. The dishes were his job, and only a natural disaster—or worse—would normally keep him from doing them before going to bed. But as he was trying to decide what to do, the overhead light switched off.

"Hey!" He looked around in time to see Joan headed for their bedroom with one of her holiday candles.

"You're not really thinking of doing the dishes, are you?" She paused inside the bedroom door and gave him a look that sent a shiver down his spine.

"Uh…no, not at all." He ran a hand over his head as he followed the flicker of her disappearing shadow like a bear following honey. "I guess they can wait until tomorrow."

Chapter 30

The key to the mystery of a great artist is that for reasons unknown, he will give away his energies and his life just to make sure that one note follows another...and leaves us with the feeling that something is right in the world.

—LEONARD BERNSTEIN

*G*ood thing they'd arrived at the concert hall early to snag some seats. No use sitting in the back row and missing everything. They claimed the better part of two rows, front and center, and as they settled in, Mallory turned to her grandfather.

"You're saving Grandma Joanie a seat, aren't you?"

He smiled and patted the empty chair next to him while he scanned the program. His eyes came to rest on Joan's name near the top, and his stomach sort of took a dive. Mallory was following right along.

"I found a typo!" She pointed to the same place he'd been reading. To her this was a great game. To him, well, he wasn't so sure. "Don't they know that she's married?"

Gerrit frowned and stuck the program in his shirt pocket as he stood. "Think I'll go see if she needs any help. Be right back."

This time T. J. was taking care of the sound booth, but you never knew. Joan would probably be running around backstage trying to get her students ready.

One of the students stood in the corner, face to the wall, hands in the air as if he was playing his piece. Man, could Gerrit identify with those nerves. Another stood behind the curtain, trying to prepare for her performance by squeezing her eyes shut and rocking back and forth. Good thing this was just a private little recital. Although come to think of it, didn't Joan say that a music reviewer from the *Chicago Tribune* was going to be here?

Sure enough, Dr. Chambliss was back there too, talking to Joan with his hand on her shoulder, leaning into her personal space the way Gerrit would never think of doing with a woman who wasn't his wife. The guy's back was turned, so he didn't see Gerrit approach, and pretty soon after that, a couple of the students came up to ask questions, so Dr. Chambliss slipped out the side door before Gerrit got close enough. Joan smiled when she saw her husband.

"Wish us luck."

"You know there's no luck, right?"

She smiled and nodded. And probably this was the wrong time to bring it up, but he couldn't help it. He pulled the program out of his pocket and held it up.

"How about telling him your name isn't Horton anymore?"

"You don't understand, dear." Joan's face turned serious. "Everybody in the music world knows me by that name."

"Or used to."

"They don't mean anything by it. To them it's just a marketing thing for the school to say they have Professor Joan Horton on staff. No one would know who they were talking about if they said it was Professor Appeldoorn."

"You're right." He turned away. "I don't understand."

And he would have just returned to his seat if Dr. Chambliss hadn't come barreling back into the warm-up area, nearly bowling Gerrit over.

"Terribly sorry, friend."

Oh, come on. How many times had Gerrit been hanging around the school, and this clown with the pricey Rolex watch still didn't recognize him? *Time to take care of a thing or two.*

"It's Appeldoorn. Gerrit Appeldoorn. Joan *Appeldoorn's* husband. Remember? You helped us move in."

"Of course it is. And thanks so much for your part in the school fund-raising auction. You know, my grandchildren enjoyed the tractor ride very much."

"I'm glad." Gerrit must have looked like he had something else to say. Maybe it was his raised hand.

"Uh…" All of a sudden Dr. Chambliss looked as if he had a plane to catch. "Anything else I can do for you, Mr. Hort—I mean, Mr. Appeldoorn?"

"Actually, yeah." Gerrit held up the program, which he'd kneaded into a pretzel by now. "I'm glad you mentioned that, actually, because I'm wondering if you can make sure you get my wife's name right when she's introduced tonight? It wasn't much of a wedding present, but I gave it to her. So I was hoping maybe she'd be able to use it in public a little more."

The headmaster cleared his throat and glanced over at Joan, but she just latched onto Gerrit's arm in a death grip and said nothing.

"Well…yes…that is, I'm sure Joan, your wife, has told you why we do it this way. Purely for marketing purposes." He chuckled nervously. "Like a pen name, right, Joan? You've never told me you had a problem with using your maiden name."

By now her grip was cutting off the circulation in Gerrit's arm, but she still didn't say anything.

"Actually, her maiden name was Johnson." Gerrit tried to lighten up his voice and add a touch of a smile to his face. Hey, the guy looked as if he was about to faint.

"Johnson." Dr. Chambliss nodded. "Yes, right. Well, naturally we're more than happy to abide by your wishes, Joan. If that's what you want. I'll introduce you as Joan Horton Appeldoorn, how's that?"

"Just—" Gerrit could hardly make himself heard over the practice pianos and the girl tuning her flute—"just Joan Appeldoorn is fine."

Dr. Chambliss blinked his eyes for a moment as if trying to clear a headache. But he nodded.

"Of course, Joan. It's simply a matter of protocol, but...whatever you prefer." He turned to go just as another student pulled Joan aside for a pre-recital question.

But Gerrit wasn't quite finished.

"Actually, Dr. Chambliss, there is one more thing. I know this is bad timing, but there's something that's been bothering me."

"Yes, of course." Dr. Chambliss was right back to his cool-smiling self again. Yeah, he recovered pretty well. "If you have a concern, it's never bad timing."

His fakey smile told Gerrit that he didn't mean a word of it. More like "Say your piece and get off my back." This time Gerrit gently rested one hand on Chambliss's shoulder, close to the back of his neck so he couldn't back away, and leaned in so that their noses were almost touching.

"I appreciate that." Gerrit did his best to soften his voice, almost as if he were talking to Mallory. "So here's the thing: I know you're uncomfortable with my hand on your shoulder like this, and even more uncomfortable with me being in your face. But I just thought I'd demonstrate for you, because that's the way I feel when I see you talking like this to my wife. And I know she would never tell you so 'cause she's too nice and you're her boss and she's giving you the benefit of the doubt. In fact, maybe she wouldn't want me discussing this with you. But I'm not your employee, so you can think I'm a prude or a country idiot or whatever you want, and it really doesn't matter. Or maybe it's just the difference between where you come from and where I come from. From what I've seen, I tend to think it's a little more than that, but hey, I'm not accusing anybody of anything. It's just that while I had the chance, I wanted to let you know. Just a matter of *protocol* between us guys, right?"

Whew. Speech over, and all Gerrit had a mind to add was some dumb comment like "And you can stick it in your pipe and smoke it," but his chest felt like it was tightening up pretty good, and Chambliss probably wouldn't have appreciated the comment much anyway. So Gerrit just caught his breath and waited for an answer.

"Listen, cowboy." By that time Dr. Chambliss had lost his composure one more time, and his face had blanched pretty good. He must have changed his mind in midstream about the cowboy comment, though he did have enough breath to mutter something about having to get back to his students. So Gerrit finally released his friendly grip, and the head-master slithered away.

Maybe it was a good thing Gerrit hadn't given that clown a pop in the nose for good measure the way he'd been tempted to do. Probably wouldn't have been a very good witness. And no sense messing with the guy's makeup before he had to stand in front of all those people.

"What else did you *say* to him?" Joan came up a moment later, her problem solved with the young musician. "He looked like—"

"Like he'd seen a ghost?" Gerrit turned to his wife. "Look, I'm sorry for putting you in a bad spot back there. I honestly didn't mean to make trouble. It's just that that arrogant clown makes me crazy, especially when he's hanging on you the way he always does, and—"

She silenced him with a kiss, and not just one of those pecks in public, but more like a CPR-approved version. And though Gerrit didn't want to be the first one to come up for air, he had to find out what was behind this public display of affection. She beat him to the question.

"You are a crazy, pain-in-the-neck farmer," she told him, arms firmly locked around his neck. "And you're probably getting me in more trouble than I've ever been in."

He was getting a kiss for being a royal, red-necked pain in the neck? Who would've thought? He tried to open his mouth, but she shook her head.

"But I love you, Gerrit Appeldoorn." She pulled back and fixed his tie the way she always did. "And I'm sorry I haven't worn your wedding present as well as I could have."

He smiled and returned her kiss. Just then they heard a familiar-sounding "Eeeuw!" from the direction of the auditorium. Gerrit looked over his shoulder to see Mallory making the announcement in a too-loud voice.

"I found him, Mom. Grandpa just came back here to kiss on Grandma Joanie. You should see 'em."

"No, she shouldn't." Gerrit took his granddaughter in tow, but not before he managed to wink back at his wife. "Break a leg or whatever you're supposed to do. We're saving you a seat."

Which turned out to be a good thing, as the performance hall filled to standing room only within the next few minutes.

"What's going on?" Randy leaned over to ask his father-in-law when Gerrit was safely back in his seat. "This is a little bit more than just moms and dads, isn't it?"

Gerrit had to look for himself, but sure enough. "Music critics." He pointed with his eyes. "And a few reporters besides. I think the word's out about Zhao Wei."

So for the next forty-five minutes they entertained themselves trying to figure out which guests were from the news media and which were just family and friends of the students. Actually, it wasn't so hard. The professionals often had more than one very expensive camera draped around their necks. Plus, they just didn't look like they were sitting with family.

In other entertainment news, Dr. Chambliss was flitting around the media, shaking hands and pointing out the best camera angles. Gerrit figured he probably wasn't filling them in on Zhao's upcoming departure— even if he knew—so he could make the most out of this publicity for the school. Or if he was trying to get himself on WGN's ten o'clock news.

Before Gerrit could worry too much about it, the lights blinked and dimmed, and Dr. Chambliss took center stage in a pool of spotlights. The bounce in his step told them he didn't mind the attention at all, no sir. He cleared his throat and tapped on the microphone.

"Welcome, everyone, to the eleventh annual Gaylord Conservatory of Music winter recital here at our wonderful Chicago campus." He folded his hands behind his back and bobbed on his toes with that smug grin of his. Gerrit had to admit the guy looked the part in bow tie and tails. "Tonight we're especially pleased to present to you the best talent our school has to offer, under the fine tutelage of our senior piano professor, Dr. Joan...Appeldoorn."

Gerrit smiled and joined the polite applause. *Good man.* Dr. Chambliss went on to say a few words about the school and its programs, about the exceptionally talented pool of young performers enrolled there this year, and about the brilliant Zhao Wei, who would be performing in a short while. But first three other piano students and a pair of violinists would take the stage.

Wow. This wasn't just a little recital for advanced music students. As the guests clapped after the first set of piano solos, Gerrit traded a glance with Warney, who looked just as impressed with his arched eyebrows. This was a full-blown concert.

And Zhao Wei would prove it, after nearly two hours of warm-up acts and Joan's short introduction. Gerrit was naturally the last one left clapping for that.

"Unfortunately, family matters force Mr. Wei to return to China at the end of this semester." Joan spoke more tentatively into the microphone, as if she wished it were a podium to hide behind. Gerrit prayed silently for his wife as the media types in the back scribbled in their notebooks or held up tape recorders as if they were at some kind of press conference. "And though we very much hope to have him return soon, we know you will enjoy his three selections today."

More applause, this time even louder. Gerrit would have given Zhao a standing-o, but of course the guy hadn't even started to play yet. But when he did, Gerrit knew all the headmaster's hype hadn't even begun to describe Zhao's talent—or the heart that went into his playing. The audience heard the music, yes, but they felt the heart. And at the end of his first number, a beautiful piece by Ravel called *Gaspard de la Nuit*, Zhao just suspended his fingers above the keyboard for a moment, the absolute calm before a storm of applause and cheers rocked the hall.

And I thought Joan was amazing. Gerrit's palms hurt from so much heavy clapping, but he didn't care. Next to him his wife had slipped into her seat and was dabbing her eyes. Well, that was a good sign, he supposed. Crying was okay. But Zhao wasn't supposed to stand up between songs and walk to the microphone the way he did.

Gerrit gulped and checked with Joan, but she just shook her head and shrugged. She had no idea what he was going to say either.

"I am very thankful you like my music." This time Gerrit understood every word. You know, you just had to get your ears tuned to the guy, and it wasn't hard at all. "But I am most thankful for my two best American friends, friends always, Professor Joan and Gerrit Appeldoorn."

Of course, "Appeldoorn" sounded a lot like "appador," but that didn't matter. Gerrit felt his face turn red as everybody clapped for Joan and him this time. He had to wave for the both of them—no way was he going to stand up—but he met Zhao's eyes and nodded, and he knew that meeting this young Chinese man had not been an accident. None of this was an accident. Not the move here to Chicago, not the homesickness, not the loneliness.

And this time it was his turn to wipe away the tears as Zhao returned to his piano.

Chapter 31

*A friend knows the song in my heart and sings
it to me when my memory fails.*
—DONNA ROBERTS

If Zhao had once been hard to understand, well, Zhao's wife made it slightly easier on them by answering Joan's questions in Chinese and letting Zhao translate. Gerrit hung on as the elevated train rocked and rolled its way around the Loop and on toward O'Hare International Airport.

"She says she enjoyed the video very much." Zhao rubbed his chin as if deciding how much to tell them. Joan hoped she wasn't prying, stepping on any cultural toes. It's just that she'd never really had a chance to speak with this shy woman who barely spoke or understood English. In fact, she hardly knew that Zhao was married. She wondered how Zhao's wife managed all day while he was in school. What had she done with her time? Now Joan could have kicked herself for not making an effort to get to know her.

"In fact," Zhao continued, "she watched it three times. And I can tell you the first time she covered her face at the end, very frightened."

"You mean during the crucifixion scenes?" Joan wanted to know, and Gerrit nodded his head too. After all, he'd been the one to give the Mandarin-dubbed DVD to Zhao and his wife. Zhao nodded and pointed to his palm.

"The nails and the sound of the hammer gave her bad dreams, I think."

"Oh dear." Joan rested her hand on Jia Li's shoulder. "Tell her we didn't mean to traumatize her."

She realized a moment later why Zhao hesitated. *Vocabulary, vocabulary.*

"I'm sorry. I meant to say that we didn't mean for the DVD to scare her so. She did see the ending, didn't she?"

"Oh yes." The smile on Zhao's face widened as his wife told him something urgent sounding. "And now she repeats all the sayings of your Jesus. My favorite is 'Therefore do not worry about tomorrow, for tomorrow will worry about itself. Each day has enough trouble of its own.' This one I like very much."

Overhead speakers crackled in their ears, though Joan didn't quite catch the words. That didn't stop Jia Li from telling the rest of her story, though, and Zhao nodded as he followed her instructions.

"She also means to tell you," he said, "that on the third time when she saw the movie about Jesus Christ, she prayed the prayer at the end, the one about following Jesus Christ in her heart."

Jia Li smiled and added a few details.

"And she means to tell you that I have not. But"—he held on as the train screeched to a stop—"but maybe I watch the movie one more time."

To Joan the train seemed like one of the most unlikely places to talk about their faith. But one look around told her that no one else seemed to notice. The kid with the headphones continued to bob, and the fellow behind the front page of the *Tribune* continued to read. Nothing out of the ordinary here.

"Even if you don't, we'll pray for you and your family, Zhao." It was Gerrit's turn as Zhao and Jia Li picked up their bags and headed for the doors. Goodness, was this their stop? Joan hadn't noticed the conductor's voice, which had probably told them more than once that the next stop was O'Hare. One look outside told her so. "Maybe you can find a good church to go to in Beijing."

"We have never been inside a Christian church," Zhao informed them. No surprise, there. "But we will write you letters when we can."

Joan stood rooted in the middle of the train compartment, and the truth of what Zhao faced hit her full force—almost like the guy with the roll-on bag who came up behind her.

"Excuse me," he grunted. "This is my stop."

Gerrit waved at her to follow and she jumped out just ahead of the closing doors.

"Sorry," she apologized, and she helped carry one of Jia Li's shoulder bags as they hurried down corridors and up moving stairways on their way to ticketing.

They could no longer keep much of a conversation going, except to say, "We'll be sure to write" or "Keep practicing the songs I gave you."

Zhao wore the cloak of sadness he'd carried since hearing about his father's illness, and though Joan couldn't blame him, her heart had split open at the awful mix of joy and mourning. Joy for Jia Li's decision and the shy happiness on her face, and mourning for the worry and concern Zhao felt for his father. Not to mention, of course, the loss of a once-in-a-lifetime student.

"I wish I will come back," he finally told her after he and Gerrit wrestled four cumbersome old suitcases onto the scales at the Air China reservations counter. Who knew how much the suitcases weighed and how much extra Zhao would have to pay? It would probably cost him a lot of new sheet music that he'd vowed to learn how to read. He stood there next to his petite wife, offering Joan his hand and his thanks. But with tears running down her cheeks, Joan enfolded both of them in the biggest hug she could manage—Zhao with her right arm and Jia Li with her left.

"Tell Jia Li that I'm sorry I didn't get to know her better. But perhaps Gerrit and I can come visit you sometime."

"You will do that?" Zhao looked shocked but pleased.

"Sure we could." Gerrit answered for the both of them as he nearly squeezed the life out of his friend. "I've always wanted to see China. The Great Wall and that great big palace, the Forbidden City—all that. You could show us around."

"I will like that very much." Zhao's grammar made the visit sound that much more imminent, which was fine with Joan. Maybe it wouldn't be such a bad idea. After all, Americans visited China all the time. For now she and Gerrit could only follow a few more steps before the two travelers would be swallowed up by security lines and inspections.

"Wait a minute! I almost forgot." Joan wiped her eyes with a tissue and reached for a little gift-wrapped bundle in her purse. She held it out to Zhao and nodded for him to take it. "This is for you."

He might have guessed what the gift was by its size and shape, but he didn't show it.

"You can open it now," she told him. That is, if he could step out of the way of a large man pressing in behind them. Zhao quickly unwrapped the little ceramic bust of Johan Sebastian Bach and looked at her with wide eyes.

"Thank you so much. Is it—?"

"Yes, it's the same one. I hope you don't mind a secondhand gift."

"It is wonderful gift. But…I don't understand why you give it to me. Was this not a very special possession?"

"It was." She smiled. "But I want you to have it. You can put it up by your piano when you practice, and…uh…maybe it will remind you of people who care about you."

He swallowed hard and spoke to Jia Li before the press of people behind them finally forced them to approach the security line. Jia Li stopped one last time, holding up the line again, and took both of Joan's hands in hers. Joan couldn't help feeling how small and fine the woman's hands were, sculpted like a Barbie doll's. The tears still glistened in the woman's eyes as she oh-so-carefully pronounced her good-bye and the only three intelligible English words she had spoken all afternoon:

"Thank you, Joan."

With one last look Jia Li turned away with Zhao, walked through the metal detector, and disappeared into the crowd. Gerrit clutched Joan's right hand while she wiped away her own tears with the other hand.

"Were you serious about wanting to go to China?" she sniffled. "It's a long ways from home."

"Doesn't matter." Gerrit shrugged as they headed back in the direction of the transit station. "As long as you want to, I do too. You know, 'Where you go I will go, and where you stay I will stay.' Right?"

"Hey, that's my line."

He laughed. "At least I left out the next verse about 'where you die, I will die.'"

"Thanks a bunch." She smiled weakly and linked her arm into his, keeping step with him as they wove through a sea of hurried people towing luggage in all directions. She sensed a strange mixture of regret and expectation. Some of the people were obviously leaving home; others were coming home. Like the little boy dragging his mother toward the arrival gates with "Daddy's almost here!" written all over his face. Or the shy little man waiting by baggage claim, hiding behind a hand-printed Welcome Nakamura Family sign. Or the young woman with slumped shoulders and eyes on the floor, shuffling out through automatic doors into the cold. Had she just said good-bye?

Joan bit her lip and tightened her grip on Gerrit's arm, pulling so close to him that she almost stepped on the side of his shoes. He didn't seem to mind, though, as they walked on toward their train.

Chapter 32

Too many pieces of music finish too long after the end.
—Igor Stravinsky

Even if Joan hadn't realized it before, the Christmas season had crept up on them. Now she could tell by the festive lights strung all over the trees and storefronts on Michigan Avenue, the bustling shoppers, and the sound of Salvation Army bell ringers on many of the corners. All they needed was a little snow. The early-season November drizzle of white stuff had been replaced with a driving wind that caused shoppers on the street to lean into the weather. She looked out Gaylord's conference-room window just in time to see one hapless woman in a fur coat and heels feebly chasing after a tumbleweed-like green and yellow Marshall Field's bag.

"Uh-oh." Latisha peeked over her shoulder, munching on a shrimp-on-a-Ritz appetizer. "There goes somebody's Christmas."

They both had to giggle at the sight of the woman flying down the avenue.

"Reminds me of the Flying Nun," added Joan, and they giggled some more until Latisha offered her one of the appetizers from her plate. They ate well at these staff holiday parties. But Joan shook her head and held up her hand.

"Thanks anyway. I'm saving my appetite. Gerrit said he made dinner reservations tonight at the Grand Lux Café. Can you believe it? We'll get a window table on the second floor overlooking all the Christmas lights on Michigan Avenue! And when a Dutchman offers to take you out to dinner at a fancy place like that—"

"Whoo, girl! Sounds like you're finally getting through to that fella. He's not going to make you pay, though, is he?"

"Well, actually…" Joan knew that Latisha had a pretty good idea how much Gerrit would probably make milking cows and shoveling manure three days a week. But really it didn't matter. "Maybe I will just have one of those shrimp."

"Here you go." Latisha held out her plate to share. "Only I'd be careful with the punch. I think Porter had it spiked."

Joan frowned and looked around the room, festive with wreaths and a garland looped around the perimeter. Clusters of staff stood around the big oak conference table, chatting or helping themselves to the snacks. Porter Chambliss himself approached their side of the room none too steadily.

"Think I'll find the little girl's room," whispered Latisha.

Joan gripped her arm and almost spilled her friend's glass of punch. "Don't you dare bail out on me now," she hissed through a smile.

Latisha stayed put, just barely.

"So, where's your cowboy?" Porter's breath confirmed all punch-spiking rumors. And though he'd been behaving himself since the recital, Joan imagined where she might accidentally poke her sharp little party toothpick if he crossed the line again. "He's late to the party."

"Oh?" Joan checked her watch as if she had no idea. "Well, maybe I told him not to come until six."

"It's six forty-five." So Porter could still tell time well enough.

She shrugged. "Oh, you know Gerrit. He's always helping out at the zoo, showing new employees how to do things. He even went out there in the middle of the night last week to help with a couple of goats that had gotten into some bad feed."

"Dedicated guy." Porter took another long sip of his punch, never taking his eyes off Joan. "Have I ever told you how much I admire him?

The farm boy coming out here to the big city, trying to make a go of it when he doesn't really have a clue? I admire that a lot. Really a lot."

"Thank you." Joan tried to smile politely, but she was afraid she might say something she'd later regret. "I think he's pretty special too."

That was all she could take, and she tried to excuse herself.

"Uh…me, too." Latisha followed her. "I think I still need to take a look at that attendance report you were telling me about."

"Not allowed, ladies!" Porter called after them, but they were already halfway to the door. "No work talk allowed. We're just here to—"

Joan shut the door behind her and rolled her eyes in relief.

"Oh, my goodness." Latisha had to laugh as she draped an arm around her friend. "This would be a great job if it weren't for the staff parties. You think Porter's going to remember any of this tomorrow?"

"I doubt it." Joan checked her watch once more and wondered.

"You really think he's at the zoo?"

"I don't know." Joan pulled her cell phone out of her purse. "It's not like him. He promised he'd be here no later than six."

"You said yourself that he gets caught up in things."

"Yes he does, but this time he promised. Still, that's probably it."

This time Gerrit was not at the dairy barn, at least not according to a college student who answered the phone. She'd talked to Jeremy on the phone a couple of times before but had never met him.

"Nah, he's not here, Mrs. Appeldoorn. In fact, he left me to finish sweeping up. Said he had a hot date, and he didn't want to be late."

Joan bit her lip. "What time was that, Jeremy?"

"Two minutes to five. I remember 'cause I was giving him a hard time about taking off early. He doesn't usually do that."

"No. Well, if you hear from him, would you please tell him to call me on my cell phone?"

"Sure thing. You don't think he's out on that hot date he was telling me about, do you?" Jeremy laughed but caught himself when Joan didn't join in. "Sorry, just kidding. If I see him—"

"Thanks, Jeremy." She hung up, closing the flip phone a bit harder than necessary. She didn't need to tell Latisha what the kid had said.

"Maybe he stopped to give somebody his coat," her friend volunteered. She knew about Avery Wilson. "Wind chill's pretty nasty out there, you know."

"That's what I'm afraid of." Joan struggled to keep her tears at bay as every nightmare scenario flashed through her mind: Gerrit, unconscious and bleeding in an alley somewhere between the zoo and their apartment. Gerrit, mugged in one of those dark pedestrian tunnels under Clark Street, connecting to Lincoln Park and the zoo. Gerrit, run over by a taxi, or worse. She thought about dialing 911, but that wouldn't do until she at least called home.

"Or maybe he just got sidetracked." Latisha meant well. "Maybe he stopped to get you some flowers, and it took longer than he expected. You know how men are. And it's only…seven."

Joan punched in their home number but only got Gerrit's recording telling her to leave a message and that they'd call back as soon as possible.

"Honey, pick up. It's me." She waited. "Gerrit, are you there?" Still no answer. What else could she do? "I'm at Gaylord. Did you forget you were supposed to meet me here an hour ago? Call me!"

She hung up again, but this time she couldn't just stand there eating shrimp appetizers and chitchatting. "If he shows up, tell him to call me right away." Joan stuffed the phone into her purse and headed for the coat tree. "I'm going home in case he might be there."

"Don't panic, girl." Latisha matched her step for step. "I'll go with you."

"No! I mean, thanks. I'm sure he's just stuck somewhere. And…and if you stay here for a while and he calls or he shows up, you can tell him where I went." She paused as she wrapped her wool scarf around her neck. "And you can strangle him for me too."

"Hey, I'll leave that one for you to handle." Latisha's big smile could put anyone at ease. But this time it didn't work for Joan. "You just enjoy your dinner, once you find him. In fact," Latisha snapped her fingers, "I'll bet that's what happened. You think he's supposed to meet you here, but he thinks he's supposed to meet you at the Grand Lux. You call the restaurant, and they'll tell you he's sitting at a window table, hopping mad that you stood him up."

"Hmm, maybe." She looked up the number before leaving the school office, then dialed it as she hurried down the stairs, bypassing the elevator. No, sorry, they told her. But they'd already crossed off "G. Appeldoorn" as a no-show.

"Where are you, Gerrit?" Joan couldn't think straight enough to pray as she hurried down Michigan Avenue in the direction of home. But at this moment she knew with certainty what the New Testament writer had meant about letting the Spirit pray for us when we don't know how to pray.

"Pardon, Miz Appeldoorn?" Freddie the doorman looked at her quizzically as she breezed in through the front lobby. She realized then that she'd been reciting the Bible verse, probably over and over, as best as she remembered it.

"Nothing, Freddie. Sorry. I'm just talking to myself." Then she skidded to a stop. "By the way, have you seen Mr. Appeldoorn lately?"

"Sure I have. Came rushing through here about the same speed as you a couple hours ago or so."

"Coming or going?"

"Coming. I ain't seen him going, 'cept I can't say I've been here a hundred percent, know what I mean? He could've left and I didn't see him. But most likely—"

"Thanks, Freddie!" Joan was already in the elevator, jabbing the button for the door to close. And by this time she had warmed up a pretty good tongue lashing for the man who had made her worry this way. *He's probably puttering around the apartment in his skivvies, talking to the cat and thinking he has plenty of time before he has to meet me at the restaurant.*

"Well, I'm going to teach that old man how to pay attention to his watch," she muttered, fumbling with her door key, "if it's the last thing I do."

Copland must have heard her first, the way he always did, and he was ready to crawl up her leg the moment she stepped in the door.

"Watch out, sweetheart." She swept him away with her foot as best she could. "You're not getting hairs on my dress tonight. Gerrit?"

She raised her voice as she stepped into the front room. If he wasn't home, he'd left the light on. And never once had she known him to waste kilowatts.

"Gerrit?" He had to be here, but he wasn't in the kitchen, either. Except she noticed that Copland's bag of food had tumbled off the kitchen counter and kibble was scattered around the tile floor. Joan's mouth went dry and her hands started to tremble. More than anything she did not want to step into their bedroom—more than anything in the world.

Latisha was right. Gerrit must have gotten his plans scrambled. He was sitting at a table at the Grand Lux Café, staring out the window at the glittery Christmas lights of Michigan Avenue and worrying his head off about her. The girl on the phone must not have realized that he had come in. And now he was probably searching his pockets for a quarter, looking for a pay phone to call her and see what was going on.

Yes, that had to be it, and she bit her lip until it bled, fighting to convince herself that it had to be true. But her legs would not believe, and they would not hold her up any longer, so she gripped the bedroom doorknob and peeked inside the room to see what she could not bear to see.

"Gerrit?" she whispered.

He'd taken off his shoes. And, of course, when she saw his stocking feet poking out from behind the bed, her adrenaline kicked in and she fell on him.

"Oh, Lord, no!" she wailed, but she knew even before she reached him that he wasn't really there. "No, no, no!"

If CPR would have done any good, she would have beat on his chest and breathed her last breath to bring him back. But he had just fallen on the floor at the foot of the bed, his free hand stretched toward the bed-stand phone. He'd not quite finished dressing, either. Two ties were lying on the bed and one was draped loosely around his collar, as if he had just decided which one he was going to wear.

Gerrit, her Gerrit, lay cold on the floor. No pulse, no breath, no life.

And as she knelt by his side, sobbing, Copland came up to lick his master on the cheek.

"No!" She swatted the cat away, regretted it, then reached back to him again for the only other warmth in the room.

"Oh, Copland!" She tried to stroke his fur, but he pulled away and she let him. Then she pinched herself. *What if Gerrit is only...?*

No. Joan hadn't seen a lot of dead bodies in her lifetime, but of this she was sure: her husband was no longer here, and his body lay peacefully on the floor, as if he had just rolled over and was taking a nap.

If only. As the world swirled around her, Joan punched in Latisha's number on her phone, barely able to see the numbers through her tears. She was afraid she might call a stranger by mistake, afraid she might not be able to say a word. And she couldn't. Only sobs and tears and groans that words could not express.

"Joan, honey? What's wrong?" Latisha sounded so far away. "Where are you? What's happening? Are you okay?"

"No." But that was the only word Joan could manage, until Latisha started twenty questions to figure out what was going on.

"Are you home? Honey, honey…just press a key if you're home."

She could do that.

"All right. You're home. You want me to call 911 for you? I'm going to call 911. You stay there. I'll be there as soon as I can. Don't go anywhere."

Joan hung up the phone and buried her face in her husband's untucked shirt. It smelled faintly of Old Spice, which made her want to believe once more that it was all a bad dream. If only she'd stayed home from that awful office party, this all might not have happened. They could have called for help in time, and Gerrit wouldn't have died here all alone.

"Oh, Gerrit," she sobbed. "What do we do now? You didn't even let me say good-bye."

And she fixed his tie, the way she'd always done, before the police arrived.

Chapter 33

It doesn't really matter whether you grip the arms of the dentist's
chair or let your hands lie in your lap. The drill drills on.
—C. S. LEWIS, *A Grief Observed*

Was there any question? They all knew he would have wanted to
be buried back in Van Dalen on the Dutch side of the cemetery
just outside of town. *And they might just as well carve my name on the head-*
stone next to his, thought Joan, *because I'm headed for this cemetery sooner*
or later too.

"Please sooner, Lord," she whispered during the opening hymn of
Gerrit's funeral service. "I'm so…"

She could have filled in the blank with a dozen words, none of which
quite described the depth of how she felt. *Heartbroken, depressed, in denial,*
empty, angry… Need she go on?

As everyone else sang about the deep, deep love of Jesus, Joan hid
behind her sunglasses, behind the widow's sorrowful look, which she'd
perfected once and hadn't expected to need again so soon. But as Gerrit
would surely have pointed out had he been there, God was in control and
they would take what He dished out.

"Leading onward, leading homeward to my glorious rest above."

And that seemed a maddeningly Calvinistic take on this horribly
hopeless situation, one which everyone else who had packed into the Van
Dalen First Dutch Reformed Church that bright December morning
probably shared to one degree or another. Could they help it? They'd been
raised that way, and sermon after sermon of blessed assurance had surely
helped them never to question, never to wonder why or how or when.

" 'Tis an ocean vast of blessing,
'Tis a haven sweet of rest."

They sang as if they meant it, in the same pews every week. And right now more than anything, except for hearing Gerrit knock on the casket to be let out, Joan wished that she had been raised that way too, in a comfortable church like this one with reassuring stained-glass sermons that seemed to provide more answers than questions.

This was honest admiration, mind you, just as she honestly admired the woman at the organ who pounded out verse after verse of "O the Deep, Deep Love of Jesus." Her timing was off a little at the coda, but she didn't seem to care, and the congregation seemed to care even less. Honestly, it was better that way, better than always hearing the music for the mistakes in pedagogy and presentation rather than just singing along with all her heart and leaving it be.

Joan was reasonably certain that when the pastor took his place behind the elevated lectern, he would not wonder why God had chosen her for the honor of being twice widowed—an honor she might have politely declined had she been asked far enough in advance. He would probably not wonder why God had taken them halfway across the country and out into such deep emotional waters, only to sink the ship and leave her alone.

No, but those were the questions Joan had already asked of God, more than once and years ago, hoping that perhaps in a place like this she would get some of the answers that these dear people seemed to possess as a matter of course. Not that she really expected instant answers, since she had already once experienced firsthand the kind of slow and subtle grace that had leaked back into her once-dry life. She wouldn't try to put the pieces back together, go on with her life, or find "closure." No, closure had already assaulted her from every side.

A closed chapter she'd thought was just opening, like a good book ripped from her hands and tossed into a fire before she'd had a chance to read the ending.

A closed heart that she could never again open up to the kind of love that had softened her so. Two times was more than enough. *Been there, done that.*

A closed casket holding the cold body of the man she'd loved, now on display, in a way, for the whole dear community to see.

Closure? Lord, she hated that word and hoped with all her heart that the reverend didn't use it in his sermon. Fortunately the word wasn't found in Psalm 23.

Beyond knowing the text Reverend Jongsma had selected—it was printed in the program—Joan didn't hear a word he spoke to the congregation. She only shivered as if mind-numbing waves of emotion were washing over her. Angry one minute *(How could he do this to me?)* and guilt-ridden the next *(If only…).*

Maybe a theologian or a good Christian counselor would try to describe the process. Someone like that could quantify her experience in a "how to grieve" book, like the one a helpful pastor here in Van Dalen had encouraged her to read. He'd even sent it FedEx to Chicago so she'd be sure to benefit from it on the plane ride back to Seattle, where a bleary-eyed Warney and Liz picked her up for the two-and-a-half-hour drive north to Van Dalen.

Did she like the book? She had no idea, really, since she hadn't opened it at all, only clutched it on the entire flight as if she could soak up its contents that way. *Never mind.* None of it would have applied to her anyway. Because even though the writer might have experienced a loss in his family or the death of a loved one, he had never lost Gerrit Appeldoorn. And now Gerrit had left her…homesick.

Homesick for the place they had made together. Homesick for the place he was now. And if God was going to keep her from being with

Gerrit, being *home,* it was His business to take her through this time of grief. Because she knew one thing for certain: she could not do it by herself.

So that left her once again with her empty question, the one she'd cried out that horrible night when she'd returned to the apartment and discovered that her second husband had left her, just like the first.

Oh, Father, she prayed, *where's my home now?*

Obviously not with Gerrit anymore. Gerrit had only promised her what was left of his heart, and he could offer no more. What about the other part of his marriage vows, the part she had memorized?

"And wherever the Lord and the music take us, that'll be our home."

Maybe...

But now she heard another voice, softer this time, quavering yet clear. She glanced up to see Mallory in a plain gray dress standing on the platform behind a music stand and a wobbly microphone.

"My grandfather was my hero," she said, her voice trembling as she read. "And he taught me a lot of things."

She paused to get her breath back, straightened her shoulders, and went on. This must have been a part of the program that no one had told her about. Of course, no one had told her much about what was going to happen, not really. There was an order to it all that she did not understand, but this was not part of that order.

"He taught me that even old people can learn new things, and that we shouldn't give up just because we're scared. Everybody knows that he took piano lessons the same time I did, and that helped me not to give up.

"But most of all, my grandfather taught me that people matter much more than stuff. Serving God and loving people matters much more than even where you live or where you go to school. 'Cause my grandpa loved God, and he would give homeless people his coat if they were cold and needed it."

Her voice cracked, but she took another deep breath and went on.

"Grandma Joanie told me about that. He never said anything about what he did, and he never bragged about it. He loved Grandma Joanie, too, and he loved his family and the people in his church."

By this time, of course, Grandma Joanie could not see a dry eye in the congregation, not that she was looking for one. She was having enough of a challenge mopping at her own eyes, and she would soon run out of tissues. But the real miracle was that little Mallory somehow continued reading.

"I really missed him when he moved to Chicago with Grandma Joanie and we moved to Olympia. But my grandpa learned how to use a computer, and he sent me lots of e-mails. I don't think he'll mind if I read you one. I didn't see it until after…after he died."

The congregation went silent as Mallory unfolded another piece of paper, a printout. Joan had no idea what would come next.

"Dear Mal," she read. "Miss you lots, and I wish you were here. Chicago's kind of big and scary sometimes, not at all like good old Van Dalen. Noisy, too. The sirens drive me crazy, but I'm starting to get used to them, and Grandma Joanie doesn't seem to mind. She's doing great in her job, like she was made for this, and I believe she was. Everybody likes her, even though her boss is…never mind. Me, I'm still taking care of cows, which I like. And you know my Chinese friend Zhao had to leave to go back home, right? I'm still praying that he comes to know Jesus, since right now I don't think he does yet. Are you making new friends too? Hope so. I think I'm learning that God never takes us away from something unless…unless…"

And that's where the sobs cut in and Mallory could say no more. Of course, no one would have faulted her if she had just run in tears to her seat. She'd already shown more resolve than anyone could have expected. A moment more, and one of her parents would surely have stood up to help her out.

But Joan—or rather, her *feet*—didn't give them the chance. Before she realized what she was doing, she stood and began making her way to the platform. Even though everything inside was screaming for her to stop, she could see nothing but a hurting little girl in tears, and she could do nothing else.

Lord, the last thing I want to do is stand up in front at my own husband's funeral. God, please no!

Still, her legs would not obey her mind, and she stepped up on the platform with Mallory, unsure of what would happen next. The only thing Joan could think of was that they would both collapse in a puddle of tears and that someone would have to scrape them off the floor. But for now, she held her little granddaughter in a tight embrace. And when she finally looked up, Mallory was holding the e-mail out to her.

"Please," Mallory pleaded, tears streaming down her cheeks. "I can't finish. You have to."

Oh no. I can't. No, no, never.

Mallory's eyes were pleading with her, and Joan didn't know if anyone else realized what the little girl was asking her to do. But Joan finally took the paper, swallowed hard, wiped her eyes, and did her best to read her husband's last note before going…home.

The only way she could get through this, she thought, was to pretend that she was standing up in front of a group of parents during a recital and simply reading a note of thanks or introducing a young student. But she wasn't. Yet her *no* collapsed in surrender, and she opened her mouth with a prayer.

"I think I'm learning…"—Joan's weak voice echoed through the church, but she refused to look out over the crowd. Thank God there was only a short bit left to read—"I think I'm learning that God never takes us away from something unless…unless He has something even better just around the corner. Even for an old farmer like me. Give my love to your mom and dad. Write again soon. Love always, Grandpa."

With that she folded the paper around an iridescent blue feather she'd been clutching all this time, the little swallow feather that had once meant so much to Gerrit. She'd never known why.

Now she and Mallory could do nothing but walk back to their seats, arm in arm. That would be enough for her today.

And tomorrow? Well, perhaps she would just let tomorrow worry about itself. After all, each day had enough trouble of its own.

⁌

At first the kids weren't going to let Joan stay alone. But by dinnertime Joan had had all the sympathy and sorry hugs she could take for one day, and she had to get out of the Windmill Inn, where everyone was staying that night. Gerrit's body lay cold now in the frozen earth, shoulder to shoulder with the bodies of hundreds of other farmers and their families, people with good Dutch names like De Hoop or Van Rejn. And, no, she wasn't hungry, although a dozen well-meaning women had asked.

"Please," she'd begged the family, and they'd finally understood, "just a little while alone."

But not really alone. Tonight she played the grand piano in the darkened sanctuary of First Church, still perfumed by the dusky smell of funeral flower arrangements, and where only the cold, bare light from a winter half-moon filtered in through austere stained-glass windows showing Jesus and the disciples, John Knox, and John Calvin. A soft drizzle drummed on the roof above. And tonight she played only for the God to whom she had once given her heart, the God who had also taken away her husband. And now if He wanted her music besides, well, she really had nothing else to give, did she?

"If You want it, Lord." And she let her fingers fly across the keyboard, faster and faster, perhaps more than the composer had once called for, but for now it didn't matter. No adjudicator was listening; no crowd taking note. Only Him, and did He like *Scheherazade,* the duet by Rimsky-Korsakov, as much as she once had?

She'd thought that surely her tears had run dry during the funeral, but when she remembered the last time she'd played this melody, they watered the keys afresh, like salty rain.

Had it been almost two years ago? Only then she'd been playing the sturdy old Steinway upright that had once belonged to Gerrit's grandmother. Joan had only gone to visit her new young student, Mallory Appeldoorn, at the family's dairy farm. The lovely old instrument had practically begged to be played, and Mallory had begged her to play too.

And then that man, that wonderful bumbling farmer, had tiptoed in through the kitchen to listen. Curious, wasn't he? He'd probably gotten a little more than he'd anticipated in the bargain. Only their time together had been cut short, just like her song. There in the dark, cold sanctuary, Joan vowed never to let herself play that piece again.

In fact, the family was probably wondering what had happened to her by now, and so she quietly replaced the keyboard cover and pushed back the bench. A small shadow moved at the far end of the room, framed against one of the stained-glass windows. Yet even in the dark Joan recognized the form.

"I didn't mean to spy on you." Mallory's thin voice echoed across the now-silent room. "But I walked over here to find you, and I heard the music, and I remembered..."

"You, too? Come up here and sit with me."

Mallory wasted no time hurrying up to the front; her young eyes must have already adjusted to the gloom. A moment later she had snuggled up next to Joan on the piano bench the way she used to do when she was taking piano lessons from Mrs. Horton.

"That was pretty funny when you found your grandpa listening in on us that day, wasn't it?"

Mallory giggled, but barely. She knew. "He thought he was being sneaky, I think. But I always wanted to ask you. Was that—I mean, you don't have to answer if you don't want to—but was that love at first sight?"

This time it was Joan's turn to giggle, and it didn't hurt quite as much as she would have thought. On a day like today, laughing and crying almost seemed like two sides of the same emotion. And coming or going, remembering or forgetting, it all ached the same.

"Well, I don't know if there's really such a thing as love at first sight the way you see in the movies or in those romance books. But just between us girls, I was pretty impressed by your grandpa that first day."

"You mean you liked him?"

"I didn't know him, but I thought he was kind of cute. And since I liked you, I thought that any grandpa of a nice piano student like Mallory, well, he couldn't be all that bad."

Mallory leaned her head against Joan's shoulder. Her silky hair, still damp, smelled of winter rain.

"I miss him."

"So do I, pumpkin. So do I."

Chapter 34

Earthmaker, Holy, let me now depart,
For living's such a temporary art.
And dying is but getting dressed for God,
Our graves are merely doorways cut in sod.

—CALVIN MILLER

*J*oan took a deep breath and looked up at the entry doors. She had done the right thing, hadn't she? A person could only take so much change, and of course the letter had changed everything. But stepping into the lobby, she knew what Gerrit would have said.

God had His fingerprints all over this.

She would have given anything to have him tell her "I told you so" in person. But she wasn't going to start crying all over again—not now. She couldn't, even with the pain of losing Gerrit still so fresh. Instead, she smiled at Viktor the elevator man and gripped her little briefcase in a vain attempt to look professional. Surely the makeup couldn't cover her puffy, red eyes, but it was too late now.

"Fourth floor, Miz Apple?"

Right. The welcome would be different this time, she knew, except for one thing.

"There you are, roomie!" Latisha greeted her with open arms and a warm hug almost before Joan had stepped into the offices. "Welcome home."

Was it? Was it home?

"Thanks." Joan would not be the first one to let go. "You know I wouldn't be here if it weren't for you."

"Hey, I just needed someone to help pay the rent, girlfriend. And since your cat was already staying with me the past few weeks, no reason why you shouldn't too."

A moment later Latisha pulled back as if she'd just realized whom she was addressing. "Actually, though, what am I supposed to call you, now? *Mrs.* Appeldoorn? Or how about Madame Headmistress?"

Joan had to laugh, despite the odd feeling of walking into this place on entirely different footing than ever before.

"Make that Madame *Interim* Headmistress. You know I'm not official."

"Yeah, yeah." Latisha waved off the comment. Joan the temporary administrator. Joan the grieving two-time widow. "We'll see how temporary you really are."

"But I really don't—" Joan stopped short of saying what she really did or did not want to do. Because if she had learned one thing over the past couple of months, it was that God's plans didn't always intersect with her own. And once more Gerrit would have told her so. At least she was learning.

"Same office?"

"Unless you want the one with his name still on the door."

Okay, obvious choice. And besides, she'd left most of her things in her old office, the room with the view…and the Bösendorfer. No way was she giving that up, even for the temporary promotion. And it *was* temporary.

"Tell you one thing, though." Latisha loaded Joan up with an armload of paperwork, then picked up a pile of books herself. "When that man decided to cook up a scandal, he did it right. You should have seen the board when they found out about the missing money. They were breathing fire, and he was a two-day barbecue."

Which explained the swift exit of Porter Chambliss. Too bad he hadn't left his affairs in better order. It might have made her new job a little easier. But oh well.

"Didn't I always tell you something was fishy about that guy?" Latisha walked with Joan back to her office. "And besides, you're going to do just fine."

"Maybe. But explain something to me." Joan stopped in front of her door, balancing the stack of papers on her hip. "Why me? And why now?"

"Why you? That's easy. People like you. People trust you. Everybody knew you were the right person for the job. What they *didn't* know was if you'd be able to take the job so soon after…"

Joan closed her eyes and sighed. "Please don't say anything about jumping right back into the saddle."

Latisha turned serious. "I wasn't going to. I know you're going to be hurting for a long, long time."

"Did anybody have any doubts?"

Latisha shook her head. "Not about you, but it was probably a good thing you didn't hear all the discussion about whether it was a good idea to have you do this so soon. Hey, I promised them you'd be okay, and everybody listens to the office manager around here, right?"

"Right." Joan had to laugh. "I know I do."

"So you just lean on the people who care about you, and we'll keep praying you through this."

Joan pressed her lips tightly together and nodded her thanks. "You know the only reason I came back so soon was because you begged me."

"What do you mean begged?"

"Coerced. Finagled. Strong-armed. But what else was I going to do, sit at home and cry?"

"That's what I told them."

"Of course, since Gerrit died, I'm not sure where my home is anymore."

She hadn't meant to say that; it would only trigger the tears again. And right now…

"Your home is Chicago, Madame Headmistress." Latisha stepped into the office and plopped her load of books on Joan's desk, right where the ceramic bust of Bach used to stand. "And it's here at Gaylord, and right now it's with me, or did you forget?"

"No, of course not." She dropped her own load next to Latisha's and wrapped her arms around the tall woman's neck once more for good measure. "But you'd better stop calling me Madame Headmistress."

"Hmm," Latisha smiled as she headed for the door. "I'll have to think about that. Don't forget the staff meeting this afternoon, Madame Joanie."

So Joan stood there trying to make sense of everything, wrestling with the pieces of this puzzle that seemed to fit—and yet didn't. In one sense everything here was as she had left it, a lifetime ago, before Gerrit's heart attack. But in another sense everything was very different. In a few minutes she would hear students hurrying past her office, probably on their way to class this first day of the new spring semester.

"Oh, Gerrit," she whispered, running her finger in a circle through the dust on the Bösendorfer. It wasn't a prayer to the dead or anything like that. Just... "You really ought to be here."

"Excuse please?" The young voice made her jump before turning to see who was at the open door. "I look for new student room."

The woman looked to be about thirty or thirty-five, dark-haired and dark-eyed. And even through the thick Russian or Polish accent, Joan could hear the clear edge of panic. How well she knew what that sounded like!

"You're a new student?" Joan smiled. "Welcome to Gaylord."

"Oh no." When the woman shook her head, her raven hair shone like someone in a shampoo commercial. But even her beauty didn't hide the obvious fright on her face. "My husband is student. I meet him, but I am...lost."

"Oh! Well, to tell you the truth, a lot of times I feel that way too."

"Sorry. My English—not so good?" The woman might have looked even more puzzled for a moment, but that was okay. Joan knew exactly what Gerrit would have done in a situation like this, and she headed for the door to show the new arrival to the student lounge.

"That's not a problem." She took the woman gently by the arm. "I'll take you there myself."

And finally the woman smiled, just a little, and seemed to relax. Her name was Varushka, she said, and she and her husband were from Kiev. He played the violin and was here on a scholarship.

"From the city, are you?" Joan asked as they headed down a flight of stairs. "Then maybe you've never seen a real dairy farm."

"Excuse? Dairy?" Of course, Varushka didn't recognize the word. *Vocabulary, vocabulary.*

"Sorry. A farm with milk cows? Big cows?" Joan put out her hands to show how big and actually gave a little *moo* for effect. "Stick with me, Varushka, and I'll show you. You never know what you'll find in a new home."

$\mathcal{A}cknowledgments$

$\mathcal{T}$he roots of this story stretch back several decades to the mid-1960s when my family moved to the Chicago suburbs. As a young child, I was fascinated but somewhat intimidated by the dazzling city just a few miles away. Yet I still have many pleasant memories of driving into the city to see the department-store windows along Michigan Avenue, decorated for Christmas. Visiting the lakeshore in the summer or the Museum of Science and Industry. Or watching Willie Mays and the Giants play the Cubs at Wrigley Field with my father.

Years later two of my children traveled cross-country to attend Moody Bible Institute in Chicago. And since I often speak at Christian schools in the Midwest, I've had a chance to visit one of my favorite cities—and my kids—quite often. As the story took shape, both Kai and Danica were more than helpful with details about the city, suggestions, and inspiration. Thanks, you two.

Of course, *The Recital* really isn't a story about a city. It's about two people who let go of their pasts to face the future together. They look forward to what God has in store for them, and that part of the story was especially gratifying for me to write. I'd like to thank three forward-looking editors who shared this vision and who helped me craft this story—Jamie Cain, Jennifer Lonas, and Shannon Hill. Also Dudley Delffs, who knew right away that *The Duet* needed a sequel.

A special thank-you to Guanglin Li for his generous and enthusiastic help, as he explained to me many of the challenges of living in Chicago from a uniquely Chinese perspective. He also enlisted the help of Chinese exchange students in the city, people who shared their stories and lives with me. Though they are too numerous to mention, their insights helped me immensely, and I am deeply grateful to them. Many thanks.

Thanks also to the staff at the Lincoln Park Zoo, who patiently answered so many of my "what if?" questions about the care and feeding of their farm animals. Their zoo is an oasis and a jewel in Chicago's crown.

Finally, thanks to my wife, Ronda, who always keeps me grounded, who encourages me, and who provides a woman's viewpoint at every step of the writing road. Thank you.

About the Author

ROBERT ELMER is the author of *The Celebrity* and *The Duet,* as well as six popular youth series. One of his favorite cities is Chicago, the setting for this book and his home for a couple of years when he was young. He and his wife, Ronda, have three grown children and live in the Pacific Northwest. To learn more about Robert Elmer and his books, visit www.Robert ElmerBooks.com.